# THREE MONKEYS

# THREE MONKEYS

Marianne Macdonald

**Severn House Large Print**
London & New York

This first large print edition published in Great Britain 2007 by
SEVERN HOUSE LARGE PRINT BOOKS LTD of
9-15 High Street, Sutton, Surrey, SM1 1DF.
First world regular print edition published 2005 by
Severn House Publishers, London and New York.
This first large print edition published in the USA 2007 by
SEVERN HOUSE PUBLISHERS INC., of
595 Madison Avenue, New York, NY 10022.

British Library Cataloguing in Publication Data

Macdonald, Marianne
  Three monkeys. - Large print ed. - (A Dido Hoare mystery)
  1. Hoare, Dido (Fictitious character) - Fiction
  2. Antiquarian booksellers - Fiction 3. Detective and
  mystery stories 4. Large type books
  I. Title
  823.9'14[F]

  ISBN-13: 978-0-7278-7636-2

Printed and bound in Great Britain by
MPG Books Ltd, Bodmin, Cornwall.

*This book is dedicated to certain friends who are so close that they are members of the family:*

*Sevin Seydi and Maurice Whitby, Mike Quinn and James Roane of Virginia and parts west.*

# Acknowledgements

I wish that I could thank the author – whoever it was – of a little children's book that I used to own a lifetime ago; it was called *Three Wise Monkeys*, and the cover showed a picture of them sitting side by side on the branch of a tree, each with its hands over its eyes, its ears, or its mouth. They were based on the three monkeys carved in the seventeenth century over the door of the Sacred Stable, Nikko, Japan, representing the motto: Hear no evil, see no evil, speak no evil. Of course when I was a child I believed that they showed how to be good. Afterwards, growing up in the real world, I discovered just what an ambivalent message they represent. To refuse to see or speak out about evil and suffering no longer seems wise – more like cowardice.

I certainly can and do thank all the people who have helped me with this book: Keith and Jo and the others at the primate house at London Zoo and elsewhere, who answered my ignorant queries about real monkeys and their habits; Abbey Hamilton, Erik Korn, Andrew Korn and Alex Wagstaff, who read through an

7

earlier version of the book and gave me their comments and suggestions; and my agent, Jacqueline Korn, who has demonstrated a truly saintly patience with me this time.

# Chapter 1

## Monkey

My name is Dido Hoare, and I hate December. Even on one of the rare cloudless days, the sun only just about manages to crawl around a tiny arc of the southern horizon, reminding us how ridiculously far north London actually is. A cranky geography teacher once snapped and made us look it up on a globe: believe it or not, this city is in the latitudes of the Aleutian Islands, southern Labrador and Irkutsk. No wonder the upper classes used to spend their winters socializing on the Riviera or conquering India while the rest of us had to stop taking baths, scavenge for Yule logs and get drunk.

It was past five o'clock, one afternoon at the beginning of the month. I was tired, and it had been as dark as night for nearly two hours. I was walking Ben – my almost-four-year-old son – home from nursery. An icy easterly wind had just blasted us across the Essex Road, and we ducked quickly into the shelter of a side street and started along the dark frontage of the

Baptist church. Ben was stamping along at my side, singing a wordless tune that sounded quite a lot like 'Hark the Herald Angels'; they were getting ready for the Christmas concert. I shifted the heavy shopping bag to my left hand and wriggled my right shoulder.

And for a moment I thought I saw a body lying across the pavement ahead of us, dark and lumpy in the faint light from the windows of the Victorian terrace across the road. Only of course it wasn't. Someone had left a plastic sack full of rubbish in the middle of the pavement. I grabbed Ben's hand as we reached it, he jumped, and I swung him over the obstruction. He crowed with laughter, and I felt better. I turned and nudged the thing with my toe, and when it shifted lightly, I asked myself what was yanking my chain today and stopped long enough to push the thing up against the iron railings, out of the way of small children and their gloomy mothers.

Ahead of us, where the street curves gently towards its junction with the main road, I could see the glare of headlights and the brightness of the Christmas decorations in the windows of the little shops.

'A, B, C, D!' Ben was chanting now at the top of his voice as he pranced. 'A, B, C, D! When are we going to put up our tree?'

'You spoke a poem,' I told him.

Ben looked at me and chortled. 'A, B, C, D, E, F! When all of us know it, we're going to

10

read books.'

'That will be great,' I agreed, paying attention but also starting to think about supper.

We stopped on the corner of our street to wait for a car that was turning in. Across from us and a little to the right was the two-storey converted Georgian cottage where I live and work. Light from the street lamp glinted on the painted sign above the ground-floor display window: *Dido Hoare ~ Antiquarian Books and Prints*. The night lighting glowed dimly behind the strings of flashing Christmas bulbs that Ben and I had stretched across the window on Sunday afternoon. They shone on the silver foil ropes and the shapes of the books in the display: old illustrated books and mounted nineteenth-century engravings of winter scenes, suitable Christmas presents. The first three weeks of December are always a busy time in the shop.

At that point I noticed that the red light of the security alarm was dark. I'd had one last customer lingering stubbornly that afternoon, and I'd forgotten to set it in my rush to get away. So I'd have to remember to pop back downstairs after Ben was in bed.

The car had gone. We crossed the road and made for the door to the flat above the shop. Home. Then I was busy juggling the shopping bag, feeling in my pocket for the keys, waiting for Ben to go in ahead of me, wondering suddenly whether any of my bids at today's book auction had been successful and whether there

11

were any oranges left, thinking about too many things, forgetting things. As usual.

I slammed the door and shut out the wind.

Already halfway up the narrow flight of stairs, Ben spoke importantly: 'I saw the monkey.'

I said, 'Did you? Where? At nursery? Are you hungry?'

From the landing, he turned to look down at me. 'It was hiding. It looked at me and then it ran away.'

'Did it?' I said slowly. Apparently I'd missed something. I started up towards him, saying, 'What monkey, Ben?'

'It lives somewhere. Can we have sausages? You said, you promised me! Sausages and chips.' I pulled myself together and hurtled up to unlock the door of the flat, and the telephone in the sitting room was just starting to ring.

Later, I woke with the impression that somebody was calling me. I'd fallen asleep in front of the television. I yawned, punched the remote, and listened to the usual night-time noises: voices in the street, a car passing, the clock ticking on the shelf above the fireplace, the faint thump of the central-heating boiler kicking in, the sound of scratching ... I'd been wakened by Mr Spock, our ginger cat, asking to be let in. I yawned again, unfolded myself, and crept down the darkened hall. From the kitchen doorway I could see the shape of the cat outside

12

the window, arching his back between the bars and the glass. In the darkness behind him, just for a fraction of a second, something else moved. My heart thumped. I took three quick steps across the room and peered out.

There is a single-storey extension at the back of the cottage which would have housed the scullery and larder in the days before the ground floor was turned into a shop and nowadays is my office. I could have sworn that for an instant I had seen a low, angular shape scuttling across the flat roof towards the wall and the damp garden next door.

All the buildings in my street and the streets around have little, overshadowed rectangles of garden at the back, surrounded by high brick walls. Whatever I'd seen could have jumped in from anywhere. I craned my neck and looked again, but there was nothing except Mr Spock rearing up abruptly on his hind legs, pawing the window pane. I pulled up the window, let him slip inside, and then shut it hard. He stood un-harmed on the counter beside the sink, stretch-ed, said something, and then landed with a thump at my feet. A scraping sound told me that he was investigating his supper dish.

I leaned against the work counter, still look-ing out at the lights in the windows opposite and the darkness in the gardens below. It had been another cat, but suddenly I remembered the time when someone had tried to break into the shop; and I still hadn't gone back to set

13

the alarm.

There was silence in the bedroom where Ben had been asleep for the past two hours. I pulled myself together, slid my feet into my shoes, grabbed the keys and crept down to the street. Here there were lights and people. I peered in through the display window although I knew that nothing would have been disturbed. Of course. Yet when I had opened the door, I stood still for a moment, listening and looking down through the open office door. It was darker in the back room, but I could see that the back door was shut. *For crying out loud, Dido!* I went in and flicked the wall switch. The overhead light glared on the littered desk and the staggeringly high pile of books waiting on the packing table: all exactly as I'd left it. The door to the garden was bolted, top and bottom, so I retreated, switching off the Christmas lights and remembering to set the security alarm this time.

There is a small triangular-shaped paved area where the side wall of my cottage makes an angle with the garden wall of the shop on the cross street. Nobody seems to own the space: it's one of those little pieces of unregistered, forgotten land that you often find in a city as old as London. Apart from the litter that blows in, only my business-sized wheeled dustbin inhabits this space. The light from the street lamp barely penetrates the area behind the bin, but I could just make out some unexpected pale shapes there.

The bell clanged in the tower of St Mary's, two streets south of where I stood wavering. Eleven thirty. No hour for street-cleaning. The wind had dropped by now, and the air was bitter. In the morning, I would put on a warm coat and clear up whatever rubbish had been dumped there. It wouldn't be the first time I'd had to do that, or the last.

# Chapter 2

## Some Days, You Just Can't Win

It had sleeted during the night. Even at nine o'clock small icy patches still lingered treacherously in the gutters and sheltered corners. I dropped Ben off at nursery and shivered back to George Street, slammed the door of the shop behind me, swept down the aisle to turn off the alarm, and went straight into the back room. The red light on the answering machine was flashing, and I listened to the messages first, because business has to go on no matter what else. This morning it had gone on to the tune of four orders from our Christmas catalogue, and three of them were still available. I wrote down the details and cast another look at the invoiced but unwrapped books waiting on the packing table. Somebody was going to have to do something about sending those off today. That somebody would be me.

The last message on the machine was more mysterious.

'Dido,' a familiar voice said briskly, 'it's Pat. I need to talk to you. You're at the shop today, aren't you? Don't go out again, I'll get back to you.'

When our mother died, my sister Pat somehow took over responsibility for our whole feckless family, including me and eventually Ben, as well as her doctor husband, her own two boys and our father, Barnabas. So I rang her number in St Albans and in turn got only her answering machine. Since I was allowing myself to be distracted, I rang my father's number and once again failed to connect with a human being. That seemed to release me from family obligations for the moment. There was just one more chore before I got out the bubble wrap and the brown paper. I wrestled the broom out of the crowded corner beside the packing table and carried it into the street, to the place where something messy had been waiting for me all night.

The thing I had glimpsed in the darkness was a big cardboard box which somebody had flattened to form a pad on the cold ground. On top of it sat a couple of torn sweet wrappers, a crushed can that had held the cheapest kind of lager, and a crumpled handful of paper that had

16

held chips, with a smear of ketchup still decorating it. It could almost have blown in from the street, except for the dirty old blue nylon sleeping bag with one split seam which sat bunched up beside the mess. I squatted down and used the handle of the broom to lift a corner of the greasy-looking thing. A lair: it was like an animal's empty lair.

I flipped up the lid of my bin to survey the bits of flattened cardboard, a slew of junk mail and some scraps of wrapping materials. I'd put those in yesterday. But there was also a plastic bag from the pedal bin in the kitchen, and somebody had torn that open. Damp tea bags, orange peel, potato peelings and an empty cereal packet lay scattered over the things from the shop: someone had ransacked my rubbish. The four-legged inhabitants of these streets are not exotic – just cats and rats, both incapable of getting into a bin like this one. Not even a monkey would be able to lift this lid. But an uneasy memory returned: there had been a monkey...

I reached for the bag.

A voice behind me said forcefully, 'Dido, what are you doing! Don't you wear any heavy gloves? There could be a ... a ... anything in that mess! Broken glass! Needles!'

I jumped violently. I'd been so absorbed in my discoveries that I hadn't noticed the arrival of my sister's big black Range Rover: Pat had sneaked up on me again. I choked back the childish impulse to promise I'd wash my hands right away, and smiled brightly. 'Pat! You didn't say you were driving into town. How are you? And John and the boys?'

She smiled back, examined me but found nothing else to complain about, and said she was fine, very busy but fine. 'I've just come into town for some Christmas shopping. Presents. For the boys, particularly. Probably some video games, that's all they seem to want these days, and John is run off his feet at the practice because of this nasty flu that's going around, and besides ... so I suddenly thought I'd better come into town. You can probably tell me a good place for getting that kind of thing. Dido, if you don't mind, I could really use a cup of coffee. I came down the Radlett Road, but even so – the traffic! And we need to talk about Christmas. Have you spoken to Dad? He isn't answering his phone – is he coming here today? We need to decide. Will the car be all right if I leave it there for a few minutes?'

She had actually parked in the residents' bay just in front of my big purple MPV, but she would probably get away with it for a while: Pat is the lucky type. I explained that the traffic wardens don't often bother with our side street on midweek mornings, but that on the other hand Barnabas would be spending the day at the British Library not the shop.

She said, 'Oh well, I'll phone him later,' and waited expectantly.

18

'You got somebody sleeping rough there,' a new voice observed.

I jumped: I'd just allowed another person to creep up on me. Ernie Weekes's face appeared at Pat's shoulder, looking sinister, half obscured by the hoodie that he was wearing under his jacket today. When she side-stepped, he moved forward. Ernie is broad, and his old black puffa jacket made him even broader, but he squeezed in between the bin and the wall with a lot more enthusiasm than Pat had shown.

'Prob'ly go away, if we clear up his stuff. You want me to do that?'

'Good idea,' Pat said promptly. 'I have to talk to Dido. Why don't you just toss everything into the bin? The broom's right there.'

Ernie and I exchanged glances. Ernie has brothers, not to mention a widowed mother who is even bossier than Pat, having coped mostly by herself with three sons as well as other problems: she is a refugee from the wars in Sierra Leone.

'If you don't mind,' I surrendered. Then it struck me: Ernie works for me on Wednesday afternoons and Saturdays, helping to finance his studies at the university up in Holloway. 'Ernie, what are you doing here? What about—?'

'Class cancelled,' he interrupted. 'Lecturer's sick. Flu, or something. Thought I'd come here, tidy up the website, enter the sales?'

I said that was brilliant, promised I'd bring

19

him a mug of coffee in a little while, hesitated, and said I thought maybe he ought to leave the sleeping bag but the rest of it could go into the bin. The owner would probably take this as a polite hint. Then I abandoned the broom and the shop to his care, and led Pat upstairs towards the coffee machine in the kitchen and an armchair in the sitting room where, as I remembered when it was too late, I'd been meaning for the past three days to tidy up a mountain of picture books and toys. And also a really only fairly small patch of cat vomit that had dried into the carpet. If my luck changed, she might not even notice it.

At four thirty I leaned back, stretched my legs, yawned, and contemplated the packing table which was empty at last, barring a few stray scraps of brown wrapping paper. I even briefly considered washing the top while that was possible. Ernie was on his way to the tube station and home, taking the final batch of parcels to the Post Office on his way. The shop was quiet. The only noise was out in the street: someone at the corner honking uselessly at the line of cars in the cross street, the distant sound of a siren, the voices of some kids walking up past the shop towards the houses. The street lights were on now. I'd close a little early, have a cup of coffee and then go and get Ben.

Then the old Nepalese bell on the door tinkled, announcing that my plans had just gone

20

adrift. I leaned forward and watched Mrs Acker slip into the shop, offer her usual vague smile, and wander up behind the far row of bookcases. I moved the chair a couple of inches and located her in the mirror that I'd installed above the display window the day after somebody had pocketed a copy of Mayhew's *The Toothache*. That's not a particularly valuable book, but the principle of the thing had sent me up a stepladder one Sunday afternoon in November to improve my security. Not that an old customer like Mrs Acker, who lived just up the road and had been buying books from me since the week the shop opened, was a problem. She never wanted my help. After six years, she was still mainly silent.

From somewhere out in the garden behind me came the rhythmical squealing of rusty metal. I ignored it. Eventually Mrs Acker appeared in the doorway, smiling tentatively and holding a book in her left hand. My first reaction was that one of us had made a mistake. She had picked out the 1927 *Winnie-the-Pooh* in a tattered dust jacket. I couldn't remember her ever buying a book that cost more than £2, and I wondered whether I'd made some kind of embarrassing error when I'd pencilled the price on the flyleaf. But when I opened the front cover I was reassured to see it was marked at a perfectly reasonable £85. I pointed that out in a tone of voice that wasn't meant to suggest anything one way or the other.

She smiled palely and started to rummage in her handbag. I noticed a grimace.

'Are you all right?'

'Yes,' she said. She flashed me a quick look from pale eyes. 'I banged my elbow last night.' She was using her left hand to pull out a black leather purse and begin extracting bank notes and laying them clumsily one by one on the desk.

Thinking of Christmas and presents, I said tentatively, 'Do you know somebody who collects old children's books?'

'Oh, it's for me,' she said. 'I mean, I love children's books, but mostly I just have paperbacks. To read. Only I remember I was given this book, just exactly like this one, when I was a child. I loved it.' For some reason, my question seemed to bother her. I glanced away casually for a moment, and then looked back and saw her hands falter. She said, 'Oh. Oh, I'm sorry, I spent ... I only have £60 here. I wonder, could you keep it for me? I'll come back.'

I tried to reassure her: 'I take credit cards.'

She spoke jerkily: 'Oh, I don't ... don't use a card much. I'd have to come back for the book, on Saturday, if it isn't too much trouble.'

I shrugged: 'Take it now. Bring me the balance any time. It's no problem.'

I ignored her whispered thanks, wrote out an invoice which acknowledged receipt of her money and recorded a balance owing, put that inside the front cover, slid the little volume gently into one of my plastic bags, and handed it over, saying, 'I used to love *Winnie-the-Pooh* too, when I was little.'

She gave me a wider smile and was gone without answering. I stopped smiling, turned off the lights and switched on the alarm system, and then followed her out the door. Before I went away, I took a few seconds to peer around my wheelie bin. The space where Ernie had left the old sleeping bag was empty.

Later, after I'd read Ben to sleep, I went on sitting in the darkened bedroom. Rush-hour traffic had stopped a little while ago; everybody who was going home from work had gone, and everybody who was out playing was still playing somewhere. I'd crammed supper, bath, reading, and even a long telephone discussion with Barnabas into the last three hours. Pat had phoned him to describe her discovery of me in my street-sweeper's disguise, and the two of them had agreed on a noisy Christmas dinner for the whole family in St Albans – which is what happens every year, basically because Pat is the only one of us with a kitchen big enough to cook a gigantic turkey, and a dining table large enough to feed it to nine or ten people. I'd confessed that I'd heard about this scheme and had no objections; but I was asking myself silently (as I sometimes do these days) whether I shouldn't grow up soon and move into a sensible little house where more than two people at a time could sit down to eat. I keep asking myself that.

When I heard the squeaking, I crept over to the window. A heavy covering of cloud had gathered after dusk, and it was very dark in the little gardens. Just enough light spilled from an uncurtained window somewhere to let me make out the lines of Ben's climbing frame. There was something – a black lump – on the seat of the little swing. A more familiar shape stood on the ground between the swing and the house: Mr Spock. He had a cat-fight in progress, or the promise of one. Spock isn't usually very territorial. I've seen him sprawl on the flat roof outside the window, watching a feline intruder with a benign eye. But he obviously didn't like this one. His back arched, and a song of challenge rose in the December darkness.

Something answered with a high screech.

Out in the street a car door slammed loudly, and Spock shot out of sight, reappeared with a thump on the flat roof, and sprinted past the bedroom window. The shape on the swing changed; the intruder dropped to the ground and slipped into shadows. A few seconds later, I caught another movement by the little storage shed. The thing swung over the edge of the roof, flattened out, and dived across the wall. It was all over. I crept away.

Mr Spock was waiting outside the kitchen window, crammed in again between the bars and the glass. When I opened the window for him, he sauntered through, thumped to the floor, and started to wash his back. Fighting is a dirty business.

I was pouring myself another coffee before it all came together: that thing hadn't really looked like a cat. And Ben had said ... There had been a monkey. I had almost forgotten it.

# Chapter 3

## The Monkey's Keeper

The monthly book fairs over on Russell Square end at six on the second day. Allow an hour for frantic packing, loading, cursing, and asking yourself what made you get into this insane way of earning a living, and then another twenty minutes (on a good evening) to drive home, and it would have been at least seven thirty on a Monday evening back in October, or maybe September, when I parked outside the shop, fell out of my van, threw a glance at the lights in the upstairs windows where Barnabas and Ben were waiting for me, and then noticed that I had a visitor. I looked again. Correction: two.

I could remember seeing him around during the summer, muffled in layers of greatcoats and scarves even in warm weather, lost in some private world as he inched along the street, or stood dead eyed on a corner: an old man, shuffling along a wall or squatting with his ragged grey rucksack on a spread-out newspaper, head bent, eyes vacant, hand out. A ghost of a voice would greet anybody who walked past him: 'Change? Got any change?'

There are people like that everywhere. Usually you try not to look at them. What made me notice this one was the monkey: a small, brown thing with a light face, big ears and round brown eyes, sitting on the man's rounded shoulder. It wore a harness with a piece of twine for a lead, and it normally sat motionless, hunched at the side of the man's head, pressing close against his neck. The begging usually went pretty well, naturally. People, especially people with children, stopped to look at the monkey and toss a coin on to the pavement. If it rolled out of the man's reach, the monkey would hop down and grab it with a quick, darting movement. Sometimes a child would try to touch the beast. Then the monkey would chatter and show its yellow teeth, and some adult would snatch the frightened child away and scold it.

So I recognized them both, the evening they visited me. Without any pleasure. I was bone-tired and they were huddled in the doorway of the shop. The monkey gave a sharp screech, and the man stirred.

'You'll have to go.' I jingled my keys suggestively.

26

The shape stirred, leaned sideways, and seemed to be having trouble getting to its feet. Without thinking, I reached out a hand to help him, but the monkey screamed and I pulled back. The bundle rose painfully, reached down for the bag and turned away.

I said quickly, 'Here.' There was a stray pound coin in the bottom of my pocket. I held it out and a hand in a fingerless woollen glove received it silently. I was tired, and I wanted to snap, 'Get yourself some food.' Pat would have. But what he did with my contribution was none of my business. I unlocked the door, propped it open, turned off the alarm and switched on all the lights, and then went out to my van for the first box.

It had been a long day, so I just dumped everything at the back of the shop until morning. I didn't bother to unload the folding wooden shelves, but I'd made some purchases of my own and packed them separately; that particular box I carried into the office. There was one book – a first English edition of Twain's *Innocents Abroad* – that I wanted to look at again, so I dug it out.

A racking cough made me look up. I hadn't locked the door, and they had followed me in. The man was standing very still, but his eyes moved over the bookshelves, the rows and rows of books. I walked slowly out of the office and stopped a few feet away.

'The shop is closed.'

The monkey stared at me. The man went on gazing at all the books.

I took a deep breath and opened my mouth again, but the grey man spoke first. 'I have a book.' His voice was light and hoarse.

I hesitated and settled for, 'You do?'

'Show yer.'

I wanted to suggest that he could come back some time when the shop was open, but I don't think that 'come back' or 'shop open' made much sense to him, and he was already squatting down and feeling slowly through whatever was inside the dirty rucksack, so I opted for polite patience. Eventually he edged something out of what looked like a bundle of rags: a book-shaped thing wrapped in a sheet of dirty newspaper. He seemed harmless, but I wasn't going to turn my back on either him or his monkey; so I moved forward reluctantly, let him put it into my hand and unfolded the clumsy wrappings.

When I saw what it was, I breathed in hard and asked slowly, 'Is this your book?'

He twitched. Affirmative. 'Pretty.'

It was pretty. And pretty rare, maybe: I'd never seen it before – a nineteenth-century octavo volume bound in old brown cloth, with lithographs of flowers, some coloured. It was in a nice, clean condition apart from a name written in ink on the flyleaf. I turned greedily to the title page: James Andrews, *Lessons in Flower Painting*. Then I turned back to one of the hand-coloured plates. It was beautiful. I was gob-smacked.

A grey hand was already reaching out for it.

I said, 'I could buy this book from you, if you like. Would you like to know how much it's worth?' I took a stab at it. 'Five hundred pounds. You could get yourself a room some-where...'

It was wrong of me, of course: reckless. It seemed impossible that he could have come by it honestly, and if I bought it I'd only be letting myself in for trouble. But just this once, trouble refused my offer. He shook his head vigorously, snatched the book from my hand and began to roll the paper awkwardly around it. His head went on shaking. No. No.

I wanted to say: 'But with so much money you could—' I stopped. Could what? Do what? A man like this? Even at the time, I didn't believe what I'd started to say. I was still strug-gling to think what I ought to do when the man, the monkey and the problem left the shop.

I just turned out the lights, set the alarm, kicked one of the boxes that was obstructing my way to the door, and left the place. He'd lose the book. He'd leave it somewhere in a fit of absent-mindedness, or lose interest, throw it away or give it to the monkey to play with.

And I told myself: too bad, I didn't care. And then for a couple of months I'd forgotten them.

# Chapter 4

## Howling

I stuck the sign on the shop door when I got back from the nursery walk – the one which claims that I'm only out for fifteen minutes – and went straight upstairs to make a pot of coffee and look at the catalogues that had turned up with the morning's mail: so I was in the sitting room, stretched out on the big settee, when the howling started. The noise made my heart thump. I clattered the mug down, scattered my notes, and ran to the window. Even there, the source of the sound was invisible, so I pulled the window up and leaned out.

The noises were coming from a greyish bundle that wavered by the brick wall of the abandoned service garage just up the street. The shrouded figure rocked violently back and forth on his heels. Anybody would guess that it was a man (though it could really have been anything on two legs) but I recognized the style: those layers of old coats and the blanket huddled like a shawl over the rounded shoulders. Today he had a brown knitted cap pulled down over his eyes and ears. I had time to see that the monkey wasn't with him. Still crazy, I thought, and getting worse. I shrank back and hid myself behind the curtains to watch.

The man staggered into the middle of the road and stopped, turning stiffly round and round like an old dog chasing its tail. A passing van brushed him, knocking him against one of the cars at the kerb. The driver braked and then accelerated. A keening sound rose in the narrow street, and my nerve broke. As I ran, I checked that my keys and phone were still in my pockets. Then I flung myself down the stairs and out the door.

The street was empty except for me and the crying man. I made myself walk steadily forward. He had collapsed on to the kerb and sat hunched between two of the parked cars. I crossed the road in front of him. His head was bowed as though he hadn't seen me, but the crying faltered.

'Are you hurt?'

For a moment I thought he wouldn't answer. Then, 'Yes. Hurt.'

'I'll help you,' I said. 'Where – how are you hurt?'

'Hurt,' he repeated, 'hurt, hurt...'

'Show me where?' I didn't believe that the van could really have injured him so badly – it had been a glancing blow, and he was well bundled up – but I waited for him to speak.

Instead, he struggled to his feet, clambered on

to the pavement, and turned toward the brick wall, gesturing.

The garage had been closed – abandoned – for so long that even the 'For Sale' sign on top of the crumbling wall was disintegrating. The wall itself had a fading painted notice which offered 'Service, Repairs, All Makes' and, beside it, a padlocked double gate where cars once drove in and out. The man edged towards a pile of weather-beaten plastic sacks which had recently started to be dumped there between the gateposts. The dustmen had been ignoring them: they only empty the wheelie bins now.

I caught up when he stopped near the heap. The keening started again. 'What?' I asked him urgently. 'What is it?'

No answer.

Puzzled, I looked for myself. He had been going through the rubbish. Several of the sacks were torn open. His rucksack lay on the ground, with the familiar old blue sleeping bag tied on with string. Maybe that was what he wanted. I edged past him and moved reluctantly towards the mess. Behind my back there was a kind of shriek, and then a hand fumbled at my arm, and a voice that sounded almost sane said urgently, 'No! No!'

Most of the bags there were gray with dust and street grime, but one looked as though it had been dumped more recently. He had torn a long rip in it. I was close enough now to catch the sweet smell, and reckless enough to look.

That smell ... Now I didn't need him to say anything. I grabbed him by the sleeve and pulled him away. As we stumbled across the road, he kept on wailing. I could see a shadowy figure in the big bay window of the nearest house pulling the curtains shut. Good for them. I hauled him on to the pavement, nudged him up against the iron railings for support, felt for my phone without letting go of him, and punched 999. Then I pulled myself together, switched the phone on, and tried the emergency services again. It took the first car a lifetime to arrive.

# Chapter 5

## Comings and Goings,
## Standing Very Still

My father marched into the shop, slammed the door with a vigour that set the bell clattering, and barked, 'What has happened?'

I stopped pretending to work and moved towards the tall, white-haired figure in the old-fashioned tweed coat and ancient striped muffler. 'Somebody found something in a pile of rubbish across the road.'

Barnabas glanced at me sharply, turned on his heel and went back outside. I followed.

Things had happened during the past two hours. By now, temporary barriers closed off both ends of the street and the police were keeping would-be sightseers back. Tapes stretched across the road in front of the garage, and most of the rest of the street was blocked by police vehicles. I had watched them break open the gates. Now a kind of tent-like white awning covered the entrance. The SOCO people in white boiler suits were still streaming in and out, and the whole road heaved with uniformed police who had been been shuffling inch by inch along the garage frontage, eyes down, searching the pavement and gutter, probably without much success, since I could remember seeing the street sweepers the previous afternoon; now they were working from one end of the road to the other, looking down into basement areas in front of the houses and examining the contents of all the wheelie bins, including mine. By now, half the population of North London was watching. To be honest, I'd been doing on-and-off watching myself, ever since I had handed the old man over to the first police officers who arrived and told them what he and I had seen.

Barnabas surveyed all this with a cold eye. 'Somebody has found something illegal over there. A corpse?'

I nodded, found myself picturing the thing again – and tried to stop. 'It was – an old man, Barnabas, one of the street people who hang

34

around. He was probably looking for food, or something to sell. When he found it, he ... flipped. I heard him howling, so I came out.'

My father looked at me out of the corner of his eye and said, 'And you...'

'Somebody had to, and nobody else was around.'

'Of course.' His tone was measured.

'I saw an arm. It looked like ... I still don't believe it. It was stinking. Some of those bags have been sitting over there for weeks.'

Barnabas said, 'Are you all right?'

I made myself think about something else and managed to nod.

After a moment he added, 'You'd think that at least some of these people would be at work.' He threw a cold glance at the crowd. 'Or in school.'

'Lunchtime?' I suggested, although it was past two o'clock. He snorted. 'Barnabas, it's freezing out here, I'm going back in.'

There is always something waiting to be done in the shop, even when police are keeping all my customers away. I settled at the desk again and tried to search a couple of websites for something to buy; but there was nothing so interesting that it could keep me from hearing the sounds in the street. I decided to try something less intellectual. Barnabas had come back. I could hear him in the shop.

'I'm going upstairs. I need to wash up from breakfast.'

'Tea, perhaps?'

'Give me ten minutes,' I said.

Barnabas grunted.

I stepped outside and hesitated. By this time, they were carrying grey bundles out of the canvas tent and loading them into the backs of two vans. Police work is full of painstaking routine – as I've been told by people who should know – and I found myself imagining the whole pile of garbage being searched routinely by dozens of gagging forensic scientists. *Stop that!* I distracted myself by noticing that the police were making door-to-door visits, presumably to ask whether anybody had seen anything; and two or three television crews had appeared behind the barriers at the end of the road. Some senior officer would probably make a statement. And I would see him, even see the front of my shop, on the box during the London evening news. Goody.

I stopped in the bedroom long enough to straighten the beds; Mr Spock came in to lay claim to my duvet for the balance of the day. Then I drifted into the kitchen. There was a small mug's worth of warm coffee left in the machine. I poured it out and was just adding a splash of milk when I happened to glance through the window.

The monkey was sitting hunched on the flat roof five feet away with its eyes shut. It still wore the old harness that I remembered, with what looked like a little address tag dangling from the buckle. There was no doubting whose monkey it was. It struck me that it wasn't very well; I could see its ribs through the thin fur, see its heart beating. I put the milk bottle down slowly, but it heard something and rose on its hind legs, staring. I froze. It dropped on to all fours and moved out of sight.

Call the RSPCA.

If they catch it, they won't give it back to the old man; they'll take it and put it in a refuge.

They could put the old man in a refuge too.

Well, he's probably been in and out of shelters for years. Maybe he needs the monkey, and it probably needs him.

You're mad! It's hungry and cold, and he can't even look after himself. It ought to be in a warm place with other monkeys.

I chose to ignore the voice of common sense.

There was a last banana going brown in the fruit bowl. I grabbed it and inched the window up. The little animal was still at the far end of the flat roof, which made me think I'd been right about its condition. I broke off the end of the banana and tossed it toward him – or her. It flinched. I threw a larger piece close to the first, then two more, nearer the window. Finally, I balanced a big lump on the frame, dropped two smaller bits on the work counter, and placed the last piece on the floor underneath. Then I drifted sideways, out of its line of sight, and froze. After a long time something scratched on the window ledge.

Barnabas thundered up the stairs, burst into the flat and found me leaning against the closed kitchen door, catching my breath. His look of anxiety changed to annoyance and he snapped, 'What in the blazes is going on up here?' He was answered by the sound of crashing and splintering from the other side of the door, and threw me one of his raised-eyebrows looks.

'A monkey,' I said tersely. It felt as though I'd been listening to sounds of destruction for hours, and I wasn't surprised that the crashing and banging had penetrated downstairs.

'A monkey,' Barnabas repeated.

'I lured it inside with a banana and slammed the window, and then it panicked and started screaming and jumping around, and there were some dirty plates on the counter, and my coffee mug and – this and that. It jumped on to the fridge. You remember that big glass bowl I keep up there? You probably heard that smashing. I thought it would be better if I left it to calm down.'

'You caught a monkey,' Barnabas said. It's not often that my father is surprised into repetitiveness.

I tried to tell him about the old man and his runaway pet. Most of my attention was on the invisible kitchen, where it had gone horribly quiet.

'You will regret your actions,' my father prophesied. 'I think we need to restrain it.'

I thought there probably wasn't much more damage that it could possibly do, but I nodded. 'It's wearing a harness. I was thinking that I could catch it by that and put it in the cat carrier. You know – that metal mesh thing I use when I take Mr Spock to the vet? This monkey is cat-sized.'

My father shrugged. 'Good. But we'll need a small blanket, or a very large bath towel. And I strongly recommend that you line the bottom of the carrier with newspapers. Go and get it. I shall take the towel and go in; you must shut the door behind me and prevent the monkey from slipping out.'

But when I approached with the cat carrier, my nose took control and led me, horrified, inside. I hadn't known that a terrified monkey will react like a terrified human being. This monkey threw something at me and I fled. In my absence, it smeared its faeces over the table and the counters, the cooker top and the shards of glass on the floor.

It was sitting on top of one of the wall cupboards, arms and tail wrapped around its body, trembling.

'You're not supposed to be in here,' my father observed quietly. 'Put the carrier down on the table and leave the top open. Stand back.'

I obeyed.

My father retrieved the floor mop from behind the door and raised the head to monkey level. The animal remained frozen. He edged it behind the monkey's body and drew it forward very gently, and in something like a second and a half the monkey screamed and hurtled through the air to the floor, Barnabas dropped the towel over it, drew back a corner from the struggling body, made a lightning grab and caught it by the back of the neck, pulled one of its arms behind its back, and then lifted it into the carrier. I slammed the lid. Barnabas fastened it. We looked at each other.

I said, 'I'd better go out and buy more cleaner and some disinfectant.'

'In a minute,' he said. 'Personally, I could use a drink. And it wouldn't hurt to leave the animal alone in here until it calms down. Wait a minute.' He spread the big towel over the pet carrier.

'Are you all right?' I asked guiltily. My father's heart is not strong, though most of the time these days I don't worry about it often.

'Entirely. However, a whiskey would be pleasant.'

'Me too,' I said. 'How did you learn to catch monkeys?'

'In Marrakech, just after the war,' he said. 'I'll tell you the story another time.'

We went into the sitting room, where I keep a bottle of my father's Irish whiskey in the sideboard. Five minutes and about a double measure later my father gave me a look.

'Explain.'

I did my best.

My father said, 'I see,' in the tone of a man who has just decided that his daughter might possibly be demonstrating some tiny method in her madness. 'You've seen the monkey with the old man? You're sure? Did he have it with him today when...?'

'No! No, and I think it's been hanging around on its own for the last day or so. Mr Spock had a cat fight with it last night.' I made a connection: 'I think the old man has been camping in the space behind my rubbish bin, and the monkey must have got away some time while he was asleep.'

'It will be upset,' Barnabas assured me. 'Monkeys are quite dangerous when they panic, you know, not unlike humans. Are you sure you're in one piece? If you have any scratches or nips, you must get a tetanus shot this afternoon. And you mustn't let Ben go anywhere near it: they often dislike children.'

'And cats,' I said gloomily. This monkey was problematical. 'Barnabas, I have to clean up the kitchen right away. After that I'll try to find out where the old man is and let him know the monkey's safe.'

'According to your description,' Barnabas began. And stopped. 'You can but try. Go and buy what you need. I shall make a telephone call. By the time you get back, the beast may have calmed down enough to allow you back into the kitchen.'

'It's shut up in a cage,' I pointed out forcefully.

'Its voice is not. Nor the – well, smell.'

'Will you go back down to the shop for a while?' I suggested.

Barnabas looked at me, obviously amused. 'In the hour since I arrived, we've had one customer, a lady wishing to return a book. There was a receipt of ours inside, so I agreed, although she couldn't explain what was wrong with it. I offered her a cheque for the refund, but she demanded cash. Which reminds me that we will need more change. You might extend your shopping trip as far as the bank.'

'Cash?' I hesitated, guessing that I knew the answer to the question but asking it anyway: 'Who was it? Why did she want a refund?'

'I've seen her before,' Barnabas assured me. 'She didn't say why she wanted to return it. *Winnie-the-Pooh*. The name on the receipt was – Asher? Shy woman. She had a black eye.'

'Acker?' I suggested.

Barnabas thought about it briefly and nodded.

I gave up on the problem and headed for the door.

Then I thought of something. 'What do they eat?'

Barnabas guessed who I meant and said, 'Fresh fruit and vegetables of all kinds. Peanuts in the shell, maybe? But don't go overboard: I may have thought of something.'

# Chapter 6

## Clearing Up

When I got downstairs, I found that the street
had been opened to traffic and the television
crews were gone, though the police weren't:
they now had a huge white van parked outside
the garage. My watch said that it was after
three. I'd need to move fast if I was going to
pick Ben up at the usual time, so I moved fast.

Returning, I stopped just across the road to
check the situation. I could see Barnabas in the
sitting room, standing by the window with the
telephone pressed to his ear. I ducked into the
shop so that I too could use a phone in privacy
to ring the local police station – a number
which is engraved on my memory through long
use. My old friend, Paul Grant, was no longer
stationed there, so I was going to have to talk
persuasively to a stranger. When a harassed
voice answered, I asked to speak to someone
about the 'incident' in George Street. There'd
be an incident room by now.

The second voice was a woman's. I took a
deep breath and plunged in. 'This is Dido

Hoare. I'm the one who reported what happened in George Street this morning. The thing is, the old man who found the – who found it: I saw him being driven away in a police car. Is he over there? I have something that belongs to him, and I want to let him know that it's safe.'

I was only slightly surprised when she checked the spelling of my name twice and then asked for my phone number, but failed to take a message. I dredged up a name from my memory, asked to be put on to Superintendent Colley, and was told that he had gone to another area last August. Right. I left the number of my mobile and hung up to think about it. In the end, I headed upstairs to my own rubbish tip.

At the head of the stairs I met a sinister silence. There was no sign of my father, but Mr Spock was glaring from the bedroom doorway. I ignored him and opened the kitchen door, releasing a wave of unspeakable smells. Spock's hair rose on end, and mine tried to. Barnabas was standing by the table, apparently oblivious to the horror. He said quietly, 'It's calming down. I've given it a section of orange.'

I enquired about coming in to clear up.

'Or perhaps I should do it?' Barnabas said. I've heard him sound more enthusiastic. 'I imagine that it's more used to a man.'

I said, 'But Ben...'

'We must try to get the animal away before Ben comes home.'

44

I caught the tone and asked, 'What have you done?'

'I have phoned Mr Stanley. My upstairs neighbour?' I knew who he meant perfectly well and waited. 'At one time he kept a parrot, but it died. He still possesses a large and luxurious cage.'

I felt a rush of relief. 'You can borrow it?'

'Better still, Mr Stanley has offered to house the animal pro tem. He seemed to welcome the idea: in fact, it was he who suggested it. I believe he may be a little lonely, and the idea of a monkey might have tickled his fancy.'

'At least we don't have to feel guilty about landing him with this thing,' I said nastily. 'You did warn him? Is he sure he wants to take on a kind of baby with teeth?'

'I warned him extensively,' my father said. 'He is expecting you to drop it and me off before you go to pick up Ben at nursery. So?'

'So,' I agreed. It would be tight, but I hoped that after I'd cleared up the disaster zone there would be nothing more to worry about, and I could relax and play with Ben, or even think about selling some books soon. I decided to move the cat carrier out into the quiet of the landing, no matter what Barnabas and the monkey said about it, clear the kitchen and maybe give myself enough time to wash my hands and brush my hair before I had to leave. I could use some time to think calmly about what to do, too. But in fact it took me a couple

45

of hours and a face on the television screen for that.

I'd been watching the six o'clock news, waiting for an item about the finding of a body in Islington, wondering whether anybody had anything to say by now. The uniformed inspector who had spoken to the reporter mentioned a woman's body. He said that investigations were proceeding. The camera slid over a crowd of onlookers at the barrier and swept the street, moved rapidly past the front of the shop, and focused on the awning over the garage entrance. The shot had been full of people, but the one who caught my attention was standing inside the barrier, ignoring both the crime scene and the TV crew while he talked intently to someone beside him. I didn't recognize the second man, but the height, the hawk-like nose and the red hair of the first made him unmistakable. It was strange to find him there. The inspector was going on in the foreground with the usual phrases. Terrible crime. All our resources. Anybody who has any information. After he had finished, they replayed the same loop of tape, and the redheaded man and his companion reappeared. I switched off when the item was finished; and after I'd made a phone call and left a message on the answering machine of the man with the red hair, I went to set out Ben's meal in the spotless, lemony-smelling, strangely tidy kitchen.

Dinnertime conversation was interrupted by

the phone. I left Ben to finish his spaghetti while I ran to answer it.

*'Dido! Are you all right?'* It was Pat's voice, very loud. Someone else had seen the reports.

I said, 'Yes, of course,' and gave her an edited version of events before I went back to Ben.

It was nearly an hour before he phoned at last.

'Dido! I nearly dropped in on you a couple of hours ago.'

I said, 'I know: I saw you on television.'

Strangely, that produced a silence. Then, 'Damn. Was I..?'

I made a guess and said, 'Not very. There was a big crowd, and you weren't very near the camera, so I don't think most people would have noticed you. Was that another reporter you were talking to?'

He hesitated. 'One of my police contacts. Somebody phoned the paper this morning and told us that an old man had found a body in a rubbish sack in "trendy George Street, Islington". It sounded as though it could be connected with my current project, so I got on to this man and arranged to meet him over there. I didn't really want to advertise the fact that I know him.'

I had known Chris Kennedy for more than a year. He is an investigative journalist working for one of the broadsheet newspapers. I tried to focus on the 'project' without being distracted by the idea that if my shop is really in a trendy area, I could probably raise my prices.

47

'Chris, I know the old man. I mean, I've talked to him before today. I was here when he found it and I called the police.' I found myself remembering everything again and had to stop and concentrate.

'I've been ringing since I picked up your message, but I keep getting either the machine in the shop, or a busy signal upstairs. I'm going to come over, all right?'

More than all right: but I said, 'Yes, but will you do something first? Or try? I need to speak to the old man who discovered the body, and I don't know where they've taken him. I can't get anywhere with the police. I want to tell him that I've found something that belongs to him, and I'll keep it safe.'

'I could probably get a message through. They'll still be talking to him somewhere. If he has no fixed address, they'll want to hang on to him for a while.'

I told him that he didn't understand, that being interviewed might be beyond this particular witness's capacity. Then I explained a little.

Chris managed not to say the wrong thing, which is one of the reasons why I like him so much. 'All right, I'll make a phone call and see if I can get a message passed on to him. Will you be there?'

'For the foreseeable future,' I said.

'In case I can do it, what do you want to tell him?'

'Just that his monkey is safe.'

'Monkey – ?'

'Monkey as in long tail, wild, "ook ook".'

I heard a suppressed laugh. He said, 'Speak to you soon,' and hung up. I stood holding the receiver, thinking back over the conversation. Something still needed explaining. I rang back, but this time I got a busy signal and gave up.

# Chapter 7

## Missing Things

It was almost ten o'clock when the doorbell rang. I went down, and Kennedy thrust a big pot of pink poinsettia into my hands. I said, 'Hello.' He nodded and scowled. I asked him whether he was coming in. He nodded again. I asked myself what was going on.

As I was turning to lead the way, he grabbed my arm. 'Wait: who's up there?'

'Ben. Asleep. Why?'

'Not Barnabas? Look, I have to talk to you.'

I looked at him in surprise. 'I took him home hours ago.' I didn't mention the monkey. 'What's wrong?'

Chris Kennedy is a tall man; but if I stand two steps up I can look straight into his eyes. Superficially, he seemed no different from, say, the previous Saturday when we'd had dinner: spiky red hair, hazel eyes, the beaky nose, black leather jacket: but he was radiating an emotion that I couldn't quite read.

I said slowly, 'You'd better tell me what's wrong, and it's warmer upstairs.'

His smile was a little hesitant. He nodded. I opened my mouth, closed it again, and led the way up into the kitchen, which still smelled of citrus air freshener, and positioned the poinsettia in the middle of the table.

'Did you find out about the old man? I wish I knew his name, it seems silly calling him "the old man" all the time.'

'Harold Terence Lewis. Sometimes answers to "Harry".'

That sounded promising. 'Who is he?'

'He's nobody,' Chris said. Now I could hear the rasp in his voice. 'The police found that name on a prescription form in his pocket. He was on their books: petty theft, begging, drunkenness. He's been living homeless in this area for at least the past three years. Somebody said he's a "character", which means they think he's a nuisance but harmless. They pick him up and deliver him to a shelter every so often, but he doesn't stay. Actually, they've pretty well given up because he refuses to be parted from his monkey. St Mungo's takes dogs, but even they draw the line at monkeys. He's supposed to be on medication, but of course he doesn't take it. They found a stockpile of pills in his bag.'

I said, 'But where is he now?'

'When they couldn't get any sense out of him, they brought a doctor in to tell them that they probably weren't going to. So they put him into a side room and told him to sit there and they'd find him a bed somewhere. One of the clerks did start ringing around, and then when she went to take him a cup of tea she discovered that he'd walked out, like the Invisible Man. They may be wondering if he's less harmless than they'd assumed.'

'He didn't tell them anything useful?'

Chris shrugged. 'They don't think he's capable of saying anything sensible, not even when he's calm. You were right: they think he found it by sheer chance because he just happened to be poking around in the wrong place.'

'He's more lucid at some times than others.'

Chris looked at me. 'How do you figure that?'

I reminded him that I'd seen the old man around before today – old, crazy Harry Lewis, if that was really his name. I even told him about the flower book.

'He's probably been living out of dustbins for years. If he ever knew anything about it, which isn't likely...'

'If he did, it would have escaped him by now.' Like the monkey, it seemed. Would he even remember the monkey? Mr Stanley might have a long-term house guest.

I was still thinking nervously about that problem when Chris said, 'When I mentioned your name, they knew it. They'll be sending some-body around to talk to you tomorrow.'

'They've talked to me already. I'm the one who called them when he found it. I already made a statement.' Then something Chris had said hit me. 'You said, "found things". It was a body, wasn't it?'

He hesitated. 'What he found were some parts of a body: the torso, a left arm. The head is is missing, and the legs and right arm. It was a young girl, a teenager.'

I turned and stared at the wall. He had just explained my impression that what I'd seen of the corpse had been all wrong – the wrong size, the wrong shape. I couldn't stop seeing the rot-ting arm lying on top of some dirty black cloth, hand flexed, fingers curled, as though it – she – had been trying to hold on to something which had got away.

'Dido – all right?'

I said, 'Yes.'

He wrapped his arms around me, and I pushed my face into his sweater because I wanted to cry and didn't want to waken Ben. After a while he lowered his chin and rested it on top of my head, and his arms tightened.

I said, 'Sorry. I'm tired. Sorry.' My voice struggled to remain level.

He said, 'It's all right, I'm crying too.' But when I pulled back and looked, he seemed angry and there were certainly no tears.

'Who is she? Was she? Do they know?'

'Her fingerprints aren't on record, and it may take them some time to find out. They say she was between fourteen and eighteen years old. They're going through piles of missing persons forms, and they'll appeal for information on television tonight. I'd like to watch the news bulletins, if you don't mind. It will be all over the papers in the morning.'

There was nothing I could say, so I made some fresh coffee, and we sat in the front room drinking it and watching the reports of the murder, flicking between three channels. Afterwards we exchanged all the facts we knew and got nowhere. Eventually we gave up.

It was after midnight when he stirred, got to his feet, and said, 'Take care.'

'Will you phone and tell me if you can find out where he is?'

'Did you hear me? I said, take care.'

'I always take care.'

'I mean it! Humour me. Do I have to say, "Sex-crazed lunatic serial killer operating in your neighbourhood?" I'm just guessing, of course.'

I almost laughed. Sometimes Chris's style can be more tabloid than broadsheet. 'Why "serial killer"? You mean there've been others?'

He looked away. 'They think so. Maybe three more.'

'I can't remember hearing about them.'

'There've been a few news items on inside pages. The other bodies weren't mutilated, just

53

dumped in the canal or on waste ground over behind King's Cross. But there are similarities. Dido, I've promised not to talk about this yet.'

I said slowly, 'If you like, I'll even keep the alarm set on the stairs as well as in the shop.' It was something that I don't usually bother with. I said it as a joke and then started to think that I meant it.

'And don't talk to strangers,' he said, and grinned at last.

I listened to his footsteps on the stairs, listened to the street door opening and closing softly, and the engine of his old Jaguar starting up and moving away. When it was quiet again I began to wonder where old Mr Lewis was spending this cold night; and while I was brushing my teeth I decided that in the morning I'd go for a walk.

# Chapter 8

## Walkabout

I delivered Ben to nursery on time, watched him skip inside, and then shoved my cold hands into the pockets of my coat and turned away.

I started by walking up the Essex Road, staring into doorways and even walking in and out of a couple of narrow passageways that I found between some of the shops and terraces. By the time I'd turned back and done the same thing on the western side, I was beginning to understand that this was a job for an army.

At Islington Green I sat down on a bench to reconsider, pulled out my mobile and rang Barnabas.

'Fine,' I assured him in response to the usual questions, 'I'm fine. How are you, how is the monkey? And especially how is Mr Stanley?'

'We are all flourishing,' my father said. Was it my imagination, or could I hear something odd in his voice? I asked about it.

'The monkey dislikes me,' he said. 'Probably it was the towel. On the other hand, he and Mr Stanley may be coming to an arrangement. It appears that Mr Stanley is entranced: love at first sight. Some relationships are beyond comprehension.'

I wondered fleetingly whether he was suggesting anything but postponed this line of thought because I had a favour to ask.

'Barnabas, did you see something on the news last night about that business down here?'

'I was upstairs for most of the time. But I have been listening to Radio 4 this morning.'

A heavy silence followed.

I took a breath. 'Well, I have to be out of the shop for part of the time today – I have some errands. Could you open up and hang on until I'm back?'

'What errands?'

'I'm looking for the old man.'

'The radio said that the police were not holding him.'

'Actually, he walked out while their backs were turned.'

'Indeed?' I could hear his hesitation. Perhaps he was trying to be tactful. 'I don't think they mentioned that.'

I grimaced. 'Chris told me.'

Barnabas avoided commenting. He is gradually coming to accept that Kennedy and I are friends and that I don't consider this any of his business. He settled for, 'You're looking for him? So are the police, I presume.'

'Not very hard. They think that he found the body accidentally, and he obviously can't tell them much, if he even remembers it. You certainly couldn't use him as a witness. They've probably asked the local patrols to keep an eye open for him.'

'And why are you bothering?'

I said, 'He's probably going to try to avoid the uniforms, considering how he panicked yesterday, but I don't suppose I'd scare him. I ought to tell him that his monkey is safe.'

'Is that all?' my father enquired, suspiciously.

I remained calm and said innocently, 'What else? It's his monkey, even if Mr Stanley likes it.'

'Yes, yes, yes,' Barnabas said impatiently, 'but...' He changed tack. 'So what, precisely, is

56

happening there this morning?'

I said meekly, 'I'm just walking around this area, because he's obviously dossing locally. I've put up a "closed" sign on the door of the shop, but this is Friday, and it seems a shame.' This was unfair pressure: Fridays are one of our busier days, especially coming up to Christmas. 'Besides, there's something else. While you're here, could you have a look online, and at that shelf of old auction catalogues, and see whether you can find out anything about a Victorian octavo called *Lessons in Flower Painting* by Andrews – James Andrews? The old man showed me a copy a few months ago. It looked fairly valuable, and I think it must be rare. Maybe we could sell it for him.'

'It doesn't ring a bell,' my father admitted. 'He owns this book?'

I temporized by saying that he'd been carrying it around in his rucksack a couple of months ago, though that was no guarantee he still had it or that he'd ever actually owned it.

'And you are merely intending to talk to him about the book and his monkey?' my father persisted. 'That's all?'

I said innocently, 'Barnabas, I should. He must be very worried about his pet, and he isn't well, and they say it's going to be a long, hard winter.'

'I'll be there in half an hour,' my father said, postponing an argument though probably only for the moment – I knew that dry tone well. If

I'd really wanted to escape an inquisition, I should have thought up a story.

It was too cold to sit for more than a few minutes. I probably ought to have gone on toward the tube station, where there is a promising area of shops, little restaurants, offices, and construction sites, but it was too much. Instead, I turned back and dived into the area between Upper Street and the Essex Road. I was trying to be conscientious, so I took the time to weave back and forth above the Green, passing along the fronts of some big, well-kept Victorian houses. I cut into St Mary's churchyard hopefully.

A couple of years ago, when I'd gone there looking for somebody I'd believed was another homeless man, I'd found a bunch of people sitting drinking on the benches around the edge of a sunken rose garden at the front of the old graveyard. It was a regular place for hanging out. There was some kind of soup kitchen in the basement of the church, which was probably why; but the man I was looking for hadn't been there. Today the churchyard was completely deserted. I stood on a path in the cold light and looked across the neatly trimmed brown grass. The emptiness wasn't surprising, considering the temperature, but I felt a pang of disappointment: this business had somehow grown in a way that was hard to explain.

I'd never known any people like Harry Lewis. I grew up in Oxford, where my father taught

English. We lived in a vast Victorian house in North Oxford, surrounded by academics and books, and my sister and I went to the best girls' school in the city. From there I got a place at Somerville College. Everything was simple. If there was a problem I couldn't handle, somebody was always there to help. I took it for granted. And if somebody like Lewis ever passed me in the street, I wouldn't have dared to look at him. The crime rate in Oxford is low, as British cities go; but that doesn't mean bad things never happen, or that there's no poverty. But when you're young, you think that everybody lives more or less the way you do.

After I took my degree I went over to New York with an American friend from college. We got jobs in the publishing firm where her sister worked, and shared an apartment near Columbia and went around with her friends, and for a while I saw and did things that I'd never known before – until my mother died and I came home. When Barnabas moved to London, I came too because by now he was nearly seventy. And while I was working in an antiquarian bookshop in Bloomsbury I met a beautiful, crooked man who married me and dumped me and gave me Ben before he was killed. It was probably Davey more than anyone else who finally opened my eyes. Nowadays they are open so wide that I can find myself looking at things too hard and being unable to ignore what I see.

I turned my back to the cold wind and started

down one of the paths that cross the old graveyard, still comparing my life to the existence of
an invisible man who lived by scavenging in
dustbins: human dirt. So I meant to give him
back his monkey.

But apparently not today. Even wearing a
couple of oversized coats, he couldn't possibly
be sitting around here. I ought to be looking in
sheltered places. I circled the church, walked
into the narrow street behind it and ducked
through the passageway that brought me out
opposite the end of my own road. I plunged into
George Street, stopped long enough to check
the handy triangular space beside Dido Hoare ~
Antiquarian Books and Prints, and saw that
Barnabas hadn't yet arrived. The police tape
was flapping in the hard wind, the tent-like
structure still covered the gate, and the big van
was sitting at the kerb but there were no signs
of police this morning.

About a hundred and fifty years ago, a speculative builder put up two rows of semi-detached
villas along the northern end of George Street.
They were shabby and crumbling when I first
came to the shop; but now the whole area has
been gentrified and they are nice, expensive
homes again with satellite dishes on the roofs
and big, newish cars parked in the street. I
trudged up one side and down the other, looking through the iron railings of all the houses as
I passed, expecting nothing.

Down at the bottom of the street, Mrs Acker

and someone else came around the corner and walked toward me. Her companion was a middle-aged man, solidly built. His greying hair was cut very short, and he wore a dark-blue fleece jacket, black trousers and heavy black shoes. From the way that she clung to his arm and trotted at his side, I could see that I was about to meet Mr Acker.

I tried to catch her eye, because I wanted to ask what was wrong with the book and tell her – when she apologized for the trouble – that it was quite all right, and to let me know if she changed her mind. But her eyes slid over my face without a flicker of recognition. His took me in casually. As we met in front of the shop, Mrs Acker passed close enough for me to touch her, but her averted face said that she had never seen me before in her life. And Barnabas had been right: she had a black eye. When they had passed, I turned around.

They stopped too. He said something, and she stood waiting while he crossed the road and rapped on the big rear door of the police van. As it opened, I could hear greetings and the casual tones of different voices, but no distinct words. A moment later, Acker raised his hand in a half salute and recrossed the road. The door of the van banged, and the Ackers continued on their way, turning in through the gate of a house halfway up the street.

Mrs Acker's escort had obviously spoken to some people whom he knew. It seemed to explain the style of his clothing: he was wearing parts of a uniform, because Mr Acker was also a policeman – an off-duty policeman. It didn't explain why Mrs Acker had decided to ignore me.

I turned into the cross street, and left at the next corner. The blind rear wall of the garage filled the middle of this street on the west side. The houses along there are terraced, a decade or two newer than in my street, and smaller. I trudged past them towards the sixties council estate at the far end, and stopped across the road while I considered the faces of the six-storey blocks and looked down the narrow roadway running between two of them. And I admitted defeat. Anything could be going on over there, but I couldn't search the whole place. I crossed the road half-heartedly and wandered around the perimeter, but it was as useless as I'd foreseen. I'm pigheaded, but not crazy, and after a moment I turned away.

When I reached the shop, shivering and red-nosed, I found Barnabas discussing an eighteenth-century edition of More's *Utopia* with a meek-looking man whom I didn't recognize. My father was listing a series of small faults at great length, so I understood that the stranger was trying to sell it to us. I crept past them into the office and stared bleakly at the old kettle on top of the filing cabinet. There was probably a little instant coffee left in the bottom of the jar.

As I hesitated, Barnabas appeared, looking

for the cheque book. 'One minute more,' he said.

I nodded and decided I'd just lean on the radiator and enjoy the warmth for the moment. Deal completed, Barnabas deposited his purchase on the desk beside Mrs Acker's *Winnie-the-Pooh*. They both had to be checked before they were shelved.

'Well?'

I sneezed. 'Too cold.'

'Isn't it also the wrong time of day?' Barnabas enquired. 'People might be more generous in the evening, out around the pubs and restaurants?'

Well, probably. I was perfectly ready to concede that it was too bright, too early, and especially too cold out there to persist. My tingling toes and fingers all said so.

'I'd better go upstairs and get a hot drink,' I admitted. 'Anything urgent?'

'No, no,' Barnabas said. 'Not for a few minutes. Go.'

I was just walking out the door when he called, 'A woman rang from the police station. There was no message. Also Mr Kennedy. He said he'll try again this afternoon.'

I waved an acknowledgement without stopping, went into the flat, turned up the central heating, boiled the kettle, and decided that I should take a hot bath. By the time I was emerging from the steam, Barnabas had come upstairs and was in the process of making some of his dubious, cool tea.

I said I'd have mine black with sugar. 'And I'll come downstairs as soon as I'm dressed,' I offered guiltily. 'You're right, I've wasted the morning. I'll just have to hope he turns up.'

'If he has any sense at all, he'll be in some kind of shelter today.'

I agreed doubtfully. Then I remembered. 'Chris didn't say what he wanted?'

'No, but he did want something,' Barnabas assured me.

I changed the subject quickly. 'How is Mr Stanley this morning?'

'I popped in upstairs for a few seconds,' Barnabas reported. 'He was so busy that his television set was turned off. He says that the monkey is in fact paper trained.'

Yes?

# Chapter 9

### Haystack and Needle

I'd finished my walkabout with a clearer picture of my neighbourhood, especially its more obscure corners – nothing more useful than that.

Barnabas left for the British Library to order

up a couple of books, and I had the shop to myself. There would be a lull before the late-afternoon customers started to arrive: we stay open until seven on December Fridays. So I stared vaguely through the glass of the door at the people passing in the street and tried to think about what I'd seen. The review turned into daydreaming. I pulled myself together and started clearing the desk.

First there was the *Utopia* that Barnabas had just bought. Despite what I'd overheard, there were no serious problems. I pencilled a price and the words 'Excellent condition' on the flyleaf. Then there was the A. A. Milne, Mrs Acker's mysterious reject. When I opened the cover, I found the original bill there with '£60 returned, sale cancelled' scribbled in my father's handwriting. I pulled that out and filed it. Then I leafed through the volume, but it seemed to be in exactly the same condition as when I'd sold it. She had seemed so pleased – I'd been sure it had made her happy. How could it worry her to owe me £25? I thought about that and then, instead of reshelving the book, put it into the bottom drawer of the desk which doubles as my personal, unofficial, 'Problem Pending' box. I found the old card file which held customer names and addresses from the time before Ernie had computerized our lists; but I'd never mailed her a book or a catalogue. I wound up scowling at the ceiling. I'd just have to go out and stop her, next time she passed.

The old man might easily wander past, too, and I'd catch him the same way. There had never been much point looking for him in an area which had more empty buildings, back doors and little triangular spaces than I'd ever before imagined. I'd wasted my time looking for a needle in a haystack, and dismantling the haystack straw by straw could take days. If I really wanted that particular needle, I'd have to try another approach. A magnet might do the trick – something to attract the needle to me.

I found the digital camera in a drawer, bundled myself into my jacket, found the sign that says 'Back in Half an Hour' and stuck it on the door. My purple van was still parked two streets over, where I'd had to move it when the street had been closed off: I sprinted all the way. Then I used up the first twenty minutes of my promised half hour creeping through heavy traffic to the house on Crouch Hill where my father lives. The top doorbell was marked simply 'STANLEY'. I pushed it, listened to footsteps slowly descending the stairs, and fixed a carefree smile on my face as they reached the entrance hall and I got ready to explain that I was here to visit the monkey.

Mr Stanley opened the door on the chain, peered through the crack and recognized me. The chain clattered down.

'Miss Hoare? Is something wrong?'

I assured him that everything was fine and followed him up the wide flight of stairs to his flat.

Mr Stanley is a retired civil servant, three or four years younger than my father but balding, round-shouldered, more rumpled, less vigorous. He led me down a short passage and into his sitting room. As we approached the door, I caught the familiar whiff.

'Come in quietly. Please don't make any sudden movements, he's still very nervous. If you'll sit down, I'll make a cup of tea. I'm sure you'll be all right.'

I nodded obediently and followed him into a room that was crowded with heavy wine-coloured moquette furniture and dusty flowered curtains. A big birdcage stood on a table beneath the window. It was now a monkey cage, just as Barnabas had reported. The monkey and I looked at each other suspiciously. It began a loud chatter and leapt to a perch at the top of the cage. I ignored it and settled in the armchair.

Mr Stanley said, 'Now, Charlie!' and to my amazement the monkey fell silent, settled on its haunches and stared. Mr Stanley said, 'Good boy, Charlie. I call him "Charlie",' and, 'The kettle had just boiled when you came.' He vanished. The monkey and I ignored one other until our host reappeared with a tray: teapot and jug, sugar bowl, two cups, and a plate of plain digestive biscuits. The monkey stood to attention.

'Would you like to give him a piece of biscuit?' Mr Stanley suggested. 'Be careful you don't put your fingers into the cage.'

I got slowly to my feet, took half a digestive from the plate, and sauntered over, holding it out in front of me as a peace offering. The monkey eyed it.

I said, 'Good boy, Charlie,' and inserted the biscuit between two bars. A strong hand reached out and twitched it from my fingers. My own hand jerked back almost as quickly and I retreated.

'Very good!' my host beamed. 'You see? He's learning.' He was so pleased that he made no objection when I told him that I wanted to take Charlie's photograph. I promised that Barnabas would bring him a copy, switched off the flash so as not to frighten the animal, and took a couple of shots in the light from the window. Then I finished my tea and explained that I had to pick Ben up. It wasn't four o'clock yet, but I had one other errand to complete before Barnabas returned and caught me at it. I stopped illegally outside the stationers to buy a new colour cartridge for the printer. By the time that the Nepalese bell tinkled and I looked up to find my father in the doorway, I had just pulled a dozen sheets of paper from the printer tray and was bundling them into a file holder. If I waterproofed each of them with a piece of the plastic food wrap from the roll in the kitchen drawer, I could tape them to lamp posts. The home-made signs that you see in the street usually advertise for lost cats or dogs. Mine read, 'FOUND' with the monkey's portrait beneath. Below that, I'd printed 'WILL THE OWNER PLEASE ASK AT THE BOOK SHOP IN GEORGE STREET'. Presumably Mr Lewis could read; if not, he would ask somebody about it as soon as he saw the picture. I was counting on it. This was my magnet, the best chance to end the monkey business.

So I excused myself to Barnabas, who called out behind my back – something which started, 'Don't forget that message...' – as I fled upstairs with the folder and a roll of packing tape. On my way to the nursery, I fly-posted George Street and the road bordering on the council estate. Ben and I put up the rest in the cross street during our walk back. This raised a lot of questions, and I was so busy answering him that the message I'd been given twice that day slipped my mind until an hour later when I went into the sitting room and noticed the red light flashing on the answering machine.

# Chapter 10

## Visitors

We were downstairs by nine o'clock on Saturday morning, which gave me time to clear up; that seemed only tactful, considering that as soon as he got here I was going to have to tell Barnabas I had arranged to take lunchtime off on one of the busiest days of the year. Ben was kneeling up on the desk chair, engrossed in the little computer game that Ernie had installed for times like this; I was checking the shelves while I kept a lookout for Barnabas, as well as for Ernie, who was also due pretty soon (although his arrival can depend on what he's been up to the night before and with whom) and Chris Kennedy. When we'd finally managed to speak, last night, he had merely said that he needed my help with something, and would arrive at noon and take me to meet 'somebody'. I'd pointed out that Ben would have to come with me. He had said that 'might not be a bad idea', and he would explain when he saw me. I'd spent time trying to interpret that statement.

Our first customer, who arrived on the dot of

the half hour, was the one I hadn't been expecting. When the bell tinkled, I threw a careless glance at the door and pulled up with a jolt. Mrs Acker sidled down the aisle, and this time she was staring straight at me. From my face, her eyes slid around the room and flickered at the sight of Ben at the computer. I smiled encouragingly. She hunched her shoulders.

'Miss Hoare, I'm sorry about the book.'

'Please,' I said, 'don't worry. Is there something wrong with it?'

She seemed to be examining my right ear again. 'No. No, but I shouldn't have taken it, not when I didn't have the money. If it isn't too much trouble...' Her voice faded, and I saw her staring at the shelf where the Milne had originally sat. 'I don't see it.'

'It's in the office,' I said easily. 'I haven't got around to reshelving it.'

She was carrying the brown handbag, and I saw her hand move towards the catch. Her voice came with a rush. 'I do want it. But only if you can keep it for me until I can pay for it. I could give you £5 a week, every Saturday. Would that be all right?'

I did some quick arithmetic and reckoned that the book would be hers some time in April. I started to repeat that I was happy to trust such an old customer, but she shook her head with determination, pulled a bank note from the purse, and held it out to me. I took it into the office, wrote up a receipt, put a 'SOLD' notice inside the front cover, and then watched her bob her head, almost smile, and turn to go. The black eye wasn't all that obvious today.

I was still asking myself what that was all about when Ben crashed the computer and shouted for help, so we plunged into a conversation about how you switch the machine off and on and usually find that everything is working, which although an oversimplification does seem to be true. Rebooting began. Barnabas arrived. The business day started in earnest at almost the same moment.

It was nearly eleven when the next unexpected visitor arrived. The man I'd seen with Mrs Acker appeared in the doorway. He wore the same semi-uniform clothes as yesterday, so I assumed that he hadn't come on official business, although he was holding a sheet of paper.

I asked whether I could help him.

He held it up – one of my home-made posters, with tape dangling from it. 'This yours?'

I nodded defiantly.

'This monkey.' He glanced down at the photograph and then back. 'It belongs to a man we're looking for. Police. You have the monkey here?'

'Oh, not here,' I corrected him. What was going on? I thought fast, made sure that my back was turned to Barnabas, lowered my voice and said, 'I think somebody caught it. I noticed it out in the road yesterday afternoon, and later on there were a couple of men with a van. They had one of those – you know, nets with long handles?' I was counting on the other voices drowning mine out so that Barnabas would miss this.

Acker looked at me so sharply that I understood there was something was wrong with my story.

'What kind of van?'

It was easy to look blank.

'Colour? Markings?'

I thought, sighed and shook my head. 'I'm sorry, I can't remember. I think it was light coloured. Maybe grey. Sort of medium grey? Maybe it was the RSPCA?'

He flapped the poster. 'Then why–?'

Good question. I decided to take refuge in fluttering. 'Oh, I put those up earlier! I hoped the owner would see it, and I could explain about his monkey being in my garden, and maybe he could catch it. He must be worried.'

He looked at me silently just long enough for me to glance down at the poster and notice that I'd been really, really stupid. It took all my nerve to stand there with a blank face.

'This man you mentioned – he hasn't been here the last day or two?' Maybe he hadn't realized. 'We're looking for him. He's a witness in a case. So if he comes in...'

'I'll let the police know of course.'

'Can you contact me personally the minute you see him?'

'I certainly can, Mr...? I'm sorry, I didn't

catch your name.'

'Acker,' he said again. 'PC Ken Acker. If he does turn up, ring my mobile and I'll get over here. Sometimes the people at the desk are too busy to respond right away.' He was feeling in the pockets of his fleece. I handed him the pencil I happened to be carrying. He hesitated and then wrote his name and a mobile phone number on the back of my poster.

'Are you going to arrest him?'

'Him? No, we just need to ask him a few more questions. This monkey...'

I waited anxiously.

'If I can just have a word with him – his name is Lewis – I'll see about getting his animal back for him. Since they passed the Dangerous Animals Act a few years ago, there are restrictions on keeping monkeys. You tell him I'll help him get it sorted. All right?'

It wasn't what I'd been expecting to hear, so I smiled and nodded, followed him to the door and watched him walk down to the corner. As he left, I turned my attention to a woman standing on the far side of the street. I thought she'd been waiting to cross the road when he appeared in the doorway, but she had turned her back sharply, pulling the hood of her jacket up over her faded ginger hair. I looked hard at her back while she went on staring at something in the window of the toy shop on the other corner. She seemed to be fascinated by the brightly painted wooden animals. I couldn't see her face, but I

74

took in the short, plump body, the sand-coloured cotton jacket with ragged fake fur around the hood, the jeans and the dirty white trainers.

I shut the door without taking my eyes off her and shifted behind the Christmas decorations. When she turned around at last, she stared at the window for so long that I thought that she must be able to see me hiding behind the prints and tinsel. Or maybe it was the beauty of our strings of lights that kept her spellbound. I was expecting her to cross over and come in; but after a few seconds she turned away and also vanished around the corner.

'What was all that about?' Barnabas had come up behind me.

I said that I didn't know. Then I realized that he was talking about our earlier visitor. 'Police,' I said, 'still looking for that old man.'

We were starting to be too busy for private conversations. I went back to staring grimly at the little snapshot I had lied about so badly. I'd been careful to shoot the monkey's picture from between two bars, so that they didn't blur the shot; but the background was in perfect focus; and despite the flowers on the curtains it was obvious that the monkey was indoors in a cage, not out in a flower bed, and just as clear that I'd been lying through my teeth. Maybe Acker hadn't noticed, but that was hard to believe. Why hadn't he said something, rather than just handing over the evidence of my whopper? I was tempted to leave Ben with Barnabas and jog around removing the other eleven telltale proofs that I'd lied to a policeman. But that could make me look even more guilty, and also the old man wouldn't know about the monkey – how would he?

I took a few deep breaths and told myself firmly that I hadn't done anything wrong except not stopping to think. I did accept that I should try to avoid a life of crime, since I am obviously too stupid to get away with it. I folded the notice, stuffed it into a pocket, and moved on to a customer who looked lost. When in doubt do nothing rash: that is an excellent motto and even had the advantage that Barnabas would thoroughly approve. I just wished that I'd remembered it sooner.

# Chapter 11

### Lunch with Annie Kelly

I was looking at my wristwatch again when out of the corner of my eye I noticed the dark-blue Jaguar. Kennedy parked it, strode across the road, and came in. At that moment there were only four customers, all male, so he easily located me in the travel section. I shelved a spare volume somewhere, stood up and opened my mouth to ask questions.

He beat me to it: 'Sorry I'm late – traffic. Are we organized?'

I said we were, but that I needed to get back as soon as possible.

'Right. I've booked a table for twelve thirty. She's supposed to meet us there.'

'Who is? And where?'

'The Granita. All right?'

I looked at him. That's one of the most fashionable restaurants in Islington, and probably the most famous. The Prime Minister and his cronies are supposed to have dined there while they were planning tactics some time before the 1997 election. Not everybody can afford it.

'Her idea,' he said. He sounded rueful. 'Annie's. My editor is paying, but I had to be persuasive. Annie Kelly.'

'Film star?' I guessed.

'You're thinking of Gene. This one's a retired prostitute.' He threw me an evil glance. I snorted. 'One of my contacts introduced us. He thinks she can help me with the project.' (Second time of mention: what project, exactly?) 'We got together yesterday and talked about an interview, but she said she had an urgent appointment, so we postponed it until today. I don't know whether she's checking me out, or just wanted a free meal, but I want to talk to her as soon as possible. I thought that she might find it reassuring to have another woman present. So when she said that she lives near here, I told her I was having lunch with you and asked her to join us.' He looked down at me with a straight face and added, 'A restaurant is a safe public place, and you're reasonably respectable.'

I made a face at him and wondered what was going on.

Chris makes his living as a journalist on one of the national newspapers. He'd been doing serious pieces on social problems for several years before I met him, and I'd known him now for over a year; but this was the first time he'd asked for my help. I had just started, 'What project? You keep talking—' when Barnabas loomed up, greeted Chris, and threw me a harassed look.

'I could use some help with my increasingly bored grandson,' he said, 'or even with the customers. And isn't Ernie due?'

Chris sprang into the breach: 'I'll talk to Ben until Dido's ready to leave.'

I called after his back, 'I still– Barnabas, I'm coming!'

Somebody stepped in front of me at that point. A long conversation and a small sale later, I checked the time and mouthed the obvious 'Sorry, just another minute' at Chris when I went into the office to dig some of our carrier bags out of the carton.

He got to his feet. 'Ben and I will be waiting in the car, if that's all right.'

I nodded frantically and went back to hand over a book, accept a £10 note for it, and say goodbye to Barnabas. Chris and Ben were going out hand in hand just as Ernie came bouncing in looking apologetic, and at the same moment I was caught by somebody looking for a Christmas present for her husband but managed to pass her on seamlessly to Ernie while I grabbed my coat.

I hissed, 'An hour, maybe an hour and a half,' to Barnabas and escaped.

The restaurant was only a minute's drive up the main road: a long room with high ceilings, cream and grey walls, and minimalist steel-and-blond-wood bar and tables. A hostess took our coats and showed the three of us to a reserved table halfway down the busy room. We were ten minutes late, but nobody was waiting there.

I helped Ben to scramble up on a chair, caught my breath and said, 'I wish you'd tell me what this is about. And at least what this person looks like, in case I spot her before you do!'

'Then look for a short, plump woman. Middle-aged. Ginger hair that she wears in plaits. In this place, she'll stick out like a sore thumb.'

Oh, that woman?

I said carefully, 'What exactly did you tell her about me?'

'Only that you're a bookseller, and a neighbour of hers, and that you're a friend of mine. She said she knew the shop.'

I said, 'Oh,' and was about to tell him that I'd

already seen her, but then I left it. If she were as cautious as Chris had suggested, she might have been checking me too. That didn't explain why she had avoided Mr Acker.

Ben said politely that he was hungry. Chris pushed the bread basket in his direction, and when I looked up from buttering duties she was coming through the door. She was wearing the same old cotton jacket. One of the staff moved quickly to intercept her.

'Chris—'

'Got it.' He stood up and took a step, but she had brushed aside the receptionist's stony-faced enquiry by handing her the offending jacket, and was marching towards us. Her eyes shot from Chris to me and then down to Ben, who was stacking up his cutlery. He'd suffered a lot of waiting around today.

A waiter arrived to pull out her chair. Chris made the introductions. She settled a pink plastic shopping bag at her feet and subjected me to a stare.

The waiter suggested drinks.

She grinned. 'Wouldn't say no to a whisky. Brass monkey weather.' She was watching me a little too closely for politeness. I returned the gaze with interest. She had a round, worn face, pink with the cold, and pale-blue eyes with lines at the corners. I guessed she was in her mid-fifties. She produced a packet of Silk Cut, offered them around, and lit up, grinning through the smoke. 'Nice place. I never been here before.' Her gaze switched to Ben. Her face softened. 'Ben, is it? I'm Mrs Kelly. How old are you then, love?'

Ben told her that he was three years and ten and a half months old and accepted his glass of orange juice from the waiter without taking his eyes off her face.

The ordering filled up a few minutes. Then she announced that she had to make a visit, got to her feet, grabbed her shoulder bag and wandered towards the door marked 'Toilets'.

I looked at Chris. 'She's playing games.'

'Like last night.' He shrugged. 'She's left her shopping, so I suppose she means to come back.'

I'd finally worked out what I was doing here and said, 'I think I need to wash my hands.'

Ben advised us bluntly that he wanted to go to the toilet.

Chris said, 'Bless you both,' and looked slightly happier.

The washrooms were down a short flight of steps and through a heavy door. Annie Kelly's trainers were visible under the door of one of the toilet compartments. Ben entered a second. I leaned against the wash basins, enjoying the musky scent of the hand soap and waiting for them both. There seemed to be something going on in the first compartment: there had been a faint whuffling noise behind the door as we entered, but it stopped immediately. I noticed that Ben was managing nicely on his own.

Growing up.

'Dido?' a voice rasped. 'I'll be right out.'

'Don't worry,' I said politely. 'I'm just waiting for Ben.'

But the toilet flushed, the door swung back, and she was there straightening her jeans. She advanced on the basins.

'You know, I did see you this morning,' I said conversationally, 'over in George Street. You went away without coming in.'

She contemplated herself in the mirror and freshened her lipstick. 'I saw somebody. Copper. I didn't feel like saying hello. Was he buying a book? I bet he wasn't: that one's a tight sod.'

I digested some implications and offered, 'I didn't know he was a policeman at first, but then he started asking about somebody I'd seen hanging around. Do you know where he's based?'

'He's local,' she said without hesitating. 'You had some trouble there in your street, Thursday? I saw it on the telly. Bloody horrible. I guess it's got them running around. They found out about that body yet?'

So we slipped into a discussion of the gruesome discovery and the lurid reports in one of the tabloids which she had read and I hadn't. Apparently the police were still looking for more of the body. They still had no head – no face, no dental records.

'Poor kid,' she said obscurely, 'it'll be one of

them buggers who thinks he owns women. Trouble is, some of 'em do.'

There was something in the words that caught my attention, and I said, 'She might have been a prostitute – is that what you mean? But she was so young!'

She looked at me in disbelief, snorted, and then looked around for a towel. 'Nothing's too young for men.' She located a pile of thick pink terry hand towels, picked one up, and looked at it attentively. 'That's what your bloke wants to talk to me about, isn't it?'

I shrugged in my turn and told her that he hadn't told me. My bloke.

'Well, look out,' she said.

I said, 'You don't sound very keen on men.'

She giggled. 'I like men all right, but they take advantage. Can't do with 'em, can't do without 'em.'

I was more or less agreeing when Ben's toilet flushed, his door opened, and he came charging across to wash his hands. I helped him with the things he couldn't reach, and found Annie Kelly standing ready with another clean hand towel to dry his hands.

'I had a kid once myself,' she said abruptly. 'A girl. Social services took her off of me. I was a real idiot.'

'Do you see her now?'

She shook her head. 'She was adopted. I thought it wouldn't be fair. They'll give her my name, if she ever asks.'

I said, 'Maybe she will. How old is she?'

'Nearly twenty, now.'

'Maybe she will.'

She said, 'Nah. It was a long time ago.' She sounded more cheerful than I would have; her eyes were bright. 'Maybe we should get back? I'm starving.'

'I'm starving,' Ben echoed, so we did what they both wanted. As I followed her up the stairs I reflected briefly that she hadn't gone anywhere near the used towel bin, and that I could see something pink where the zip fastener of her shoulder bag was slightly open.

Chris and our food were waiting for us.

She started things off by putting a chip into her mouth, stabbing her steak and mumbling, 'So, Mist— Chris, what do you want?'

'You know DS Johnson gave me your name.'

'Over King's Cross, course I know him. But you been talking to the local coppers, over here? Somebody called Acker?'

I speared a stalk of asparagus with my fork and focused my eyes on the butter dripping from it without missing even a twitch from either of them.

He was looking at her, frowning. 'Who's Acker?'

She shrugged slightly. 'Local plod. Never mind. Well, if you're looking for that stuff, you'll still find it over King's Cross way, even if they say they cleaned it up. I have friends over there. *He* knows – Sam Johnson. So, what d'you want to talk about?'

'Sergeant Johnson said you might fill me in from the – the personal point of view about how it was?'

'I can tell you some stories,' she said, 'if that's what you're on about. What – you want stories about the girls?'

I was getting impatient and decided to protest. 'I've been seeing articles like that in the newspapers for years.'

'I'm concentrating on new talent,' Chris said evenly. 'Dido, there are girls being brought here illegally from abroad. Smuggled in. Understand?'

I said, 'Oh.' I'd seen the news items all that autumn about young women, illegal immigrants whose fates were nothing like what they had been hoping for when they left their homes seeking fame and fortune, or maybe just a job with a living wage, in England. So he wasn't doing the old human-interest piece about King's Cross vice, but something specifically about people trafficking; I couldn't see why he was being so evasive.

'Good idea,' Annie said cheerfully. 'Let's say £100 an hour, all right? You ask me questions, I'll tell you what I know. Maybe remember some good human interest stories? It's ten past one, right? And you might want some more names, people to talk to?'

Chris pulled a tiny recording machine out of a side pocket, pressed a button and set it down on the table. Ben knelt up on his chair to have a closer look. Chris grinned at him absent-mindedly, produced a notebook and opened it to a page of notes.

'And I'll need cash,' she added.

'No problem.'

Annie sighed. 'Bugger it, I didn't ask for enough.'

I tried not to giggle.

A thoughtful voice at my elbow was saying, 'Bugger it, bugger it.' I interrupted by wiping Ben's mouth with my napkin and asking what he wanted for a sweet.

Annie let out a howl of laughter that made both Ben and me jump. 'All right,' she said. 'All right, ask away. I'll keep it clean. Sorry, Dido.'

# Chapter 12

## Speaking of Evil

A helping of chocolate ice-cream pudding had exhausted Ben, so I was carrying him home, propped on my hip with his head on my shoulder, nearly asleep. We had almost reached the top of George Street before the Jaguar caught up and slowed. When I ignored it,

Kennedy accelerated and turned in, and by the time I caught sight of the car again it was parked outside the shop and he was striding towards us.

Despite my burden, I managed to side-step him and keep on going.

'Dido?'

I said in a low voice, 'I'm taking him upstairs for his nap now. If you want to tell me something, you can wait in the sitting room.'

We completed the walk in silence. I went past the door of the shop and upstairs. In the hallway, I threw my keys down and carried straight on into the bedroom. Chris turned into the front room, and while I was taking Ben's shoes off and settling him on his bed, I heard the murmur of a telephone conversation that ended abruptly when he heard me shut the bedroom door. When I reached the sitting room, I was still feeling cross.

'Are you going to let me in on the secret?'

'What?'

'What this whole thing was about?'

I caught that old flash of evasiveness in his eyes. I'd had to deal with it before, and I glared at him.

'Dido, just say what's bothering you.'

Why not? I sat on the desk chair and faced him straight on. 'I don't like being used. Let's start with all your talk about a "new project", details left blank. You involved me in this meeting with Annie Kelly for no very good reason that I can see – she's certainly not shy enough to need a chaperone. Incidentally, I think I liked her. Then you insisted on driving to a restaurant that's four minutes walk from here, despite the fact that parking in Upper Street is impossible on Saturdays and we might still be going round and round if a taxi hadn't happened to pull away from in front of the door just—' I stopped and looked at him. 'And it was just luck that taxi left at the very moment we got there? Yes? Then Annie Kelly turned up, and you did a deal and paid her £100.'

'Two hundred. We went over the hour.' His face was solemn.

I refused to laugh, and returned to the attack. 'For that, you got her life story. I couldn't see anything in it that would be worth £10 to a newspaper: it was just a rant about herself, her needs, the way men have always taken advantage of her – nothing new there, then – and what it was like to be on the streets fifteen years ago, or five years ago, before they cleaned up King's Cross; and ramblings about how she's a reformed character who spends all her time regretting her past and wandering around the shops in the West End – shoplifting? Hand towels, that kind of stuff?'

'She does have a couple of convictions,' Chris said meekly. He was pretending to be penitent and trying not to laugh.

Time to finish winding him up. 'When I finally walked out, she was telling you lots of things you can read about in newspapers any day.'

'You walked out very stylishly,' Chris commented. 'You didn't throw your coffee at me. Thanks.'

I stuck out my feet, crossed my ankles, and suggested that in return for my restraint he might try giving me a stylish explanation of what was going on.

He hesitated. 'One condition?' I looked at him. 'All right, not a condition, just a plea to be careful about anything I say. You may like Annie Kelly, but I'm not so sure. She has a past, and she still has some funny friends. What was the first thing?'

'The project.'

'Of course I'm not doing another bleeding-heart piece. This is – an angle on the current illegal-immigrant panic, if you like. Do you know anything about Eastern European gangs that are moving into prostitution and drugs here? Traffickers? When my editor decided to run a series, I went straight to an old friend in Scotland Yard, who hinted that there's something simmering in King's Cross and parts of west London. He sent me to a detective called Johnson who's stationed at King's Cross – the man you saw with me on television. I believe he's all right, but my friend at Scotland Yard made it pretty clear that any information I can get from Johnson is fine, but that if I happen to dig up anything new, it goes straight to him and nowhere else.'

I interpreted: 'You more or less trust Johnson, but Scotland Yard think the local police may have their fingers in whatever is going on?'

Chris looked at me. 'You have the suspicious mind of a true journalist.'

I thought I'd take that as a 'yes'.

'So I'm wandering around with my ordinary and outdated human-interest project on behalf of one of the major newspapers. Everybody knows that there's nothing new there, as you so rightly pointed out. I'll get a little background piece without too much trouble, and it'll be published one Saturday soon, and everybody will assume that's that; but if I'm careful and lucky, I may get the inside track on something much better.'

I was starting to calm down, but I couldn't help saying, 'I wish you'd just trust me not to gossip.'

'And I wish I thought that nobody might be in danger just because she knows me.'

I looked at him. He was staring at a spot somewhere in the middle of the ceiling. There wasn't any point my saying to him, 'What about you?' so I asked him, 'Why did you want me along today?'

'You and Ben? Smoke screen. I did think about it very hard before I decided it would be safe: nobody is saying that Annie Kelly herself is involved. Look, Johnson gave me her name as somebody who might have a contact with the gangs through a minor local criminal who's an old boyfriend of hers. When she and I were introduced yesterday, she was evasive, but I did think that Johnson was probably right about her, mostly because she was being so cute. I was pretty sure it would take something else to get her to relax enough to give anything away or introduce me to – people. She's an occasional drugs user herself, living on benefit, so she's vulnerable to my bribes and other people's threats and presents; but she's very careful of her own safety and, God knows, she probably has the right idea. I'd say she's a survivor. Apart from that, I thought she'd be more comfortable with you and Ben around.'

I said slowly, 'That's what she was doing in the toilets. I wasn't sure at the time, but she was taking something.' I wasn't talking about the two pink hand towels.

Chris said, 'I noticed it when you all came back. What else? The car – we drove there so I'd be able to offer her a lift home, because I'd like to know where she's living at the moment. Incidentally, so would Sam Johnson. I made a mistake, and she shied away. And yes, of course I'd hired the cab to sit there and keep the space for us. I needed to have the car handy in case she accepted.'

'The advantage of owning a conspicuous car,' I muttered. 'What do you mean, a mistake?'

'When I offered her the lift, I asked whether I could arrange for one of our people to photograph her. I thought she'd be flattered, but she took off like a scalded cat.'

'She didn't want to see her face in the newspaper?'

'It was a big "no".'

'All right: what happens next?'

'I have the number of her mobile, and I'll ring her tomorrow, thank her, and ask her if she can introduce anybody else who'd be willing to talk to me.'

I'd been making connections. I said, 'What does all this have to do with the body across the street?'

'Who says it does?'

'You do. You and your policeman friend rushed straight over here, remember?'

'We happened to be together when he got a call about it. There may be nothing to it.'

I hesitated. I couldn't think of a good excuse to push this, so I gave up for the moment and said, 'I'd better see what's happening in the shop.' It was after three o'clock, and it would be chaotic from now until closing time.

'I want to do some thinking and scribbling and phoning,' he said. 'Maybe I could baby-sit?'

I got to my feet, leaned over and kissed him lightly on the cheek. 'He was so tired that he probably won't wake up for an hour or two. Let me know when you need to go.' The unspoken message was that I'd forgiven him but that I didn't like people playing games, even if or especially because they thought they were shielding me from the facts of life. I need to make my own choices.

At seven o'clock I locked the shop door and fled into the office. Barnabas had gone upstairs to rest, drink tea and read to Ben, who by now had presumably finished his supper and was waiting for me, playtime, bath and bed. Chris had been gone for hours. Ernie had just left with a pocket full of cash to meet some friends who would help him spend it. Saturday night. Dido Hoare, feeling glad that Christmas comes but once a year, was trying to be enthusiastic about tomorrow. We'd decided to open on the first three Sundays of the month, mostly on the grounds that all the other shops in this area were doing the same, and that had to mean it was a good commercial idea, probably.

Saturday night. And I just wanted to go to bed.

My last task of the day was to count the cash, list the cheques, and take everything around to the night deposit box at the bank. I sorted, counted, wrote. The total cheered me up briefly. I pushed everything into the deposit envelope and slipped that into my shoulder bag. Then I found one of our rubbish sacks and stuffed it with the contents of the waste bin plus a dismantled cardboard box. I was on automatic by now: office lights off, alarm set, keys in one hand and sack in the other. But the wheelie bin was full and they weren't due to empty it until Tuesday. I pushed down on the scraps of brown

93

paper and bubble wrap and encountered resistance.

For a second my mind flashed to bin-liners and bodies. I couldn't just ignore it.

The street lighting shone into the bin. I pulled aside some wrapping paper to look underneath it. Not plastic, but heavy canvas, a strap, something soft. I grabbed the strap, heaved the old man's rucksack out and let it fall at my feet.

He must have left it there. That would have been some time in the past twenty-four hours, because it hadn't been there the previous night. He must intend to come back for it. If I could catch him, then we could get the monkey sorted out, and maybe even the business of the flower book. I could sell that to somebody in half a day at this time of year, and he would get enough cash to carry him comfortably over the new year. Just for a moment, I wondered whether that would make any difference. Anyway, I couldn't just leave the rucksack where it was, or he'd sneak up and take it and disappear.

I exchanged my rubbish for the rucksack and shut the lid. I didn't want his things in the flat, so I had to go back into the shop, dump my find in the office and reset the alarm. Then I set off up the street towards the night safe. I kept my eyes peeled. There was somebody sitting on the pavement beside the cash machine. He was just a young boy. I dropped a coin on to his blanket and hurried back to George Street where the lights and warmth that were waiting upstairs.

94

# Chapter 13

## Getting My Hands Dirty

I spread the sports section of the newspaper on the floor of the office and knelt there with the old man's rucksack at my side. I hesitated, but only because of the smell of sweat and grease hovering over my find.

First I undid the strap around the grubby nylon sleeping bag and turned it inside out. Apart from grit, some possible dead fleas and a half-smoked cigarette, there was nothing in the bottom. I emptied the outside pockets of the rucksack: two bottles of prescription pills – one antibiotic (three times a day with food, no alcohol), and one with a name I didn't recognize – a plastic pouch holding a few shreds of rolling tobacco, some Swan Vestas, and the wrappers from two chocolate bars. So far, just as expected. Rather than plunge a hand into the main compartment, I turned the whole thing upside down and shook it over the newspaper: worn socks, a tea towel full of holes which looked as though he'd been wiping his nose on it, a bundle of plastic sheeting, a couple of unravelling sweaters, one small sized T-shirt with roses on the front, a dirty old chocolate box with an elastic band around it, a disposable razor, a grubby red fleece jacket with one sleeve ripped off, one dirty-white trainer without a lace, and a pair of underpants which I would rather not have seen. No book. Unsurprised, I examined my finds and reflected that my meddling had brought me exactly what I deserved – a pair of dirty hands. The only thing to do was put everything back and pretend this had never happened.

Although I was in a hurry to finish and get back upstairs, I shook the shoe upside down before I threw it back. I added the clothes, piece by piece. There was no point folding anything. The old chocolate box rattled, so I opened that and turned it upside down too. A small cascade of coins and papers scattered across the floor. I picked them up bit by bit and replaced them, counting £7.23 in assorted coins, a couple of those unfilled prescription forms I'd been told about, from a clinic over Hoxton way, and a fragile slip of paper which turned out to be an old birth certificate: Harry Lewis had been born in Southend on May 1st, 1954 – he was a younger man than he looked. His mother's name was Alice; his father was also a Harold Lewis. There was a creased and faded black and white snapshot of a woman with two little boys. Judging by her hairstyle, one of the children was probably my crazy old man. There were no letters, notes, receipts: nothing that would tell me anything about where he was coming from nowadays or where he might be hiding.

I secured the box with the rubber band, added it to the mess in the bag and tightened the cord at its mouth. Part of me kept thinking about the pretty little book. He had probably dropped it into some bin as he tottered past, or left it sitting on a bench. Except – I half corrected myself – he had seemed to value it that day when he showed it to me.

Something glinted among the bits and scraps of unidentifiable rubbish. It looked like an earring, a tiny, tarnished disc engraved with a fine leaf pattern on a chain, with a hook for a pierced ear – delicate, easy to miss. When I looked closely, I realized that it was just one part: a hole at the bottom of the disc still held one link of a fine chain to which something else had once been attached. I held the little thing in the palm of my hand and wondered what it was doing here – where he had found it, why he'd kept it. A souvenir? In the end I put it on the desk under the computer keyboard to think about.

With the repacked rucksack sitting on the floor beside the door, I asked myself when Lewis was likely to return. The shop would be open until six, so he had some time to come in and ask for his possessions, including his monkey and the even more essential warm sleeping bag. He seemed to have thought he could manage without it last night.

I went upstairs to check on Ben and put in a restless phone call to my father to make sure that he would arrive before we opened at one o'clock. That gave me time. It was probably the vivid memory of the old man's filth that decided me to spend the next hour at the launderette around the corner. It's a place where I can take Ben, with a couple of his storybooks too; there's something soothing about watching a fortnight's dirty clothes turning round and round in bubbles behind a porthole while I read aloud. While a second load was flopping around in the dryer, I decided to spend the remains of the morning on essential, efficient things connected with life and business. In pursuit of this, I pushed two more coins into the slot and took the first load home.

Coming back, we turned north to circle the block. I wanted to walk past the Ackers' place because I'd been thinking about my evasive old customer. In fact, as we sauntered up to the house hand in hand and I threw a furtive glance through the railings, it was Mr Acker whom I discovered, standing beside the path with his back to us, washing out his wheelie bin with what smelled like bleach. Two full bin liners waited beside it. It looked as though the body parts in our street had freaked everybody out. Mrs Acker was probably unreachable while her husband was there. Never mind, I still had things to do.

I was staggering home with the second load of clean clothes when I decided that the time had come to clear up the other business, too. I dropped the bag in the bedroom, left Ben with a glass of milk and a biscuit, and went downstairs. My wheelie bin showed no evidence of new rummaging, and nobody was hanging around in front of the shop looking for something. You might wonder how Harry Lewis was managing without any of his belongings. Or you could wonder whether something had happened.

I phoned the police from the flat. The switchboard put me through to a woman who introduced herself as DS Laura Smiley and listened to my tale without interruption.

When I ground to a halt she said, 'Miss Hoare, aren't you the person who rang us last Thursday?'

Just for a moment, I couldn't remember Thursday. Oh: this was the same harassed soprano I'd heard when I asked about getting a message to the old man. I agreed faintly that I was me.

Her response was sharp. 'Will you wait where you are, please? I'm coming there.'

The note of urgency in her voice was so interesting that I was waiting by the window when she arrived: a plump woman my age, with short-cut ash-blond hair, a tailored blue coat and a businesslike manner. I fled downstairs, let her into the shop and introduced myself. And the rucksack. But she ignored it.

'Ms Hoare, I'm sorry: we really should have got back to you before this. There are some problems about the statement you made the other day. You knew Mr Lewis personally?'

It almost felt as though I did by now, but I explained: he had been wandering around the neighbourhood for months, he had sheltered behind my wheelie bin sometimes, I had noticed him particularly because he had a monkey – I left it at that – and I had heard the old man howling when he made his discovery. Then I had found his rucksack in my bin yesterday, where I assumed he had hidden it himself, and so far he hadn't come back for it.

She listened attentively. I pointed out the waiting rucksack again. She said, without looking down, 'I'm afraid that Mr Lewis is in hospital. He was found by a passing motorist in a street just off Balls Pond Road last night. It looked like a hit-and-run accident.'

I asked slowly, 'Was he badly hurt?'

She gazed at me without any particular expression. 'He's regained consciousness, but they're keeping him in for a while. Why do you ask?'

'No reason,' I lied. I was thinking that Lewis had hidden the rucksack just before he hurried off into the evening darkness towards his accident. It made me wonder whether something was chasing him. It would be nice if this could all make sense. I hoisted the rucksack. 'I want to give you this. There might be something in here that will help. I'd better get back upstairs. My son is alone. But – could I visit Mr Lewis?'

She hesitated and said, 'Maybe in a little while he can have visitors, I don't know. Do you know him personally, then?'

I said, 'I've talked to him a few times. He was in the shop once.'

'Yes.' I watched her thinking about it. 'We'll interview him about what happened as soon as he's well enough.'

'You said it was an accident?'

She said, 'Would you know any reason why it shouldn't be?'

I blinked.

She scowled; obviously she didn't either, but she wasn't going to say so. I saw her come to a decision. 'Miss Hoare, I'll take the bag off your hands now, and thanks for contacting us. You say you found it yesterday in your wheelie bin?'

'At about six in the evening. We'd just closed.'

'Right. Then – just to be on the safe side – I'm going to send somebody over here to empty the bin. They'll be in a marked police van, and they should get here within the next half hour. They'll want to bag the contents, and please don't touch anything, don't put anything in or take anything out, before they get here. They'll give you a receipt, if you wish.'

I said I thought I didn't wish. All that I wished

was to understand what was going on. I said tentatively, 'I'm sorry about what happened to him.'

She shrugged and nodded. 'What lives those people do live! Look, you ring me in a couple of days and I'll let you know about visiting, all right? I'll be back if I have any more questions. You aren't going away for Christmas or anything like that?'

I decided that Christmas dinner in St Albans didn't count, and told her I wasn't. She left with the rucksack and all its smells. As soon as she had gone, I remembered that I'd forgotten to mention *Lessons in Flower Painting*. But it didn't seem particularly important now. We were due to open in a few minutes, Barnabas hadn't arrived yet, and somehow all that seemed more urgent.

# Chapter 14

### And Clearing Up

In the morning, I was opening the mail when it jolted me: the monkey. I hadn't been thinking about the animal since I'd visited, but this was Monday, and it seemed to me that I should explain to Mr Stanley that he was probably going to have a lodger for longer than we'd expected. I might have left this to Barnabas, except that when I rang my father's number there was no answer. Mr Stanley's phone was not listed. On the other hand, he had been at home the last time I'd dropped in, and I had a suspicion that he was usually there. It was tempting to get even one small thing cleared up; so I went out to the car and set off toward Crouch Hill.

I was right. He was wearing rubber gloves when he answered his door bell; I'd obviously interrupted the washing-up. The smell in the front room was no worse than before, and the monkey – Charlie – reacted calmly to my arrival. I looked at the pale face and alert hazel eyes, and saw that the harness had gone. Apparently everybody had been making progress. I turned to Mr Stanley and caught him smiling.

'He looks happy.'

'I gave him a bath,' Mr Stanley said. 'He was scratching. I'll leave the harness off, now he's living indoors. Were you coming to tell me ... some news?'

I nodded. 'His owner, Charlie's owner, is in hospital. I haven't had the chance to tell him about the monkey, so ... do you mind keeping him a while longer?'

He walked over to the cage and opened the door. The monkey scarcely hesitated before he leapt out and landed on Mr Stanley's shoulder. A hand grasped his ear. Mr Stanley beckoned,

103

and said, 'Just don't stare at him.' I strolled over and noted from the corner of my eye how the little animal watched me without any real sign of fear. I stopped a couple of feet away. 'He's changed.'

'Changing. You have to respect monkeys,' Mr Stanley explained in the tone of an expert.

I was saying that I thought everything would be just fine, when my eye fell on the old harness lying on the table behind the open cage. A little disc was fixed to the buckle. I'd noticed it the other day but hadn't looked closely enough. If it was an address tag, like the ones dogs wear on their collars, then I ought to hand it over to Sergeant Smiley with my grovelling apologies. I reached around and picked it up, and it was just a coin: a worn silver coin, slightly tarnished, with the head of a man and lettering in the Cyrillic alphabet, which I can identify though I can't read it. A short piece of dull wire was threaded through a hole in the coin and twisted around the buckle of the harness. I put the harness down and said I hoped everything would be all right, and that I'd leave Mr Stanley to get on with his washing up.

'You must come again,' he said formally. 'You're welcome to visit us at any time.'

I thanked him just as politely and left, thinking that this had worked out pretty well, and crossing one thing off my mental to-do list.

I was squeezing my MPV into a tight space outside the shop when my mobile phone rang.

The screen said that the call was from Chris. I switched on, said, 'Give me a moment?' and put the phone down until I could turn off the engine and climb out.

'I'm here.'

He said, 'Have you seen the news?'

'What? You mean ... What news?'

'There was another find yesterday. It was in a plastic carrier bag that somebody had dumped in a shop doorway on Upper Street during the night. The manager found it in the morning when they came to open up.'

'What?' I repeated. My voice sounded strained, even to me.

'A head.'

My first reaction was that they would identify her now. My second thought was that now I could understand Sergeant Smiley's distracted air.

'They've done some work reconstructing the face, and I think they'll be appealing for somebody to identify her. They'll probably start by asking you and other shopkeepers in the immediate vicinity.'

I snapped, 'There's no reason to assume she lived around here!' The idea of yet another police visit was making me edgy, and the fact that there were things I'd forgotten to tell Sergeant Smiley – or decided not to mention – was starting to look reckless.

'I'll give you a statistic,' Chris offered. 'Ninety-one per cent of all murder victims are found within half a mile of where they were killed.'

I could have pointed out that this left another nine per cent; but the figure was unpleasantly suggestive. 'Wouldn't a murderer dump the body as far away as possible?'

'Witnesses. Accidents. Dead weight.'

I suggested that when you dismember a body, it should make the bits more manageable, not less ... I couldn't believe what I heard myself saying.

'But,' he said in a tone of exaggerated patience, 'the more body parts that you cart around the streets, the bigger the chance that somebody will see something. They were at two different sites over there, and the police are assuming that the killer must live locally. Damn! Dido? Listen, I have a call waiting.'

I said I'd be around, dropped everything and went upstairs to turn on the television. There was a short item on a news bulletin; but it wasn't until the end of the main evening news nearly five hours later that they screened a computer-manipulated portrait. The dead girl had been dark, with a long, unmarked face and high cheekbones. She looked very young. I listened absently to another plea for anyone who recognized the victim to contact the police.

I might have seen her myself. *Anybody* might have seen her, anywhere. Her face looked stiff and empty but very ordinary.

I was about to switch off when another picture

106

filled the screen and the word 'earring' froze my hand. It appeared that the victim had been wearing one dangling earring of tarnished silver, made up of a small disc on a fine piece of chain, with a bigger disc at the bottom: an old coin. I didn't need to go downstairs to make sure; the hook and the small disc with the engraved leaf pattern were identical to those on the earring that was still sitting under my keyboard. Worse, the bit that was missing from the one on my desk was identical to the one I saw on the screen – the voice was describing it as an old Russian coin – and I'd just found its mate attached to the monkey's harness.

This of course was impossible.

I reached for the telephone but then stopped. Sometimes I do pause and remind myself of the vow I took just before Ben was born: *From now on, I will always look before I leap.* Half an hour's delay couldn't make any difference, except to give me a chance to think through the problems I'd been making for myself. I could imagine the police being awkward about my withholding evidence, because this had concealed a link between Harry Lewis and the corpse. *He had known her.* How else could he have got her earring for his monkey's ornament? A thing, as I had just remembered with a sinking feeling, which had been attached to the harness since some time *before* Lewis and I had seen the torso. I went through the whole sequence of events twice, but it always came down to one thing: the monkey had escaped, wearing this harness, at least two days before the old man had found the body. I kept trying to find an explanation, but couldn't.

The monkey had one earring of the pair, and the body had the second. Well, there might be more than one pair of those earrings around. But I couldn't quite make myself believe that many identical pairs of rare foreign earrings were knocking around the streets. Had he known the girl before she was killed? Did he also know who had killed her? Could he conceivably have killed her himself, just to steal an ornament for the monkey's harness? I was juggling coincidences: the coincidence of there being two identical pairs of those earrings, against the coincidence of Lewis having innocently picked one up off the pavement somewhere the way he would pick up a ten pence piece. If he hadn't killed her himself – for such a little thing – had he been there when she was killed? I could imagine him lurking in some shadowy corner, watching what was happening and being too terrified to move. I closed my eyes. Night time. Dark, freezing. The old man huddled somewhere on the streets, asleep: a car stopping, a struggle, a scream, and Lewis creeping out again when it was quiet, crawling towards the dark shape on the ground...

Yes, it seemed possible except for one thing: when had it happened? You couldn't dismember a girl's body unnoticed on a London street, not even a quiet street, not even in the middle of the night. So Lewis must have been wherever it had happened, and maybe he had seen who did it. It could mean his 'accident' hadn't been genuine. My head was spinning.

Fact: there was a link between the dead girl and the crazy old man. And I'd have to talk to Sergeant Smiley again, to persuade and explain and apologize and—

Right away.

# Chapter 15

### Something Fishy

But I put off phoning, because I had worked out that it might be best, for damage limitation, to make an unsuccessful but recorded attempt to tell Sergeant Smiley first of all. Hoping she was still on the day shift, I left my name with the switchboard just after nine o'clock, then hung up and claimed the comfortable end of the settee from Mr Spock, who was too sleepy to resist, and checked my strategy. As a result, I phoned Barnabas, confessed as little as I could get away with, and said I'd explain when I saw him.

The doorbell rang just before ten. I wasn't

expecting trouble, but my teeth were gritted when I got over to the window, looked down and found Kennedy standing by the door looking up. I noticed that he was holding a carrier bag. I threw the key down and went along the hall to meet him, softly shutting the door of the bedroom as I passed.

He was surrounded by a fishy aura. I breathed it in greedily.

'Relax – there's enough for two.'

'I ate with Ben,' I said firmly. I sniffed. 'I might have a couple of your chips. I'll get the vinegar.'

'And the paper towels,' he said. 'And the bottle opener – I brought beer.'

We settled in the front room, and while he was unwrapping two slabs of battered cod and two bundles of thick potato chips, I turned the television on, lowered the sound, and joined him on the settee. I was a little hungry after all. We raised our bottles and toasted one another silently, and then I turned half my attention to the nothing new about what they were calling the 'Body in the Bag' case, and naturally there was no mention at all of a traffic accident involving a homeless man. When the presenter returned with the national summary, Chris grabbed the remote and switched the set off. I picked a big piece of batter out of the wrappings and said, 'Do you have any idea what's going on?'

'Maybe. There are some things that they

110

haven't made public. The body shows signs of heavy sexual activity. And she was a heroin user. They assume she was working as a prostitute somewhere locally. You remember I told you about some other, similar bodies? They're using the media heavily, trying to find somebody, anybody, who might have met her. If you want the blunt truth, they're afraid that they may never know who she is or what happened to her.'

I licked the last of the grease off my fingers and thought about it. 'That's why you and what's-his-name – Johnson – are so interested in Annie Kelly? Is that what this is really about? They think that she might know something about the girls? She's an informant?'

Chris shrugged, leaned back and yawned. 'Not really. She still knows people in the business, though she's supposed to have retired. That's why the police over there are thinking she might be a way in. Personally, I'd say there isn't much hope.'

I said slowly, 'She knows a lot of policemen from the old days, and she probably still feels that they're the enemy.'

'Yes, but it's mainly that she's a drug user herself, and that makes her vulnerable. She's known to some dubious characters, and she can't afford to rock the boat.'

'But why should she talk to you? Can you convince her that you'll be a kind of, of guarantor if she'll just agree to talk to your contact?'

He yawned again. 'Johnson – I phoned him. He says that they've been gnawing on this problem for months. It's well known that there's a trade in economic migrants who pay to be smuggled into the country. The girl you found was probably one of them. The tabloids are making a campaign out of this killing, and there will be be a lot of media pressure to come up with answers.'

I wondered whether that answered all my questions, but I left it for the moment and said, 'There's something I want to tell you. A link between my old man and the body he found.'

I explained about the coin on the harness.

Chris frowned. 'Maybe he picked it out before he noticed what else was in the sack?'

'No! It was on the monkey's harness, but the monkey ran off days before, remember.'

He scowled. 'So where and when did he find it? You're right: this is important. What do the police say?'

'I left a message for the detective who contacted me before, but she hasn't rung back.'

When he looked at me I started to repeat myself, but he interrupted: 'There's something I haven't told you yet. The pathologist has reported that the body had been frozen. You understand?'

No, I didn't think so. Or did I? If there had been a longer interval between the murder and the discovery across the road, then it threw the timing out of whack. Did that make the earring more problematic, or less?

I said, 'Lewis might not even know anything.'

'And the earring could be a coincidence. Even so, the accident – another coincidence? They'd want to trace where he's been since he walked out of the police station. We should get things moving.'

He was awake now, on his feet and also on his mobile. I listened to him speaking to somebody who had recognized his voice and didn't need to be told his name. I leaned against the cushions, closed my eyes and eavesdropped. Johnson – he was speaking to Johnson, of course – passed him on to somebody else after a sketchy explanation. I was glad I'd phoned Islington. Chris was telling them about the monkey, the coin, my role in the business. There were many silences, and even a point at which I might have fallen asleep for a moment, because it had been a long day.

When the conversation was winding down, I opened my eyes.

'Dido, they want to know where the monkey and the harness are now.'

I yawned and gave him Mr Stanley's address, but protested, 'They aren't going around there now, are they? He'll be in bed. They'll give him a heart attack!'

'They'll send somebody who'll be tactful,' he said impatiently. 'Don't worry.' I listened to him pass on the address.

As soon as he had switched off, I made my

own phone call. It was answered after a single ring.

'Barnabas?' I interrupted him when he started to speak. 'Listen: the police are on their way to talk to Mr Stanley about the monkey's harness. Could you warn him they're coming, and not to go to bed yet, and can you maybe stay with him until they've gone?'

'Of course.'

I had the impression that he wanted to say more. 'And then phone me back? Chris is with me. We'll be waiting.'

'Ah? Excuse me, I shall go upstairs now.'

I returned to my seat. Chris said, 'Good idea.' I edged closer. He laid an arm across my shoulders, and we waited.

It was more than an hour before the phone rang.

'They have been,' Barnabas reported abruptly, 'and gone. They took the harness away with them.'

I said, 'What about the monkey?'

'They wished to arrange for the monkey to be picked up, as it is an illegal animal. But it was missing. I must be insane to go along with this. However, my neighbour has become quite fond of him. There is really no accounting for tastes.'

'What did Mr Stanley say?'

'That he left a window open,' my father said drily, 'and that presumably the animal had squeezed out, but won't last long in this weather.' It sounded like a semi-permanent alibi.

114

I breathed out. and said maybe it was lucky I'd forgotten to pick up my cat carrier when I was over there?

Barnabas grunted noncommittally. 'I don't suppose they'll return. So perhaps I should bring the carrier with me when I come down there in the morning?'

I thanked him and asked whether he and Mr Stanley would be all right now.

'Probably,' he said. He managed to make it sound as though I still had a lot to answer for.

As I hung up, I noticed Kennedy watching me, with a grin starting to spread across his face.

'They put the monkey into the cat carrier and hid him somewhere, probably in my father's flat, and they told the police it had escaped. As far as the authorities will know, it's gone for good. My father doesn't know whether to be cross or amused.'

This solved the problem of Mr Stanley's unlicensed keeping of a dangerous animal, and now they'd probably stop asking about it. They wouldn't have anything to tell Lewis, when they finally caught up with him, and that would be best for everybody. I'd tell the old man myself, when I got to see him, if it was safe by then. That was the plan.

# Chapter 16

## Looking and Seeing

Nobody who knows me well has ever believed that tidiness is one of my virtues. Despite that, I made a circle around the streets next morning on my way back from nursery and tore down my home-made posters. I dumped them into my empty wheelie bin when I got back, and let myself into the shop where my father was waiting. He looked gloomy. I felt a little cranky myself this morning, so I spoke before he had the chance.

'We did the right thing about the monkey.'

Barnabas grunted. 'The monkey itself is irrelevant to police inquiries. If you were thinking that I agreed as a kindness to Mr Stanley, that's true. However, there is a perfectly acceptable monkey sanctuary down in the West Country.'

I looked my question.

'I phoned the primate keepers at the zoo on Saturday in case a backup plan were required. My bathroom still smells. The cat carrier apparently has unhappy associations for the animal.'

'I have air freshener,' I offered meekly.

'So do I. Dido, enough chitter-chatter: what is going on?'

I said, 'A lot. I don't suppose you were watching television last night?'

'Just tell me.'

'That will take a little while.' I moved a pile of catalogues off the visitor's chair so that I had somewhere to sit down, thought back to the moment when I'd pulled the rucksack out of the wheelie bin, and set about bringing Barnabas up to date. By the time I'd described my actions on the previous evening, he was thinking hard.

'Let me make sure I understand you. A young girl was murdered, and her body frozen, then cut up and – in part – rediscovered later in various plastic bags that have been dumped throughout this neighbourhood. Though very young, she was a prostitute. They think that her death is probably connected with the murders of several other similar girls in the area over the past ... how long?'

I tried to remember what Chris had said. 'I don't think anybody's sure whether they are connected.'

'An autopsy should either confirm the connection or rule it out?' my father speculated. 'The *modus operandi* will be revealing. Now, the next point is whether your old man was in some way involved.'

'Coincidence? Or he picked something up when it happened to turn up across the road

117

here.'

'No: you told me he already had the earring then.'

I said slowly, 'I've been trying to work that out all night, but I don't see how anybody can be sure. You see, there's no proof that he got it from the girl, either before or after she died. He was always looking through dustbins, you could see that from the kind of things he was carrying around. He might have come across it in some rubbish that the killer had dumped. It *might* originally have been with some of her clothes, but since he'd had it for at least a couple of days before he found ... her ... then that's that. The dustmen come around once or twice a week, so if there was anything in the rubbish that hasn't been noticed yet, it's gone.'

Barnabas considered my reasoning, sighed and shrugged. 'However, about the dismembering of the body: you say that only a torso, head and one arm have been found so far? That means there is at least one more "discovery" pending, unless of course the rest of the body has already vanished into some landfill site. Very well, that leaves two questions. First: *why* was this poor child treated so? It is reminiscent of what you hear about serial killers. You recall that unpleasant married couple some years back, who filled the garden with the corpses of young women, including their own daughter?'

'Are you saying that the old man could have been collecting victims? Barnabas, he was homeless! He had nowhere to hide them.'

But my father had the bit between his teeth. 'The police should be searching empty properties, though considering the number of derelict sites between Euston Station and the Angel, I suppose it could take them an extremely long time.'

'And if Lewis wasn't involved?'

'But another thing which suggests that he might have been,' Barnabas persisted, 'is his "accident". Anyone else involved would think him dangerously unreliable. What a shame that the police didn't manage to keep hold of him when they had the chance.'

I pointed out that it had been a traffic accident.

Barnabas threw me a withering look.

I said meekly, 'I could try to find out.'

'Wait! Think: why was the body dismembered? You said there may be a connection with other killings, but she – the one in the street here – is the only one to be disposed of in this way as far as anybody has noticed?' He frowned at the ceiling. 'There must be a reason. It could lie in the mental state of the killer, or it might involve someone else entirely.'

'Or it could just be easier to hide the body this way.'

Barnabas snorted. 'Hide? I would suggest that placing the victim's head in a split carrier bag and abandoning it on the doorstep of a shop in Upper Street is scarcely the most effective way of hiding anything, short of waltzing into Scotland Yard waving the evidence in the air and reviling the Lord Chief Justice.'

'Somebody wanted it to be found?'

'I should think it follows.'

It did seem possible; but why? We looked at each other.

'I could ask.'

'Ask Mr Kennedy?'

'I'll phone him in a minute. Or even...' An idea struck me, and I glanced over at the answering machine on the desk. My father pressed the button. There were two messages: an order for Cholmondeley-Pennell's *Sporting Fish of Great Britain* and a request for me to call DS Smiley, with the number of her mobile phone; it sounded urgent. Both had been left that morning.

We changed places, and I dialled.

'DS Smiley.'

'It's Dido Hoare. You wanted to speak to me?'

'Miss Hoare, you left a message for me last night.' She sounded preoccupied.

'Yes.' I'd almost forgotten about it. 'I wanted to tell you that I'd seen a part of the earring – the missing one of the pair that belonged to the murdered girl. I recognized it when they showed it on TV last night: Mr Lewis had it. When you didn't ring back, the ... somebody who was with me called a friend at King's Cross, and they went and got it. But I still have one part of it here in my shop – I'm terribly sorry, but I put it down on the desk when I found it, and I forgot about it when you came for the rucksack, and I imagine that you want it?'

'How long have you had it?'

I thought fast. Oh, of course – Saturday night. I explained that I'd forgotten to put it back in the rucksack. It was all perfectly true.

Her voice grew resigned. 'Listen, Miss Hoare, I'm very near you at the moment, so I'll come straight by. Are you in the shop?' I mumbled something. 'All right, then I'll be right there.'

'She's coming at the gallop,' I told Barnabas as I hung up.

'I'll be getting that parcel wrapped,' my father said. 'The fish book. You can concentrate on working out your story.'

'I don't have to,' I said. I was telling the truth today – most of it. I went out into the shop again and hung around for about two minutes until a blue light flashed outside and a car pulled up conspicuously at the kerb.

As she came through the door, I said, 'Coffee?'

She shook her head. 'I have to get back. We're still searching the – We're doing a search at the moment. Do you have the earring?'

'In the office,' I said, and introduced Barnabas.

She refused his offer of a chair, received the earring part when I pulled it out of its hiding place, and slipped it into a plastic envelope.

I explained one more time that I'd only gone through the bag because I was trying to find a clue to the old man's whereabouts.

She nodded, giving an impression of not paying much attention. 'I don't suppose there's any harm done. Thanks, and I'll—'

I interrupted her. 'I don't suppose this means anything, but there's something missing that should have been there. He had an old book, a flower book. He showed it to me a few months ago, but it wasn't there when I found the bag.'

'What about it?'

I explained as far as I could: that it had been an illustrated nineteenth-century book about painting flower pictures, and that I'd tried to buy it from him for £500 but he'd refused.

Her eyebrows rose. 'He refused £500?'

I explained that maybe he hadn't understood, or he'd loved the book too much to sell it. It wasn't convincing. 'I don't suppose it's very odd. I mean, considering how vague he usually was. But I thought that I ought to mention it.'

She looked doubtful. 'He probably traded it for a can of lager. He's in a parallel universe half the time, poor old sod.'

'I suppose it's not surprising he walked out in front of a car – if that's what happened.'

I waited for a nod or a shrug. I got what looked like a sideways glance.

Barnabas caught it too. He asked innocently, 'How did it happen? I don't believe I've heard anything about it in the news?'

122

'It looks like a traffic accident.'

Barnabas gave her a paternal smile. 'You're saying that there was something odd about it?'

'Professor Hoare, I'm not saying anything like that. We won't know until he can talk to us. Thank you for reporting this, Miss Hoare. Before I go – I ought to ask you whether you've remembered anything else odd or suspicious in the last week or two that might be connected with the body across the street?'

I shook my head.

She said, 'Thanks again.' Then she nodded at my father and left.

I said, 'What do you think?'

'Something about this accident is worrying them.'

I thought so too.

'Did you notice? She started to say something about searching, searching "the" something, and then she stopped herself.'

I had noticed, but then they ought to be searching the whole area, for what it was worth. It made me think about doing a search of my own: getting on the computer and looking for a copy of *Lessons in Flower Painting*. It was an uncommon book. If there were a copy being offered for sale at the moment, I should show an interest. I might even circulate a query. The booksellers' associations are good about publicizing missing books.

By the time I'd spent half an hour online without any luck, and another hour dealing with the morning's mail, Kennedy still hadn't rung. His mobile was switched off, of course. But when he did ring back at last he started by asking what was wrong.

I said, 'Nothing,' and then contradicted myself. 'I was talking to DS Smiley this morning when she came to pick up the earring bit that I had here. She told us, I mean she implied, or...'

'I know what you mean,' Chris said. 'Go on.'

'All right, I think there's something funny about Mr Lewis's accident.'

'I can try to get something on it. Dido, are you busy?'

'Well, the shop isn't open today and Barnabas is here, but – you know?'

He grunted. If he didn't know, he hadn't been paying attention. 'I'm looking for Annie Kelly. At one time, she was staying up near the Caledonian Road, but she's not there now, and she isn't at home. It's urgent.'

'You want me to look for her? I know she told you she lives near here, but that doesn't mean much.'

'I only meant for you to keep an eye open, please. Presumably she goes out to buy teabags and cigarettes, and I need to talk to her as soon as possible. I've been leaving messages on her mobile, but I can't risk saying much in case somebody else picks it up. If you see her around, or she comes into the shop for some reason, try to persuade her to contact me – that's all.'

124

'Where are you?' I was hearing the noise of traffic in the background, and what sounded like heavy machinery.

'I'm over to the east of you. Do you know where Southgate Road crosses the canal?'

He could have been talking Chinese.

'Dido, haven't you heard the news? All right. They've found a car in the water, with a body inside. The diver says it looks like another of these girls. They're hoisting the car out now. If you see Annie, just say I'm very anxious to contact her again, and I have money.'

'Why would she know anything about this?'

'Don't jump to conclusions. I want to tell her that the police think she's in danger.'

But she already knew that. It explained her behaviour.

'If the wrong person hears that she's been talking to the newspapers...'

'Not as bad as talking to the police,' I supposed. 'All right, of course.'

As I switched off, Barnabas looked up from the chair where he was reading through a catalogue and raised an eyebrow.

I supplied a rough outline.

He scowled. 'I can't help thinking that things are spinning out of control.'

True, and I hoped that the spin would at least slow down soon, because I wanted to get off. I suggested a pot of tea, and we went upstairs.

When I went for Ben at five, I took the MPV instead of walking. There was a street atlas in its glove compartment, and I looked up South-gate Road. But when Ben and I got down to the canal half an hour later, the place was dark and there was nothing left of the activity that Chris had described a couple of hours before. We parked and stood for a while on the bridge, looking down at the black water. The wind had dropped, but it was bone-numbingly chilly by the canal. It might freeze over this year.

'It smells,' Ben observed. 'It really, really smells here. Can we go home?'

There was nothing to see, not a hint of anything wrong. I agreed that it really, really smelled, and we went back to the van, hand in hand. Ben was telling me about his day, and about the rehearsals. I listened and asked the right questions. At the main road I turned left and drove down towards Old Street, turned along the City Road, hit the heavy traffic flows, and struggled towards the Angel. It occurred to me for the first time that this route actually skirted three sides of an area of crumbling brick commercial buildings, trading estates and dark stretches of water. And that this whole place lay right next to the lights and money of my trendy Islington, waiting for some of that money to spill over and for redevelopment to obliterate its dark corners. And that Annie Kelly or any-body else who knew the place could slip from the one side to the other every day, and never be seen.

# Chapter 17

## Diversions

It was ridiculous, of course. I hadn't been able to locate one more-or-less immobile rough sleeper when I'd gone looking for him, and finding Annie against her wishes would depend on the sort of coincidence that you shouldn't expect. I also had a sense that it wouldn't happen if she saw me first. Even so, the idea took me over to the display window from time to time to look outside. It was raining again. I switched on the Christmas lights.

I'd trudged back after delivering Ben to nursery, where they would be busy all day with important rehearsals, and went into the shop without much enthusiasm. My father had gone to the British Library and Ernie wasn't due. I dealt with the day's post, which consisted mostly of Christmas cards from business acquaintances. The wind had veered around to the west during the night and brought heavy cloud cover with the rain. It was a little warmer today, and almost dark enough for the street lights to switch themselves on.

I also cleared the answering machine. Chris

hadn't rung, but I dealt with some messages and wrapped a book for posting. Then I pulled open the bottom drawer, got out Mrs Acker's *Winnie-the-Pooh*, opened it at random and started to read. I could still remember all the words. After a few pages, I noticed that I was starting to feel like Eeyore, so I put it back and wandered over to the window again. The street was absolutely deserted.

I'd posted quite a lot of money into the night deposit safe yesterday. In normal times, this would have inspired me to buy some more books. Today, I seemed to need short-term first aid. I remembered seeing something in the new little dress shop opposite the launderette. It was a red dress with spaghetti straps and a skirt made from layered triangles of gauze sewn at angles to the lowered waistline and ending in points that fluttered around knee level. I could still picture every detail of it twenty-four hours after I saw it. It would knock their eyes out at Christmas dinner in St Albans. The fact that gravy would almost certainly be spilled on it at some point seemed irrelevant.

Thirty seconds later I was rounding the corner with my credit card. The shop – it was called Glad Rags – was open, and the red dress was still there in the window. My first glimpse assured me that I hadn't been wrong. I plunged inside. Ten minutes later I came out again, breathing hard, with a shiny black and gold bag in my hand and a new credit card slip in my pocket.

Mrs Acker was there ahead of me, just turning the corner into George Street. When I got to the same spot, I found her standing in front of my display window, head bowed and one hand on the window sill. I ducked back. After a moment she straightened up and went on slowly. When she hd got well ahead, I ran to my door and deposited the red dress safely inside. Then I went after her. I had nearly caught up when she stopped again and clutched at the railings.

When I called, 'Are you all right?' she turned her head.

'I don't know.' It was just a whisper. 'I'm suddenly ... dizzy...' Her face was white, and the yellowing bruises stood out against the pallor.

I said, 'I'll get you indoors,' and put a hand under her left elbow.

'Next house,' she whispered. We stumbled through a gate and up a wide set of steps to the front door, and I supported her while she dealt slowly with the three locks. When the door swung open, she said, 'I'll be all right now,' and then caught hold of the door frame.

I grabbed her again. 'Is your – Mr Acker in? Or should I phone him?'

'No! He's on duty. I'll be...'

I said, 'I'm putting you to bed. I'll make you a cup of tea, if you like, and I'm going to wait until you decide whether I ought to call your doctor.' I didn't actually say, 'Or an ambulance,' but I didn't count it out. 'Don't talk, wait till you're indoors.' We wobbled inside. I kicked the door shut.

We were standing in a high-ceilinged hallway, empty except for a worn hall runner, a small, scratched side table pushed against one wall and some closed doors. A wide flight of stairs stretched ahead of us to the gloomy top-floor landing, and I pushed her towards them. I took her shopping bag out of her hand and left it there. In the upstairs corridor, we turned and wobbled over to one of the doors which opened into a room furnished with an old-fashioned beech bedroom set and a big double bed. The blinds were drawn. I got her over to the bed and sat her down.

'How's that?'

'I'm sorry to be a nuisance.' Her voice was a little stronger. 'I skipped breakfast. I'll be better in a minute. I don't want to bother you.'

'You aren't,' I said. So all this was brought on by skipping breakfast? I decided to act as though I believed her. 'Would you like to rest while I go down and get you something to drink, a cup of tea and maybe a biscuit or something? Where's the kitchen? Is it downstairs, or in the basement?'

She hesitated and nodded. 'Thank you. The kitchen is just downstairs at the back. But I ought to put the milk and the fish into the fridge.' She was fumbling her shoes off and swinging her legs up one at a time. She sank back against the bolster, still wearing her coat.

That was probably a good move: the room was freezing.

'I'll do it. I'll be back in a minute,' I said and left her there.

I carried the shopping bag into the kitchen – another big, cold, plain room, with wall cupboards and a little Formica-topped table – bare and clean. The first thing that I did was to find the boiler on the back wall and switch the central heating on. How could anyone bear coming home to such a freezing house? There was an old electric kettle on the work top, with the tea caddy and a pottery sugar bowl beside it, and the cupboard above provided a clean cup. It was all immaculately tidy. Empty. Apart from an old kitchen clock above the fridge, and a calendar from a takeaway in Upper Street, the walls were bare. Two plates smeared with what looked like tomato sauce sat in the washing-up bowl in the sink; but of course Mr Acker might have needed two breakfasts before he went off to do some hard policing.

I filled the kettle, plugged it in and, as it heated, looked for food. For a moment I thought that all I was going to find was the six-pack of lager in a bottom cupboard. Then an open packet of chocolate digestives emerged. The Ackers were living in a nice big maisonette converted from the top floors of a nice big house with nice big rooms which contained nothing but the barest necessities. I grabbed a paper napkin from a holder beside the cups, put it on the tray, and crept out into the hallway.

I saw nothing. Like the kitchen, everything was clean and bare. No hall mirror, no picture. There were two doors in the wall to my left. Moved by naked curiosity, I crept to the nearest and pushed it open. This was a dining room: polished dining table sitting on another worn rug, chairs, sideboard with an empty pottery bowl on it. Chandelier over the table with little candle bulbs. Tidy. Dust-free. Empty.

I pulled the door shut and tried the next one, which opened into a sitting room. Curtains were drawn across the bay window, but I could see enough. The little television set was almost an antique. There was a poinsettia already going leggy on a table by the window. What kind of people have no family pictures, no little china figurines, no copies of magazines or yesterday's newspapers lying around? No books. I'd sold Mrs Acker lots of books. She must have them upstairs.

A cracking sound made me jump, but it was just the heat expanding the metal radiator, not an outraged Mrs A creeping downstairs to find me poking my nose into her business. I shut the door quietly. By this time, even that old kettle would have boiled.

When Mrs Acker's eyes finally closed, I whispered goodbye and left her to sleep. I left the tray on the kitchen table: a bit of mess. But I'd suddenly imagined the burly police constable coming home and finding me there, and that picture pushed me hastily out of the room and the house. I pulled the front door shut behind me, listened to the lock snap, and hoped she would be all right.

There was an estate agent's board fastened to the railings a few doors up the road. I memorized the name and phone number on it before I turned back.

No customers were queuing at the shop door. I went to take my new dress upstairs. Unpacking and hanging it distracted me again for a few minutes, but something was bobbing up and down just under the surface. I went and made the phone call. Yes, the period upper maisonette in George Street was still available, although two couples were coming to see it that afternoon. Yes, it was a conversion in the top two floors of a house, three bedrooms, two baths, clean decor, shared use of the garden. Presumably the same as the Ackers', although it sounded nicer. Yes, and the asking price was £455,000. I said that was a little more than I could afford at the moment and agreed that they could send me their future lists. Why not?

It was time to do some work; but first I went into the kitchen where Mr Spock was dozing and switched on the coffee machine. Then I leaned on my elbows at the table. Spock came, bunted my nose with his forehead, and sat down, looking attentive. I obliged by rubbing him behind the ears and asking whether he knew how a police constable could afford to rent such an expensive place, even if it was only half furnished and horrible? According to the newspapers, the big rise in London house prices during the nineties means it is now almost impossible for public-sector workers in central London to find affordable accommodation anywhere within miles of their work.

Spock listened politely to my theories: the Ackers had rented the place twenty years ago on a lease that, curiously, didn't specify any rent rises? Mr Acker was a royal duke? Mrs Acker had a secret night job as a brain surgeon?

My companion opened his mouth and gave one of his silent miaows. I poured myself a mug of fresh coffee and took it downstairs. Having removed the sign which said that I was 'out on business', I settled down to checking the accounts which Ernie was entering into our computer spreadsheet. From time to time I broke off, made a fruitless phone call, and dusted some shelves. Kennedy still hadn't answered his voicemail.

At four fifteen I stopped, put on my coat, grabbed my umbrella, and went out to buy some milk. And bananas. I had wandered all the way to the tube station before I noticed that I seemed to be keeping my eyes open for Annie Kelly after all. So I turned around and headed straight over to the nursery. I was at the gate fifteen minutes early, standing under my raised umbrella, looking at the rain, failing to make sense of anything.

# Chapter 18

## What Dreams Are

Somebody had used a knife or an axe on her. It must have been an axe. The door had sprung open, banging against the display case, and then Mrs Acker stumbled into the shop, her eyes wide and empty. There was a deep wedge cut into the side of her skull. She had bathed in blood. I stared at her breathlessly until there was another bang, louder than the first, and I opened my eyes and saw Ben tiptoeing into the bedroom. In the background, I heard the toilet flushing. It was still dark.

Ben told me, 'It's seven-something-o'clock.' He's good at the hours now, though the minutes are harder.

I pushed back the duvet, groaning. The alarm on the bedside table began to peep. I whispered, 'Good morning, love,' and struggled upright, slowly starting to think about breakfast with a brain that wasn't working yet.

When I got back from the nursery walk, Barnabas was in the shop, frowning at a shelf of children's books.

I switched on the Christmas lights and said, 'Barnabas, what are dreams?'

My father is always more than equal to these questions. 'Merely the brain processing things, processing one's daytime experiences. Should I assume that you didn't sleep well?'

I told him I'd slept all right, and we spent a minute or two comparing our sleep, our general health, and our contentment or otherwise with life. It seemed we were both all right, as was Ben. I took my chance to remind him that we were both booked as audience for the nursery's Christmas concert. It seemed like a long time ahead, but wasn't. Then I told him I felt a burning need for caffeine and went away to make it.

By the time I got downstairs again with two mugs of coffee, I had thought of a plan. It involved taking one of the shop's nice blue-and-gold carrier bags, dropping a reading copy of a Roald Dahl into it, and putting on my coat. I drained my mug and informed Barnabas that I was going out to do some research.

'You spend more time out of the shop than in it these days,' he commented. It almost wasn't a complaint. 'Will you be coming back?'

I nodded vaguely. In the street I turned left, walked past the first couple of houses, and stopped just opposite the crime scene. The police van had gone, although the awning over the gate looked like becoming a permanent street fixture. I started ringing doorbells. The first three went unanswered. The fourth brought a spaniel and an old woman in a tracksuit to the door.

I recited my prepared speech: 'Hello. I own the book shop just down the street, and I hope you can help me.' I held up the bag. 'Somebody left a book in the shop yesterday, and I'd like to deliver it to her. Mrs Acker. I know she lives along here somewhere, but I don't know the number. I think she's married to a policeman. Do you know her?'

When the lady with the dog looked blank, I apologized and went on.

Some of the doorbells brought no response: working hours. I criss-crossed the street, getting a response at a few of the doors and repeating the same speech a dozen times. When I reached the right house, I rang the bell of the basement flat and stood close against it, listening. A little sign by the bell said it was '21B' – so this was a separate flat, all right, and the most likely place to find someone who had heard suspicious noises upstairs. Nothing happened. I rang again, a loud peel, and started using my eyes.

The wooden shutters inside the window were closed, as they had been yesterday. Now that I looked more carefully, I doubted whether the shutters made much difference, since the windowpanes were thick with dirt, as though nobody had cleaned the glass since the house was first built. The window ledge was covered in street grit, which also darkened the ridges on the door and made me think that the place might be uninhabited. When I looked down at the cement doorstep for a clue, the dirt on it showed signs of feet and of wheels – a shopping trolley, maybe. More confidently, I pressed my ear against the narrow glass panel and listened to absolute silence.

This had been my best hope. I'd try again later.

Upstairs looked equally lifeless. I made sure that there was no face at the window, then retreated briskly with my fingers crossed. From the gate, I zigzagged back and forth across the road, visiting the immediate neighbours. Now I asked about the Ackers directly.

On the third attempt, a woman who was summoned to the door by her little girl said a man and woman did live in that house.

'I nod to them in the street,' she explained, 'but they keep themselves to themselves. I took in a parcel for them once, but I can't remember their name. Sorry.' I thanked her anyway and went on a little further.

It seemed that nobody really knew the Ackers. I had hoped to hear a little gossip, even if I had to tell someone a part of the truth, but I'd got nothing better than the phrase about 'keeping themselves to themselves'. We're often like that in the middle of a big city with a restless population.

I went home wondering whether I had the nerve to return in the early evening when more people would be at home, and trying to think of a better way to get a sense of my customer's life. Especially the bruises and the black eye. I hadn't needed my father's explanation of dreams to tell me that I had been brooding over Mrs Acker's bruises for days.

# Chapter 19

## Hints and Tricks

Sometimes I pretend to myself that I have to look up Paul Grant's phone number, rather than having it ingrained in my memory. I suppose that one day he'll change it. We go back almost five years, from the days when he was a DI stationed here in Islington. He'd moved on to one of the Met's special units, and we weren't in regular contact any more.

I sidled past the shop window as inconspicuously as possible and went upstairs to use the phone. He answered immediately.

'It's Dido. How are you?'

With barely any hesitation he said, 'I'm fine. Busy – you know. What about you? And the family?'

I told him that Ben and Barnabas were flourishing and worked my way around to admitting that I had a problem.

'Can I help?' I caught the tinge of amusement in his voice, and had to remind myself that it wasn't the first time I'd done this kind of thing.

'Can you tell me anything about a man named Acker? He's one of the uniforms at Islington, and I'm pretty sure that he was there before you left.'

I caught an interesting hesitation. 'I think I remember him. Is there a problem?'

I tried the truth, if not the whole truth – that Mrs Acker had been a customer ever since the shop had opened, and that I was worried about her. 'She's been injured recently, I think more than once. When I asked her about it she said she'd hurt herself.'

Silence. Then, 'You mean she claimed she'd walked into a door?'

'There's something furtive about how she reacts if you ask about it. Or ashamed.'

'Maybe she's embarrassed by her own clumsiness.'

I was hearing the old advice to mind my own business. I ignored it, as I always do. 'I know she's embarrassed, but that doesn't mean I'm wrong.'

'Dido, look: domestic violence, if that's what you're talking about, is difficult. If you want my personal opinion, don't get involved. If you're serious, you'd better contact the person at Islington who's in charge of this work now. I don't have a name, but you can phone the switchboard and ask.'

140

I said, 'But Acker is a policeman, and he's *stationed* there.'

More silence. Then he said, 'Ken Acker? He arrived a little while before I left, but as it happened I never worked with him. PC Ken Acker, right? I think he transferred there from somewhere south of the river – Bermondsey, maybe?'

'Isn't he too old to be a constable?'

'A lot of people don't go any further – it isn't just seniority, you know.'

'Are you saying there's nothing unusual about him?' I listened to more silence. 'Paul! why can't you just tell me? Isn't it on the record?'

'I don't know about records. We heard he'd been demoted when he came to us. He'd been a sergeant.'

'Why?'

'It usually means that his superiors suspected something incompetent or shady, but either there wasn't any evidence or it wasn't enough to take disciplinary action on. They could have suggested he should apply for a transfer. I didn't get the impression that he was stupid, but he wasn't particularly matey. There was a complaint once, I think, that he'd roughed up a suspect, but nothing came of it. If there was anything really off, they'd probably have caught on to it by now. He seemed to do his work all right.'

I thought about asking whether he could find out more, and decided not to. It was probably enough.

'Dido?'

'Mmm?'

'Why don't we get together for a drink?'

'Why not?' I agreed. 'Some lunchtime, perhaps, if you're over this way?' I could manage that much.

'Good. Dido, one other thing.' I waited. 'If you're right that he's beating up his wife, you should expect it to be ugly. Abusive relationships always are; and yes, it's awkward because of what he is. You could get her hurt.'

I breathed in. 'I've thought about that, but she's being hurt now, and I don't just mean her feelings. I ought to get her talking to me, shouldn't I?'

'And then?'

'Then,' I said slowly, 'what I do is persuade her to make a formal complaint.'

'Yes,' he said, 'exactly. Not easy.'

I said, 'I know.'

He said, 'Well – see you later.'

He left me with some questions. I was curious to know what Ken Acker had done to merit demotion and transfer – if that was what had happened. 'Too physical' with suspects? That would fit his getting too physical with his wife. But how could I persuade Mrs Acker to be open with me, when even in normal circumstances she was one of the least talkative people I'd ever met?

I considered the welcome option of forgetting

142

about it: chin up, polite smile, eyes straight ahead. I visited the sideboard, poured myself a shot of Barnabas's Tullamore, wondered briefly whether it was all driving me to drink, and sat down to take a breather and consider my options.

Barnabas asked, 'Are you sure? Dido, the evidence is circumstantial. Even if Mrs Acker has been showing signs of injury, she did tell you she'd had an accident and accidents can happen. May I offer the phrase "mountain out of a molehill"?'

'There was the book: *Pooh.* They live in an expensive area where you wouldn't expect a police constable to be living anyway, but he is, so they must have some money, and she has a problem with £85?'

'Are you suggesting that he objected to this purchase and hit her in order to persuade her to return the book?'

Stranger things happen, maybe.

Barnabas sighed. 'Is there more?'

'Not really.' Only there was. It had no connection with the other thing, but I suddenly remembered Acker's arrival in the shop carrying one of my monkey posters. I'd probably been trying to block out that embarrassment, but I'd assumed at the time that he had seen I was lying. Lewis had been hospitalized soon afterwards, so they had both the old man and the earring now. They could go straight to him with their questions, assuming he was awake and sober and making sense. Maybe that was it.

'The whole argument is flimsy,' Barnabas commented, 'although I know this is bothering you. Why don't you take advice?'

'You mean the police? Mr Acker is police.'

'I meant the social services,' Barnabas snapped. 'Or a women's support group, whom you could locate with the assistance of the social services or the police.'

I looked at him suspiciously. 'I thought you were advising me to mind my own business.'

My father smiled faintly, turned away to reach for the pile of books he had been working on, and threw over his shoulder: 'I would always prefer that, but on this occasion I only advise caution.'

'Research!' I said slowly. 'I think I need to know a little more before I call in the army.'

Barnabas said placidly, 'Let me know if I can help.' He is always in favour of research.

A couple of women who looked like mother and daughter drifted in and put an end to our conversation. I smiled at them and watched them get on with browsing. Their conversation made it clear that they were looking for Christmas presents. I made a few suggestions, hung around the rear shelves doing a little tidying and thought about Mrs Acker.

When I need legal advice, I usually contact Leonard Stockton. He is a solicitor with offices a short distance away on the Essex Road. The firm deals with civil matters (although he did once take the trouble personally to bail me out of a problem with the Thames Valley Police) and this was what I needed. As soon as the women left with two illustrated dog books, I looked at my watch and decided that it was worth trying to catch him before lunch. I waltzed into the office.

Barnabas looked up. 'Are you all right for a while if I go do a few errands?'

Shopping, presumably. I nodded. 'Ernie's due soon, so I'll manage. I'll ask him to put in some extra hours.' Christmas was hurtling toward us, and I ought to do some present shopping too.

When he had gone, I flung myself on the address book, found the phone number I needed, and asked for Mr Stockton. He and I exchanged pleasantries. Leonard Stockton seems to like me even though I get myself into trouble so often. Maybe I amuse him.

I took a breath. 'I'm phoning to ask you how I can find out the name of the freeholder of one of the houses in this street. It's divided into two flats, and I'm interested in the upper maisonette, but any information...'

'Are you thinking of buying?'

I said cautiously that I might be.

'Of course all that will come up in the title search. You don't want to wait?'

I dug up the memory of a conversation I'd once had with Ernie about his mother's housing problems and said, 'I've heard that there's an absentee freeholder, and there might be problems with structural repairs and insurance, so there might be too much hassle. Before I make an offer I'd like to know the worst. Can you tell me what I should do?'

'You should ask me for help,' he said promptly. 'I'll get back to you. You're right to be careful. Give me the address. It shouldn't take long.'

I stammered my thanks, he said it was nothing, and I smiled to myself and said goodbye. Then I fiddled around and waited. By two o'clock, Ernie was already an hour late. I wrapped a couple of books, dealt with a customer, and was alone and just trying to persuade myself that I didn't need food anyway, when the street door crashed open and two figures fell inside. One of them was Annie Kelly, her plaits standing out at right angles to her head; the second was a lanky blonde girl in a red padded jacket whom Annie was dragging along by the wrist.

I opened my mouth.

Annie slammed the door so hard that the window rattled, screamed, *'Dido! Hide us!'*, flung herself past where I stood gawking, and dragged her companion into the office. The girl squealed as she banged against the door frame. I went after them. The girl was making rasping noises and Annie's face was bright red. Then the weird girl fell to her knees and tried to wriggle under the packing table where I keep my boxes and bubble wrap. There wasn't enough room for her. I stopped thinking, flung myself at the door into the garden, unlocked and yanked it open, and waved them through. It didn't really need comment, but I did hiss, 'And *keep quiet!*' Annie gasped and nodded as they squeezed past. I shot the bolts, then turned the key in the lock and tossed it over the filing cabinet where it clattered on to the floor. When I turned around, two shapes were sprinting in front of the display window. They paused for a second at the door and then walked in. The idea that they were policemen lasted just long enough for me to wonder what kind of mess I'd got myself into now.

Once inside, they moved apart and looked along the aisles. I watched a kind of uneasiness sweep over their faces. Books, so many books, it seemed to say. The nearer one spotted me. He was a short, middle-aged man with a narrow, lined, acne-scarred face and straggling dark hair. The other was one of the biggest people I've ever seen, well over two metres tall, with a bodybuilder's muscles. Or a thug's. His head was shaved, but not his chin, and it was a toss-up whether his scalp or his face showed more hair. They both wore leather coats and jeans, and 'Muscles' sported a pair of thick-soled brown boots that looked as though they were designed for stomping dogs to death.

Options, Dido?

I took a deep breath to stop myself whimpering and felt at the desk top behind me until my fingers closed on my mobile phone. I raised it furtively to my ear and said to it loudly, 'Yes, yes, of course I remember you, Sergeant. Just a minute, please, some customers have just walked in.' I looked directly at the little man and called, 'Hello! I'm on the phone – have a look around, and I'll be with you in a minute!'

Neither of them seemed to understand me. The big man blocked the street door, while the smaller one stepped forward, looking uneasily from side to side. I moved toward him, since I had nowhere to run, and held up my hand. He hesitated. I held the phone to my ear.

'Yes,' I said to the phone, 'yes, I can answer a few questions of course. You said your name is – ?' I stopped. 'Sergeant Smiley, yes. Just a second.' I said to the small man, 'I have to talk to somebody for a minute. I'll be right with you. Go ahead, Sergeant.'

I saw the small man turn and throw a glance at his companion. Then he nodded blankly at me and turned his face to the row of shelves. He was trying to act like a customer, but I didn't get the sense that he was actually reading the titles.

At the front of the shop, the big man shifted. 'Miss? We are looking for two ladies, two friends. They come in here?' It was meant to sound like a polite question.

I asked my phone to excuse me for a moment and called, 'When was that? When were they here?'

'Now,' the little man said.

'They aren't here now,' I pointed out accurately. 'Wait: there were two women here about half an hour ago. They bought some dog books.'

'I don't think so.' He took another step forward, and I couldn't keep from edging away. Now he was at the door of the office, looking inside.

I said, 'I'm sorry, that's my office – it's private.' When that seemed to make no impression on him, I spoke clearly to the phone: 'I apologize for keeping you waiting, officer, but a couple of men have just come in; they say they're looking for some women. No, no, it's quite all right, I'll be right with you.'

I stopped and looked haughtily from one of them to the other. The little man finished his survey of my desk and packing table, threw a glance at the other, and shook his head almost imperceptibly.

Then the door opened, Ernie bounced in, and I noticed how fast my heart was beating. Something about the look of the men stopped him in mid-stride. He closed the door slowly, slid the strap of his rucksack off his shoulder, and hefted the bag thoughtfully. Then he looked with a blank face from one to the other. His mouth straightened into a line. He said lightly, 'Hey, Dido; busy?'

'No,' I said. 'These people came in asking

about two women, but I haven't seen them, so they'll be going.'

Ernie opened the door again and stepped to one side. His eyes were focused on a point between the two intruders, looking at neither, seeing them both.

I said firmly, 'I can't help you.' Then I said to my phone, 'No, hang on a minute: my assistant has just arrived, so I'll be right with you, Sergeant.'

The smaller man moved suddenly, edging past me and up the aisle toward his partner.

'Thank you,' he said as they walked out. Ernie closed the door behind them and snapped the lock before I had time to suggest it. I slid the phone into the pocket of my jeans where it would be at hand.

'Who were you talking to?' Ernie asked. 'Coppers?'

'Nobody,' I said.

Ernie caught on and chortled. He sobered quickly. 'You know them? One had a funny accent, or did I hear it wrong?'

I didn't bother answering him. I was shivering. The reaction sent me back into the office to sit down while I got over the shakes, and that brought Ernie in after me.

'You all right?'

'In a minute,' I said. 'I was scared.'

Ernie said, 'Scared? You were OK, just outnumbered. What happened?'

'They were following a couple of people who

came in just before them.' That was clear enough; I intended to find out why as soon as I was sure my knees would hold me up. Before that ... I grabbed an adhesive address label that was lying on the desk, fumbled a marker out of the top drawer, and carefully printed 'PLEASE RING FOR ADMITTANCE'. I held it out. 'Ernie, stick this on the glass of the door just level with the bell push. We'll keep it locked for a while. While you're outside, have a quick look up and down the street and see whether they've really gone. Don't let them see what you're doing.'

He was back in a second with the news that there was a car parked just up the road with its engine running. 'Old grey Ford,' he added. 'Better keep looking.'

I nodded.

He stared around us. 'I don't see two strange ladies in here.'

I jerked my head at the locked and bolted door leading to the little yard. 'I don't want them inside until we're sure the men have really gone. If it were me, I'd come back again to make sure.'

He said, 'Good thinking,' and went to lurk behind the window display. I leaned back and closed my eyes, concentrated on breathing slowly.

'Coming.'

I jumped and looked in time to see a car rolling slowly past the shop. 'Ernie? Can you see whether they're both in it?'

'Yeah, it's all right. I'm just gonna stick my head out and make sure they don't stop again.'

All right. I waited until he turned and nodded. Then I tried to wrestle the filing cabinet away from the wall, handed the problem over to Ernie, who wouldn't have as much trouble with the dead weight as I did, and wriggled down to feel behind it until I located the key. I unlocked the back door with it and stepped out into the rain that was starting again. Annie was standing by the storage shed, her eyes fixed on me. The strange blonde was attempting to cram herself between Annie and the shed wall, to Annie's obvious impatience.

I said, 'They've gone. Come on, we'll go up-stairs.'

Annie moved forward, but the girl froze where she stood. I went and held out my hand. The tears were rolling down what was left of the bright makeup and she seemed too fright-ened to move, so I picked up her hand and pulled her across the yard. When I'd locked and bolted the door again, Ernie ran interference to make sure that we got upstairs without anybody seeing us, but it did seem as though their pursuers had left.

# Chapter 20

## Teatime

The women slumped side by side on the long sofa under the windows, clutching mugs of sweet tea. In the girl's case it was half a mug of tea, because she was shaking so hard that this was the most liquid I was ready to risk. I wanted to slump, too, but that would give the wrong impression; so I'd left the armchair to Mr Spock and gone instead to the upright chair at the desk. It meant that I was sitting straight and tall. An authority figure, I hoped.

I sipped my tea, deposited the mug carefully on a catalogue that was lying beside the phone, and said, 'Who were those two?'

Annie's eyes focused on some internal calculation. 'The little one? Georgie? That's an old mate. The big one is a mate of his.'

'They're friends of yours?' I asked disbelievingly. 'Then why were you running away?'

Her eyes flickered to the girl sitting beside her, then slid down and focused on her mug.

'And who is she?' The girl's face remained as blank as though she hadn't heard the question.

'Her name is Nina. She's some kind of a foreigner. Russian, or something, I think. Her English isn't that good, you know?'

'Is she the one they were after?'

Annie looked at me significantly and nodded. One step at a time. 'Why?'

'She owes them money. Them and some other people.'

'What?'

Annie looked annoyed and sat up straighter. 'Bloody hell, Dido, where've you been? She's an asylum seeker, right? She got herself smuggled into England so she could work and make some money. Only what can a kid like that do? Washing dishes, or piecework in a sweatshop, or maybe domestic work, looking after kids, something. One or two quid an hour, if you don't have papers? She owes the people who brought her here, and she has to work it off somehow. You with me? They own her until she pays them, and how can she pay off nearly three thousand quid by working in a caff?'

'She's a prostitute.'

Annie looked at me and said, 'Well, at last! There's lots around, you know – it's no big deal. Well, it depends who you're working for, but some of them aren't so bad.'

'But she doesn't want to?'

Annie shrugged. 'They gave her a bad time at first.'

'Why doesn't she give herself up to the immigration authorities? They'll send her home.'

The girl stirred, and I saw her looking at me. Her eyes were almost black. 'No!' she said hoarsely. Her voice was thin; I realized it was the first time I'd heard her speak. 'No home! I given to men.'

'They'll catch her if she goes home,' Annie translated, 'and bring her back again if she's lucky, or do something fucking nasty if they're too pissed off. She's gotta pay them, that's the answer.'

Surprise. I said, 'So where did you meet her?'

'She was at Georgie's place when I dropped by this morning.'

'He's one of the men? The traffickers?'

'The what? Yeah – no! He's got a friend who sells him ... Dido, I don't know where to start. I just felt sorry for her is all. You see what she's like. She was crying, and I felt sorry for her, she's fifteen, what the hell ... I see she's going for a pee, so I go after her and pull her out of there before anybody sees – and I need my head examining. I still don't know how, but we run out of the flats, and then we see two coppers standing near the bus stop out front, so we just stand beside them and jump on the first bus, and Georgie can't stop us with them standing there. They come after the bus in Georgie's car, and I was gonna take her to my place, but they'd've found us there. So when the bus stops out in the main road by the church there, and I see that the car's stuck back at the lights, we hop off and run here. That's all.'

155

Something clicked: something I'd been seeing ever since Annie had helped her out of the
quilted jacket. I got to my feet and sidled
around the coffee table to the settee. Nina
looked up at me and shrank back. I held the
hand with the mug steady and pushed up her
loose sleeve. There were half a dozen small
round bruises in the skin inside her lower arm,
and the tracks of old punctures: needle scars. I
pulled her sleeve back down.

'She's an addict?'

'It takes the pain away, Dido. Inside. They
hurt her a lot.'

I wanted to shut my eyes. I said, 'Your friend
– the little man...'

'Georgie?'

'He's a dealer?'

'No! Well, sometimes he has something for
his friends.'

Oh. So Nina was his friend. All right then.

'Why did you come here? You don't even
know me.'

Now she sounded more confident. 'Well,
that's easy. Your mate, Chris. What I was thinking while we was on the bus is, he's the one
who can help. She's just what he's looking for,
right? Big newspapers got a lot of pull. So he
can talk to her and pay her thousands of quid.
Do a feature? I hear the papers pay thousands
for a good interview. So then she can pay them
off. Or he'll take her and hide her somewhere,
get her her papers, see about getting her work?

156

So when we run out of time, almost, I thought we'd come here and you'd tell him. Does he live here?'

We both looked around the room for signs of male habitation, but I couldn't see it myself – barring three of Ben's shoes.

'I'll phone him.'

'See, I better not take her home with me. Georgie, he might know where I'm living just now.'

'If they turn up at your place – then what?'

'Georgie isn't a problem. I'd tell him she climbed off the bus somewhere and ran for it. I might get a slap, but he won't let them hurt me.'

I looked at her. 'Are you sure?'

She nodded; but I wondered.

I tried the phone; Chris's mobile was switched off. I tried his extension at the paper and got his voicemail. I left the same message on both phones: Trouble. Phone me. Urgent. I hoped he'd pick it up soon, and I hoped he'd take it seriously. I wondered for a second whether I shouldn't try to locate the policeman, Johnson, Chris's contact; but I had no idea how to find him, and Annie wouldn't react well to the attempt – I knew that much.

'All right,' I told them. 'He'll phone back as soon as he's free. You should be all right up here, because I have Ernie downstairs – you saw him. He's used to these things.'

But Annie was growing more and more edgy. 'I oughta get on.'

I wasn't putting up with that: not until I knew this woman a lot better – knew exactly how far to trust her. 'No: you have to stay until we've spoken to Chris.'

She looked at me. 'Yeah. All right. Then what about some more tea, girl? You got any chocolate biscuits?'

I nodded. As I was passing the door to the stairs, I turned the key in the mortise lock: nobody in, nobody out, not without my agreement.

We were sitting with the empty pot and a plate of crumbs when the phone rang. It was Barnabas.

'Dido, Ernie tells me you're upstairs with some people. Are you—'

'Barnabas, where are you?'

'The library. I was just—'

'Good,' I said. 'Good. Barnabas, can you go and pick up Ben? Grab a taxi – you should get there by five easily. Take him back to your place. Give him supper. Let him see the monkey. Wait until I phone you, all right?'

'Do you want me to send the police?' His tone was quiet, almost casual.

'No!' I said quickly. 'Definitely not! Ernie's here, and he's looking after it.'

'So he told me.' My father sounded unconvinced.

'I'm getting in touch with Chris.'

'You wouldn't like to tell me...?'

I said that I didn't have the time right now but

I would as soon as possible. I couldn't claim I had a strategy, but I was beginning to work out a few tactics.

There had been no sign of the two men since they had driven off. I knew that because I'd been leaning out the window every five minutes to scan the street. There was no sign of the Ford, or anybody lounging around in the cold drizzle instead of walking on briskly. I was starting to think that we'd got away with it.

A couple of customers straggled up towards the end of the working day, rang the bell obediently, and entered the shop. Ernie was coping. At six o'clock I phoned downstairs to tell him to lock up and set the alarm.

'Dido, are those two ladies still there? You wan' me to come up?'

I said that would be a good idea.

He said, 'No problem,' sounding eager.

Ernie has worked security at some of the clubs in Holloway. It's not that he likes trouble, but he knows about handling it, and I wanted him with us in case Annie had been lying, and Muscles and Georgie came back. I'm used to assuming that I can just call the police when I need to, and I could get them here simply by pushing the panic button on the security system. But what about Nina? Not that I was giving it that much weight, because it would take months for them to deport her, and at least she'd be safe for the time being, and we might even work out a way to square the authorities.

We should think about it when there was time.

The first thing was to get us safely through the next few hours – all of us. I looked furtively at the two silent women. Annie seemed to be sunk in her own thoughts, and if her face was anything to go by, they weren't pleasant. And there was something wrong with Nina: she was still shaking. I hoped that I couldn't even imagine what she'd gone through.

I needed to talk to Chris right now. I was reaching for the phone again when it it started to ring.

# Chapter 21

### Musical Chairs

Ernie and Nina were lost in the episode of *Buffy the Vampire Slayer* which was playing on my TV with the volume turned down. I couldn't help wondering what Nina made of it. Annie had been more interested in eavesdropping on my sequence of telephone conversations, mostly with Barnabas. I'd given him an outline of events to explain why I had Annie Kelly and a strange teenager – who spoke very little English and seemed to be ill – in my sitting room. We'd had a long argument about what to do, with

Barnabas favouring a rational option. Annie must have been able to make out enough of this, because her restlessness was growing. I'd give her about five minutes from our final conversation before she exploded. It took ten before she pushed herself out of my comfortable cushions and leaned forward, glaring.

'Dido – I'm going home.'

Instead of telling her she wasn't, not unless she wanted to climb out the window, I said sweetly, 'I'd better call the police.'

'No way! What are you trying on?'

'Annie, we have to *do* something. Right? I'm going to get the police here. You'll be safe. We'll all be safe.'

Annie glared with an intensity that almost gave off sparks. 'You don't know nothing! Dido, you get the fucking coppers here and it'll be worse. Nobody'll be fucking safe! And you can just unlock that door, girl. You think I'm an idiot? You call the coppers, and I'm off outa here, even if I have to kick your door down!'

She had got Ernie's attention. I looked at him and shook my head slightly. Then I looked back. 'They can keep her safe.'

'Dido, will you fucking *listen*? They'll send her back, and the same people will get her all over again. If they're feeling nice, they'll just do things to her and then send her somewhere else. Only maybe she'll be dead. I'll be in bad with an old mate anyway, you know? And you – maybe they'll take it out on you, too – or the kiddie. Some of them are nasty men! You hear the message?'

I heard it. It was a loud and impressive rant. 'Then we'll have to get the two of you away to somewhere safe. And we have to make sure that your two friends don't know where she is, and that they do know that you two aren't here. I didn't like their faces, and I don't want them coming back. My father thinks we should call the police. I agree, but I'm trying to find another way.'

She almost smiled; it was touch-and-go. 'All right, so us two are a fucking nuisance. But I don't see what you're up to.'

I said I'd explain, but the phone was ringing. When I picked up the receiver, a voice exploded in my ear.

'Chris! Everybody's all right.'

Silence. Then, 'I just picked up your message, and then Barnabas phoned. It sounded...'

I said, 'It was serious, it is serious. Annie Kelly turned up a couple of hours ago with a girl called Nina – she doesn't speak much English. They were being chased by two men. Annie says that one of them is a friend of hers, but I don't think she can count on it.'

Chris said, 'Have you called the police? I'm coming.'

'I may need to, but will you please just get here yourself? Now? It's complicated: we need to talk. You have your car with you? We'll need that too. We're all upstairs in the flat, and I

162

don't think we're in any immediate danger, but we might be when we try to leave.'

'I'm there,' he said in a voice that promised mayhem on the roads.

I dialled my father's number once more. He answered so quickly that I knew he'd been sitting with his hand on the receiver.

'Dido?'

I said, 'Chris just phoned. He's on his way. But I need you here too. What can we do about Ben? Is he all right?'

'Of course he is.' My father sounded offended, as though I'd accused him of a grandfatherly failure. 'He'll be asleep in another few minutes.'

I scrambled to find a way around this, because I needed another body. After a moment I could only suggest, 'Do you think maybe Mr Stanley would look after him? Or I could ask Susie Bates to put him up. I could phone her, and you could take him over in a cab and then come straight on.'

Barnabas was silent for a moment; then he said, 'No. I will stay with Ben.'

I wouldn't really have wanted it any other way, but I was going to have to think of something. I needed more help. I needed somebody to take charge of the women: somebody reliable, somebody who was not a policeman or involved in this situation in any way. I started considering possibilities, and it struck me that I was seriously short of manpower. I was so desperate that I even wondered about enlisting Ernie's younger brothers. But they are teenagers, and I calculated that Annie Kelly could probably demolish them both with one look.

'I need another man,' I told my father helplessly. 'A big man with lots of authority.' My mind skittered uncontrollably in the direction of Paul Grant, who fulfilled both of those criteria but was unfortunately disqualified by his profession.

Barnabas said, 'I may have an idea. Give me twenty minutes.' He hung up.

Annie and I spent the time arguing in an unenthusiastic way. Occasionally one of us would throw a look at Nina. She was watching television but seemed not to see it any more. At one point, Annie muttered, 'We got a problem, Dido.'

Doorbell. I inched the window up and leaned out. The old Jaguar was at the kerb, and Chris stood beside it, looking up. I gave him a wave and went down to the door. He wanted to talk, but I whispered, 'I have to get back,' and led the way. When I locked the mortise behind us, he grabbed my arm, eyebrows raised.

I leaned against him and breathed the words, 'Annie. She's ready to make a run for it.'

He nodded quickly and hugged me for a second. I hugged him back, then grabbed his sleeve and pulled him into the kitchen.

He shut the door behind us and leaned on it. 'Who's here?'

'Annie and this girl she brought, and Ernie. The girl is one of the ones you were talking about. Annie says she's Russian. She's run away from the people who smuggled her to England, and Annie thinks you can help her. Chris, she's about fifteen, and she doesn't want to be sent home. Annie says she could be murdered, and I keep thinking that she's like those girls you were talking about, the ones who were killed.'

'So Annie came through after all?'

I disillusioned him by explaining what had happened while I was spooning ground coffee into the machine and switching it on.

'Go in and talk to Annie,' I suggested. 'I don't think you'll get far – she's having second thoughts. I'll bring the coffee in a minute. If the phone rings, yell for me.'

When I joined them a few minutes later, Chris and Nina were staring at one another in mutual incomprehension while Annie pouted. A lot of people on the television screen – some of them werewolves – were engaged in a Kung Fu fight, which was keeping Ernie amused. I distributed the coffee, and the doorbell rang.

This time it was Chris who looked out and drew back quickly. 'Dido? It's a car with two men – I don't recognize them.'

I gulped, squeezed between him and the arm of the sofa and peered down furtively. An estate car sat in front of the Jaguar, lights and engine off. I could see one person behind the wheel, and a second man standing at my door, leaning forward as though he was listening for footsteps. I needed to see his face, so I cleared my throat. Mr Stanley looked up at me and nodded politely. I cursed Barnabas's idea of a big man with authority, smiled wanly, and said I'd be right down.

The sitting room now became crowded. Ernie slid on to the floor without taking his eyes off the TV, which freed up a seat. The rest of them stared at Mr Stanley, who was neatly dressed in a blue suit. I'd been looking at it all the way up the stairs. He glanced from one face to the other, and finally at me.

'Your father asked me to come. He told me to bring a car and to have it wait.'

I waved him into the seat which Ernie had just vacated, because he was going to be here for a while. 'That was very nice of you. To offer to help. The car...'

'It will be there,' said Mr Stanley. 'Don't worry. "For as long as it takes", Barnabas said, "even if it's all night." Before you ask, Charlie is improving hour by hour.'

Good. All right. I surveyed my forces. They looked pretty motley, and I thought I caught a flash of incredulity in Chris's eye. There was no time to explain.

'Ernie? Sorry – time to go.'

Ernie shook his head and rose to his feet. 'I gotcha. Anyway, it's a repeat. So I'm going downstairs to walk around the block and swing back from the other end of the street. I look out for a parked car, that one from this afternoon with the two heavies in it. I come straight back and make sure nobody sees me coming in.'

I nodded and he shrugged himself into his old black jacket and let himself out. While he was gone, I told the rest of them what to do. As I went through it, I wondered for a moment whether the plan wasn't over-elaborate, but everybody seemed to approve.

The doorbell blipped. I didn't believe that Ernie could have come back so quickly, but when I went down and called through the locked door it was his voice that answered. I let him in. His eyes flashed in the dim light.

'Dido, they're here. Car's on this side of the road facing this way, and they're both in it.'

'Did you check the street for any other suspicious cars?'

Ernie looked at me reproachfully.

I said, 'Good! Let's get the show on the road.'

He said, 'All right, but I don't see how they're going to think I'm that girl.'

I said, 'Trust me.'

Three minutes later, we hurried across the pavement to the Jaguar. Chris led the way, a lanky figure whose identity was unmistakable even in the dim lighting. Ernie followed. He had thrown a blanket over his head and shoulders, clutching it around himself, eyes on the ground and footsteps faltering, doing his best to totter along like a sick young girl – my fingers were crossed. I came last. I put an arm around his shrinking waist as additional camouflage. I was wearing Annie's padded cotton coat, the raggedy hood pulled well up over my head and my face turned down to the pavement. I was counting on the watchers to jump to conclusions. We reached the car. I stuffed myself into the little back seat, and Ernie got into the passenger seat and shut the door quickly. I sat sideways watching out behind as Chris started the engine and we moved off. Their sidelights came on. I said, 'They're coming. Don't get too far ahead.'

Chris muttered something under his breath. We shot into the cross street and turned right.

I hissed, 'Slow down! Don't lose them.'

'Wouldn't dream of it,' he said.

We cruised down the main road, stopping virtuously at every yellow light and every zebra crossing where anybody showed the slightest intention of wanting to walk. It wasn't hard to keep in touch, not just because the traffic was heavy, but because this car was so conspicuous: the low Jaguar shape and especially the light-coloured soft top were easy to identify. They were just behind us at the Angel, where we drove straight across towards Clerkenwell and then turned right, heading up to King's Cross. The northbound traffic was heavy at this time of evening, and I lost sight of the grey Ford at one point, but we dawdled until Chris spotted it in his wing mirror two lanes to the right as we were heading up towards Camden Road. I dug my mobile phone out of Annie's breast pocket and rang home. The receiver was picked up.

I said, 'It's me.'

Mr Stanley's voice sounded calm. 'Is everything all right?'

'Yes. You?'

'Yes. Should I ring now? Professor Hoare said he will answer my phone.'

I said that I'd do it, because he and the two women should leave quickly. I wished him a safe trip, and hoped that I hadn't alarmed him. But his voice remained calm.

'The little girl – Nina – is poorly. Mrs Kelly says she may be having withdrawal symptoms from a drug and might have problems tonight.'

I wasn't surprised. We'd just have to cope with that too. I switched off.

When I rang Mr Stanley's number, a cautious voice answered.

'It's all right, it's me. We've done it – so far. Is Ben...?'

'Sound asleep in the next room,' Barnabas said. 'I've promised him that he can see the monkey in the morning. That should be an excitement for all. When will you get here?'

'We're on the way, but we need to make sure they don't realize that they aren't following Annie and the girl. The others are leaving now, and Ernie will start up there in a few minutes.'

'Keep to the main streets,' was all that Barnabas said. I spent some time worrying that he sounded strangely calm.

At Finsbury Park, Chris timed his approach and made a quick left around the station just as the lights were turning red. He made two more lefts so fast that I slid from side to side, and then did a skidding turn in the short, empty road leading into the bus terminal, which left us facing the way we had come with our lights off. Ernie scrambled out and said, 'Should be there in ten minutes if there's a bus,' and trotted towards the stop.

Chris slammed the door and got us back into the main road. There was no sign of the car.

'Food?' he said.

That sounded good. 'If we follow the one-way system, we could turn back towards Upper Street, in case they're still with us.'

'The kebab house?' he suggested, and drove off at a stately pace. He pulled up just across Highbury Corner. I stuffed Annie's coat under the seat and emerged wearing my own leather jacket, dawdling elegantly and acting carefree and out for an evening's fun. Chris locked up and joined me on the pavement.

I said, 'I haven't seen them again. I think it worked.'

He held my hand, and we walked like actors across the road to the restaurant. The traffic was lighter by now, but I couldn't see the Ford, or anybody taking an interest in us.

There was an empty table at the back. We needed to take half an hour, make sure we really had lost our pursuers, and give them time to argue about it and decide to go for a beer. I was ravenous. 'I'll have the chicken kebab,' I said thoughtfully. 'A double.'

'And wine?'

'And wine,' I sighed. 'A glass of red.' It seemed that we'd got away with it.

# Chapter 22

## Hurts

By nine thirty we were all together in Mr Stanley's sitting room. Annie had backed Nina into a corner of the settee, where she was sinking into a kind of silent anxiety. I watched her shifting restlessly. Annie muttered the occasional word in her ear. Watching them, Chris had taken the corner beside Annie, and Barnabas was in the armchair by the door, watching us all. Mr Stanley served instant coffee and squeezed himself in between Ernie and me on the smaller settee. The absentees were in the kitchen (Charlie) and the spare bedroom. Ben had wakened for a moment when I went in to see him, told me he was asleep, and then demonstrated that. I'd wanted to crawl in beside him, but there was the clearing up to do first.

My father found space for his cup and saucer on a side table and coughed. 'We have been playing musical chairs all evening, and I should quite like to know why.'

I leaned back, closed my eyes, and babbled, 'Annie and Nina turned up at the shop this afternoon followed by two thugs.' Somebody gave a little protesting cough, but I ignored her and went on with my summary, ending with, 'While they were after us, Mr Stanley brought Annie and Nina here.' I considered this picture. 'Maybe Annie and Nina will be safe now.'

A nearby voice suddenly whispered some words which made no sense. I opened my eyes again. Mr Stanley was leaning forward, looking hard into Nina's face and speaking to her. He noticed the silence and looked around. 'I was asking her if she's all right. I think that the little girl needs a doctor. She said that she hurts. I'm not sure...'

Annie said crossly, 'I told Dido she's an addict.'

She had; but more to the point, Nina had been whispering her problems to *Mr Stanley*? 'You understand her?'

He smiled and straightened up slightly. 'Naturally, I've forgotten a good deal over the years, but I was on the Russian course.'

The 'Russian course'?

Barnabas was reminiscing, 'The Russian course! National Service?' He looked at our blank faces. 'Oh, good heavens – the course of

172

language studies for potential spies and inter-preters which was run in Cambridge at the end of the war! We were preparing for a Soviet invasion, you know. Many studious boys did the course during their two-year national service; they may have thought that studying Russian was preferable to learning truck maintenance or even marching about and being shot at by Cypriot independence fighters or the Mau Mau.'

We all looked at Mr Stanley. I was trying to see him as potential spy material. He smiled back brightly.

'You can understand her,' Chris said, getting straight to the point. 'Can you ask her—?'

'Not now,' Mr Stanley interrupted firmly. 'Somebody should put her to bed and call a doctor.'

'Bed where?' Annie asked pointedly. 'I'm going home in a minute, and I don't have a bed for her.'

I said, 'We need to discuss that.'

'Nothing to talk about.'

'Do you think you'll be safe?'

My question made her hesitate. She sank back against the cushions and scowled.

My father said slowly, 'I could take Ben downstairs again and give him my bed. I don't suppose they are likely to appear at this point.'

Mr Stanley saw what he was getting at. 'Then there would be a spare bed here. But I would really be happier if a doctor—'

'I know what to do,' Ernie interrupted. 'I helped a mate at college, coupla months ago. Me and his friends. He di'n't want any questions asked, so we – we helped out.'

'An offer worth considering,' Barnabas said seriously, 'though even better would be to phone for an ambulance.'

He and Mr Stanley exchanged a glance. Mr Stanley seemed resigned but nervous. Two down.

'I'm going,' Annie said. 'She'll be all right with you. Not as if she knows me or anything, not before today. I'm off.'

I said, 'I'll take you home. I want to get back to my place, too. We'll go in a minute.'

Barnabas said, 'Dido...'

'I'll set the alarm in the flat. In fact, I might keep the shop locked up tomorrow. Customers can ring the bell to be let in.'

Chris said, 'I'll drive you both.'

I shook my head. 'Not in your car. You'd better leave it where it is for a while.' I looked at him seriously until he saw what I was getting at: there are times when you do want to be noticed and times when you don't.

Barnabas announced he was sure we would all regret this. He was being polite, probably because there were strangers present.

We dug Annie's coat out of the Jaguar and then sped down to Islington in a black cab, Annie beside me, Chris facing us on the jump seat. Nobody spoke. The cab swept past the church, ran through the lights at Angel a lot faster than we'd done earlier, and turned left on the City Road. At Old Street Station we turned left again and then, following Annie's directions, entered a tangle of little streets, made a succession of turns, and stopped in front of an old block of flats.

'Do you want us to come with you?' I offered. 'See you safe indoors?'

Annie sent a knowing glance in my direction and said, 'Thanks, love, and no thanks. See you later.'

We watched her walk through a gate, turn left and vanish into a passageway. There were a few dim lights along the footpath, but the place was full of shadows.

'Wait a minute,' Chris said abruptly. I watched him climb out and follow her. Perhaps I fell asleep for a few minutes, but I'd started to think about ambushes by the time he returned. He climbed in; the driver made a U-turn and headed back to the main road. Chris slid the glass partition shut behind the man's head.

'You think she'll be all right?' I asked.

'I didn't see anybody hanging around. She walked straight through the estate and out the other side, and I lost her two streets over. Maybe she intends to get in touch. Dido, what was going on? Why did she walk away with a girl she claims that she'd never seen before? She must have known she'd be in trouble with her friends. And why didn't you want to call in the

175

police?'

I said, 'I'm not sure. Barnabas is going to have a go at me about that, so please don't you start. I was tired, I didn't like the look of those men, everybody was scared, I felt sorry for Nina – even Annie was sorry for her. Maybe it was stupid, but something had to be done, and I decided to do it. I'm too tired to talk about it.'

He slid over, put an arm around me and pulled me closer. He probably thought I'd been as reckless as Annie Kelly. I leaned against him and closed my eyes, feeling as though the day had been going on forever.

I'd made some mistakes. I still wasn't sure that I shouldn't have called the police. Annie had objected, and I'd understood that Nina must be terrified. People had been telling her to come here, go there, do that. She had arrived in a world where nothing was what she had ever known before, and everything was different and meaningless – every detail, from the design of the street lamps to the language people speak. She was helpless. Nothing made any sense to her. But Annie? I couldn't read her at all. She was certainly on home ground, and asking for trouble.

But considering everything, I thought that I hadn't done too badly: quick-acting, tough, no squeaking ... not much squeaking, anyway. Made everybody do what had to be done in circumstances that were too strange. We'd probably be all right now for a while. Even

Annie, if she were lucky.

Then I remembered something that made sense after all: Annie'd had a daughter, and she was lost somewhere too. I think we're all haunted by our old mistakes.

# Chapter 23

## Wake Up

The silence woke me. I opened my eyes in a flat where nothing breathed except me and Mr Spock. After a flutter of panic, I remembered that Ben was safe with Barnabas and then everything else flooded back. The illuminated numbers on the clock said it was five past six. I closed my eyes but found that I couldn't shut down my brain, so I gave up, made coffee, ran a hot bath, lay in it, and decided that almost everything I'd done last night – and for the past two weeks – had been a bad mistake.

Barnabas arrived by taxi, late and preoccupied. I'd been downstairs for a couple of hours by then and was wasting time straightening the books on the shelves and sweeping grit off the floor. He walked straight past me into the office. When I went in to put the broom away, I found him staring at the dark computer screen.

'I must be getting old. Presumably the "big seven-seven", as you might say? My reason is faltering.'

That seemed unlikely. I moved the second chair to a position near the desk from which I could watch the street door, sat down and and said, 'Too much has been happening. Yesterday...'

'I must have been dozing.'

'How are they?'

'I went back after I'd dropped Ben off. That girl is on the spare bed, occasionally crying loudly but mostly just thrashing about. Mr Stanley is shaken; he has taken refuge in his sitting room with the monkey. Ernie does appear to know what he's doing, I will grant you that; he is at the bedside offering damp face cloths and chatting to her. I imagine she finds that comforting. I wonder what will happen when he needs to go home? By the way, you will have to bring Ben back here this afternoon; I did find him a spare toothbrush, but he would like to see his mother.'

I nodded and waited.

'Dido, you have dug yourself into a hole. You know the advice to those in a hole?'

I did.

'And I arrived here just now to find that the door of the shop is not locked, as you promised it would be, so that anybody could just walk in.'

I decided to interrupt. 'I tried. Three customers in a row stopped and read the notice,

178

looked confused, and walked away. One rang the bell and came in to ask what our problem is, so I had to say we'd been getting shoplifters, and then he said it was because there are so many asylum seekers around these days, and I had to stop myself throwing the sticky tape at him. He didn't buy anything, so I couldn't even overcharge him. It's no good – we can't run this place like Bond Street jewellers.'

I could see my father considering. He grimaced. 'Then I'd better stay here with you.'

I offered the opinion – which was almost the only clear thing that had come out of my morning worry – that they wouldn't come back: too much time had passed, and they should have decided that pushing things would only bring them trouble.

He started to say something but caught himself.

'What?'

'If I were they, I would find Mrs Kelly and persuade her to assist me. I'd be extremely worried about that were it not for two facts. One is that all the houses along our stretch of Crouch Hill are identical, and I very much doubt that she was in any state to notice the street number. She may not even have seen the name of the road, given the adverse conditions last night. The second is that I have warned Mr Stanley not to answer the doorbell under any circumstances. I thought of exempting uniformed police officers from this caveat, and then decided not. Dido, we must talk.'

I agreed. 'Things have been happening,' I told him feebly. 'Things, people ... they all seem to be tied in together. Maybe not everything. I suppose the police might know what's going on, but I don't.'

'And you have been deliberately evasive,' my father noted.

'About Nina – yes.'

'And a variety of other things, starting with the monkey, the old man, the—' He stopped abruptly and frowned, looking into the middle distance. When he spoke again, he had changed direction: '...with the result that you have painted yourself into an embarrassing corner. You must stop and consider. Explain these women to me again: where they come from, how Mr Kennedy became involved, how the two thugs knew them and why they were pursuing them, and precisely why you made the assumption that the police could not be brought in. I understand that the girl is addicted to some illegal drug: but addiction is an illness, not a crime. Perhaps I am naive, but I should have thought that a full and frank confession could only help. You should aid her in the most sensible way possible: you, Ernie, and Mr Stanley. The three of you must gain her confidence and explain the situation. She may well fear the police; but she is the victim here, is she not?'

It sounded so reasonable that he almost convinced me. 'Kennedy says...' My father waited for me to go on, both eyebrows raised. I said slowly, 'Maybe drug addiction is a crime when you're an illegal immigrant, because everything you do is a crime.' I told him what Annie had said. 'Nina could go to the police anyway, and maybe somebody would help her to stay in this country if that's what she wants. But if they send her home, she'll be in danger. The people who brought her are organized. They have agents over there. She doesn't know how to get away from them either here or at home. And girls like her are being killed. That body across the road, for example.'

'She needs help from qualified people, not well-intentioned amateurs,' my father said cuttingly. 'If she is a potential victim like – well, like others, then all the more so.'

There was something uncomfortably convincing about the argument. I probably did need input.

Chris Kennedy's mobile was switched off. Mr Stanley's phone wasn't, and was answered hesitantly by Ernie, yawning.

'How is she?'

'Sleeping,' he said. 'The old man's been talking to her, an' now she's asleep, but when she wakes up she's gonna be worse. It'll be a couple more days before she can leave here, Dido.'

I said cautiously, 'Does Mr Stanley know about that?'

'Sure. I think he's OK. He likes talking to her. He says he's practising his Russian language.

181

Dido, my mum just phoned. I've gotta go home soon.'

Of course that was bound to happen. 'How soon? Now?'

He said, 'Well,' which meant as soon as possible.

I promised to ring back as soon as I'd worked something out and passed the facts on to my father. Then we both pretended we were working while we thought about it. A few customers drifted in and out. Barnabas was busy with one of them when Kennedy rang, so I mouthed, 'Five minutes,' at him and went upstairs with my mobile; I had heard something in his voice.

'Chris, what is it?'

'Sorry to take so long to get back to you. I had my phone off. I'm at the hospital. Annie Kelly was attacked last night. They dumped her on the street when they were finished and somebody called an ambulance.'

I paused long enough to notice that Barnabas had judged this absolutely correctly. I hoped that he was also correct about the rest of it: that she hadn't been able to tell them much. 'Will she be all right?'

'She was lucky. She has a cracked rib, a broken arm, and concussion. The doctors say she'll be fine.'

'What do the police say?' I wondered.

'They say it was a punishment beating by somebody who knew her. Dido, are you — ?'

I said quickly, 'Barnabas is here, and I'm

182

keeping my eyes open. But somebody has got to go up to Crouch Hill, because Ernie has to go home. Chris, can I come up there later?'

'They won't allow visitors.'

'You are.'

'Just keeping Johnson company, trying to find out what if anything they're thinking of doing about it. How is – you know?'

'Ernie says she's going to be sick for a couple of days, but she's talking to Mr Stanley a bit now.'

'I haven't mentioned her to them, but I wonder?'

'I know. Barnabas and I are trying to work something out. He's worried about the men.'

I could almost hear his brain working. 'I don't think you're in danger. People like this don't want to get involved with outsiders. It's different for Annie. They may think she's talked to the police, and they're taking precautions. Her so-called friend might drop out of sight for a while. He's probably used to moving around regularly as a precaution. If we're lucky, they could decide that Nina isn't worth bothering about. There are lots of Ninas. They might just cut their losses.'

I thought about all that. There was a lot of guesswork in it. 'The reason I was phoning you – do you think I should talk to your – to Johnson?'

'Honestly? Yes. Do you want me to set it up?'

I said, 'Give me his phone number,' wrote the

digits down on a supermarket receipt that came to hand, and sat looking at it.

Thinking about the things I'd been hearing, somebody had been killing girls like Nina, presumably as each in turn had become sick, or rebellious – a liability instead of a money-spinner. Now Annie Kelly had been hurt – not too badly, so she might have saved herself by telling her attackers about us. If I could talk to her, if she were well enough to talk to me, I'd find out.

At this point I noticed two things. One was that somebody was yelling: Mr Spock was on the wrong side of the kitchen window again. I'd forgotten to feed both of us: he was glaring at me through the glass and I was sick with hunger. I opened the window and apologized as I scraped a tin of cat food into his bowl. It smelled delicious. I pulled myself together and looked into the bread bin. Stale crumbs. Cereals? Hah! Tins of baked beans? Gone. It might be time to visit the supermarket. In the end, I opened a tin of tomato vegetable soup, emptied it into a saucepan, heated it up quickly, and then took the saucepan and a soup spoon over to the table. The soup was only just warm, but it tasted good.

I'd finished most of it before I remembered what Barnabas had said about digging myself into a hole. I had agreed with him at the time; but suddenly I was wondering whether a hole was so bad – a nice, empty, private hole where

I could hide. Sit at the bottom and have time to think. Dig a ramp and walk out when I was ready. I looked at what was left in the saucepan. There wasn't enough left to keep. Tomato vegetable soup. Little coloured bits of vegetable, so small that it was hard to make out what they were, hid in the thick orange-red liquid and bobbed into sight whenever I gave it a stir. Being in the soup is much worse than being in a hole, because you can't see what's in there with you. You notice that there are lots of little, mysterious, disconnected things: beans maybe, oniony bits without much flavour, green pieces, yellow things, blobs.

I was in the soup. For days now, things had been bobbing up around me: crazy old men, thugs, books, monkey, earrings, corpses, abused women ... Lots and lots of dangerous people and knobbly little things swirling around in the December darkness.

That was the exact point at which I remembered something. I'd been talking to a senior policeman some time during the previous spring: Paul Grant, to be precise. I can't even remember what we were discussing. He said that amateurs always try to prove the things that their instincts tell them, whereas professionals (meaning himself) dig into the facts – all the facts – examine them rationally and then, only if they hold up, position them carefully against other facts until the jigsaw is completed and the unarguable picture is revealed – and, essentially, becomes capable of prosecution. I'd ignored him at the time on the grounds that this was just Superintendent Grant telling me, as he always had, that I should mind my own business. But it didn't sound like a bad analysis. Furthermore, there is a man who has always been skilled at just that kind of patient, rational examination of the facts.

I scraped the last pieces of celery, or something, out of the saucepan, left it soaking in the sink, and went downstairs to talk to my father again.

Eventually Barnabas said, 'Go out. Do some shopping. Christmas is nearly upon us. Ben. Why don't you go over to the West End and buy toys?'

I blinked at him. It wasn't the reaction I had expected. But the idea was tempting: Regent Street, crowds of ordinary, frantic shoppers, Hamley's toy shop, Liberty...

'Somebody needs to go up to Crouch Hill so that Ernie can go home. And I don't like leaving you here alone.'

Barnabas snorted. 'Should two cowboys come to the door with smoking six-shooters, I shall assume a blank expression and tell them we're closed. You say they caught up with Mrs Kelly. In that case, why would they come here? The one thing she would have told them with assurance is that the little girl is no longer here. As for Ernie ... Let me see ... I shall phone Mr

Stanley while you keep an eye on the shop.'

The shop at the moment held one customer. I went and hovered until he left and I saw Barnabas beckoning. 'Arranged. The girl is asleep, and Mr Stanley is there now. He felt that it is improper for him to be alone with her...' He quelled my snort with a wry look. 'However, I have persuaded him that it is an emergency, and have promised that I will return within four hours. You will take a break, get away from here, do a little shopping, and clear your head. I find that a change of scenery often brings new insights. I should take a bus, if I were you. Sit on the top deck, look around you, empty your mind. Ideas often come to me in such circumstances.'

Fair enough. I picked up my bag. 'I'll drop the cheques in at the bank, and then I will. I'll be back at three thirty.'

'One thing,' Barnabas said. 'You might want to stop off at Charing Cross Road – Crow Hall Books in Cecil Court. You know the name of course?'

He slid a sheet of paper across the desk. I looked at the address he had printed on it. And at him.

He cleared his throat. 'You mentioned this, I seem to remember, though presumably you haven't had time to do anything about it. I found it on the Abe site while you were upstairs. Crow Hall are offering a copy of the Andrews *Lessons in Flower Painting* at £450.

187

You might want to take a look before they sell it on? The owners are called Lane. You would be interested to know where they got it, I presume?'

Yes, I would. I thought I'd give him something in return. I told him that I would be back as soon as possible and that in the meantime I had a question for him to be thinking about. 'Why,' I asked him, 'is this all happening? At first it didn't strike me, but I've started to wonder: why are parts of a girl's body being dumped all around me? The prostitution seems to have been based over in King's Cross, and that's where Georgie is supposed to live. There's lots of waste ground over there, railway lines and the canal. According to Chris, similar bodies have been found over there. But somebody's been dumping parts of a body around *here*? What kind of sense does that make?'

'It had occurred to me,' my father admitted softly. 'Once, perhaps, might have been chance, but two or three times must be significant.'

I tried to picture a murderer storing body parts in his kitchen freezer until he had the time to dispose of them, piece by grisly piece, in the street on his way to work.

'I'd better just go,' I said.

# Chapter 24

## And Georgie

It was raining when I came out of the tube station, so I stood for a moment in the shelter of the entrance, letting the crowds push past me. It didn't seem worth trying to get on to one of the buses crawling towards the roundabout, although I was loaded like a camel. But home was a short walk away, and I was still buoyed up by shopping frenzy as well as the carefully wrapped book which was hidden in my shoulder bag. I had five large carrier bags of presents, each of them weighing a ton or two. Either I'd been easy to please, or too desperate to be fussy, but the warm feeling of accomplishment gave me wings.

I turned south, crossed at the lights and set off. When I reached the side road which would take me to the top end of George Street, I turned left and was nearly at the corner when I noticed the taped-off area inside the gate to the council flats. I stopped. When had Sergeant Smiley had let slip a phrase about searching – searching 'around'? Around the grounds of the council estate, maybe? So there had been another of them here? Things kept on happening in my familiar streets.

I turned right into George Street. I wanted to take another look at the enigmatic face of the Ackers' house. In fact, I still had a few minutes before I needed to go for Ben, so maybe I'd just ring the Ackers' bell and ask whether she was feeling better. But when I got to the house, its dark windows said that the place was empty. I looked into a sunken area in front of it and wondered fleetingly who lived downstairs, if anybody did. The whole house looked forlorn. I switched the bags between hands, wriggled my shoulders and went on.

But there was a familiar shape leaning against the wall of the garage across the road. I stopped. Just enough light came from the nearest street lamp to confirm my impression. Running away with big shopping bags didn't seem to be a realistic option, so I did the opposite: strolled diagonally across the road towards him. The waiting man straightened up and stared at me. The end of a cigarette flared and faded. He coughed, shifted from one foot to the other, and tossed it into the gutter.

Keeping my voice flat, I said, 'I thought I recognized you. Why are you hanging around?'

Georgie said hoarsely, 'Look, I don't want no grief.'

I didn't even try to muffle an incredulous snort and said flatly, 'All right.' Now I could see a couple of people walking towards us, so I

190

decided to stay where I was. I put my bags down on the wet pavement. 'So what *are* you doing here?'

He looked straight at me. The heavy folds of a habitual frown deepened between his eyes. 'Thought you might be working today.' He nodded slightly in the direction of my lighted window.

I said, 'Time off. Christmas shopping.'

'Ungh.'

I went on waiting.

He coughed again. 'Look – Annie.'

'Annie who?'

'You know Annie. She knows you, anyway.'

*Thank you, Annie Kelly.*

I shrugged. 'What if I have met somebody named Annie?'

'She had 'n accident.'

I wondered whether I should just kick him.

'Last night. I got the ambulance, don't know where they took her to.'

I said, 'Really,' making it noncommittal.

'Really,' he echoed impatiently. 'Look, will you give her something?'

'What?'

'A few quid.'

I swallowed. *'What?'*

I think he swore, but he kept it muffled. 'Just take it!' He stepped forward and dropped a little roll of paper into my disbelieving palm. I managed to grab it before it bounced to the ground. I didn't take my eyes off his face, but it *felt* like money.

'She'll need it when she gets out. Tell her I'll see her later.'

I was just opening my mouth when he dodged around me and strolled off up the road. I shoved the notes into the pocket of my coat, picked up my bags, and started briskly in the other direction, keeping my ears open. When I was opposite the shop, I turned around. He had crossed the road, and I could see a shadow sitting on a low wall in front of one of the houses now. A cigarette lighter flared. No wonder Georgie had a bad throat. I waited until he moved off again. He was in no hurry. I lost sight of him when he reached the top of the street.

So I went upstairs, pushed the bags well back on top of the wardrobe where Ben wouldn't be likely to see them, and pulled out the roll of cash: £20 notes – ten of them. All right. No, I didn't know what was going on. I pushed the cash into a compartment of my wallet and went to make sure that Barnabas and the shop were all right, hide something in the filing cabinet, and go for Ben. I thought I should walk. I might get there wetter and a few minutes late, but it would give me time to think. To be honest, I felt too preoccupied to be safe behind the wheel of a car. Barnabas's advice about getting away from things, riding on buses and giving myself space had been spot on, though a few more problems had turned up too. I had even formed a sort of provisional plan for getting myself into

Annie Kelly's presence: that was an obvious priority, and talking to her about Georgie's gift should prove interesting. That was for tomorrow. I was pretty sure I could talk my way in to see her, since she wasn't under arrest and they certainly couldn't consider me a threat.

I locked up, plunged down the stairs, and found Barnabas there alone. I rushed past him into the office and opened the third drawer of the filing cabinet, which for some reason tends to be less crammed than the others. I took the package and pushed it furtively out of sight.

'I'd better go straight off to get Ben.'

He said, 'Mr Stockton phoned.'

Stockton! I'd forgotten.

'He left a message: the freehold of the house about which you were worried is in the name of Acker – Mr K. Acker. He also says that there are three charges on the property, which "seems significant", and it may be that the owner is in financial difficulties and likely therefore to accept an offer. Dido, should I understand that you are at last considering buying a place large enough to house a growing boy?'

'I was asking about it. Barnabas, there's something I want to show you, but I have to leave right now.'

He said, 'Of course. And I must relieve Mr Stanley. I'll put the sign on the door as I leave. We can continue this later.'

He meant, of course, that he would make sure we did.

I said to the telephone, 'Have you heard anything more about Annie Kelly? I have to see her.'

On the other end of the line, Chris cleared his throat. 'I don't think you can. She's getting better, but she isn't supposed to have visitors. It's for her security.'

'Chris,' I said from the security of my belief that some things had to be done quickly now, 'who's going to think I'm any kind of a threat? She knows me. I'm a respectable citizen – as far as the police think, anyway. So if you'll just tell me what ward she's in, I'll get there.'

'Dido – all right, she's in a side room off the St Catherine's ward, fourth floor. But the nurses and the security staff have all been instructed to keep people out.'

I stopped long enough to picture myself being carried kicking and screaming down the escalators by two or three fat, uniformed men with bad breath. I'd better have a back-up plan.

'Then will you get Sam Johnson to tell them to let me in?'

'Dido...'

'And tell him that after I've spoken to her, I'd like to meet him, if he can spare the time.'

I heard a barely muffled laugh. 'All right, we'll try that. Will you tell me why it's so urgent?'

I said, 'Georgie was hanging around outside the shop this afternoon.' I carried on talking through his exclamation: 'He didn't seem to want any trouble. In fact, he gave me some money to give to her. I thought that I'd do that and ask her what happened, especially whether she told Georgie and his friend anything about Nina. Ernie says that Nina won't be fit to leave Mr Stanley's place for a few more days, so it's important to find out just what Annie did say to them. She hasn't told the police anything, has she?'

'No. They're getting impatient, but I hear that she keeps pretending to be asleep when anybody turns up.' There was another, shorter silence. 'All right, it might work.'

'And what is going to happen to Nina? And to Annie, when she leaves hospital? Where can they go?'

'Holloway?' Chris suggested acidly. 'They'll be safe there.' Obviously he was thinking of the women's prison, not the area.

I said, 'I've heard that the food there is really bad. I bet the Christmas turkey will be dry. Look, can't your paper do something for them?'

He groaned at me. 'I'll phone Johnson in the morning. I should be able to reach him at about eight thirty, and I'll let you know the answer.'

'Call my mobile,' I said. I'd be heading to the hospital straight from nursery. 'Goodnight. And – you know? I'll do something for you some time.'

Ben said, 'Are you going to visit Mrs Kelly? Can I come?'

195

He had Mr Spock in a stranglehold on the settee, apparently listening to my every word.

'You'll be in school,' I said. 'Maybe next time, if you want to.'

He yawned, 'All right.'

'Bed now,' I said.

# Chapter 25

### Display and Pay

I walked through the swing doors under the sign that read 'St Catherine's Ward' and found myself in a cramped waiting area with three waste bins, four plastic chairs, and a nurses' station straight ahead. There was one person behind the counter at that moment: a short, brisk, blond man who was jabbing at a computer keyboard and juggling an armload of files.

During my trek across the visitors' pay-and-display car park, I had used my mobile to run Barnabas to earth in Mr Stanley's flat, ready to report that Nina seemed unchanged and that Ernie would be relieving him at lunchtime, at which point my father promised to turn up and open the shop if I hadn't returned. So far so good. I'd also noticed a voicemail which I had chosen to ignore. It was from Chris, and it would tell me either that he had arranged for my visit to Annie's bedside, or that the police had vetoed it. I'd prefer not to know. In certain situations, acting out of ignorant innocence can be quite successful. So I slipped up to the counter and waited politely.

He said, 'Yes?' without looking up. I checked his name badge and gave him my own name. He scrutinized my face.

'I'm here to see Annie Kelly, Mr Hull.'

His eyes strayed to a piece of paper tucked under the edge of the counter, but he was already saying, 'I'll show you where she is.' So I was expected. I smiled prettily and followed him into a side passage. At the first door, he stopped, tapped, opened it, and ushered me inside.

'Mrs Kelly seems to be asleep.'

I said casually, 'That's all right. I'll wait.'

He threw me an amused glance which said that he could recognize a try-on as well as the next person, then slipped outside and closed the door firmly at my back.

I surveyed the room. There was an empty bed by the window and an inhabited one behind the door. A Christmas cooking programme was flickering silently on the little TV set on a shelf. Annie had probably been watching it before we came in, but now she lay under the blanket with her eyes shut, her plaits spread out on the pillow. I expected snoring.

Her face was the wrong shape, swollen and

bruised. Apart from that she looked peaceful. But I caught a glint between her eyelashes. I crossed to the visitor's chair; by the time I was seated, her swollen eyelids were shut tight. I remembered what Kennedy had said.

I brought the roll of bank notes out of my pocket, pulled one off, and dropped it on Annie's chest. Followed by another.

She made a show of stirring, blinking and yawning. 'Mmmmmggh, uh, Dido! What are you doing here? What's this?'

Her left arm and wrist were splinted, but her right hand had snapped shut on the money. I handed over the rest of the roll. She looked at it. And at me. Her eyes were bloodshot, and she could only open them halfway, but they hadn't lost their sharpness.

'How are you?'

'Better. A little better.' She looked significantly at the money, then at me. 'What's this for, then?'

I said, 'A present, maybe? A friend of yours gave it to me to deliver.'

'Mr Kennedy?'

'Georgie,' I said, watching her. A shadow crossed her face. Then her lips twitched. I could hear a faint musical theme coming from the silenced TV set.

'Bloody hell,' she said. 'When?'

'He was hanging around outside my place yesterday afternoon, so I stopped to talk.'

She thought about it. 'Did he say anything?'

198

'Not really. Just that you'd be needing some cash when you got out of here, and that he'd see you some time.' I'd been thinking. 'Was that a threat?'

'Maybe. Nah. I told you, we're old mates.'

'Funny kind of mate,' I suggested. I let her see me surveying her: one bandaged arm, two classic black eyes, and quite a lot of bruising if you assumed that some of it was out of sight. She wriggled a little, grimaced, tucked the money under her pillow, and closed her eyes again. I waited.

'I better get some rest,' she said. 'All this stuff they give me makes me sleepy.'

'Who did that to you? Not Georgie? Really? So was it the big man who was with him the other day?'

When she didn't answer, I got up, took my coat off and tossed it on to the foot of her bed, sat down again, kicked my shoes off, and put my feet up on the edge of her mattress. Then I leaned back and closed my eyes. Together we relaxed for a while.

After a few minutes, she said, 'He's called Andry. He wanted to know where the girl is.'

'And you said?'

'Told him the truth. Said I left her with a friend of hers, up Holloway, and no I didn't know the address, never been there before. Georgie believed me anyway, and the other one stopped when I started to yell and some kids shouted at him from one of the other flats.'

'So they know where you live.'

She hesitated again. 'Georgie brought him. I better get out of there. It's all right, I'll have to get my things, and then I'll go stay with a girl-friend for a while.'

'You'd better not go back there alone.'

'I'll work it out,' she said.

I said, 'That's good. Now, tell me what you said to them about me.'

She glared. 'About you? Nothing!'

'Then what was he doing at my place yester-day? And what about the other one? Are they going to come for me next?'

She looked shocked. Maybe it was genuine. 'You? Course not! Why you?'

'To find Nina.'

She thought about that, and when she spoke again her voice had become sober. 'Dido, I don't think so, honest. Why'd they do that? They already got their hands on me, and I didn't tell them anything they didn't know already. I wouldn't! Far as they know, you don't know nothing anyway. They ain't crazies!'

She seemed to mean it. I wasn't so sure, but I had to leave it there.

'Annie, do you need anything?'

She hesitated. 'Better not. I'm taking so many pills, they're coming out of my ears.'

I didn't bother to ask her what it was that she'd better not. Instead, I scribbled on a page of my notebook, tore it out and placed it neatly on the bedside table beside her water carafe.

'I'm leaving you the number of my mobile. If you need anything, you can phone me.'

She blinked. 'Thanks love, I will.' She yawned, her eyes closed, and she said, 'How's that little girl?'

'Nina? Not good. We thought she'd be a little better by now, but she's having a hard time. Annie, I know she was injecting heroin. Was there something else too?'

'I think so.' Her eyes had opened again, but she didn't look at me. 'Yeah, they prob'ly got her on crack. That stuff is bad. I'd never touch it, but the kids are on it more and more. It stops you hurting, but it grabs you right off and there's nothing you can do then, you do anything just to get the next hit because it stops you feeling like crap. It all stops hurting for a while.'

I left her lying there silently with her eyes shut and her good hand under the pillow where she had put the money.

Mr Hull was at the desk, still engaged in the war with paperwork.

I leaned on the counter. 'When will she be well enough to leave?'

He looked up at me. 'Probably Monday.'

'Not today or tomorrow?'

'I'd say Monday. She isn't anxious to leave us.'

I thought I could guess why. I said, 'If I phone at nine in the morning, will you be able to tell me if there's any news? Then I'll ask her if she wants me to give her a lift home.'

'The police will be making arrangements for her, but you can phone.'

I said, 'She might not want to bother the police.'

He let out a snort of laughter. 'That one knows her own mind. You ring at nine, any morning. I'll be off for the weekend, but I'll leave a note for my relief. Unh, and there's somebody waiting for you.' He indicated the row of chairs behind me, and I straightened my back, took a resigned breath, and turned around.

It wasn't Sam Johnson. I'd looked at him curiously during those seconds when he had been on my TV screen. This was a different man: taller, as tall as Chris, but more solid – and greying at the temples. He wore a respectable dark-grey suit which said that this was a senior police officer. My first instinct was to make a run for it, but considering how long it had taken for the hospital's elevator to come on my way here, it might be more trouble than it was worth. I marched forward. It had worked with Georgie.

He stood up as I approached. 'Miss Hoare? I'm Superintendent Allan Barker. I was told you'd be here this morning.'

I put on my polite, businesslike face. 'May I see your identification, please?' I held out my hand, palm up, received the usual leather folder, and let him watch me comparing the photograph inside with his face, point by point. I handed it back. 'I was expecting to see somebody else. In fact, I asked to see somebody called Sam Johnson. I wanted to talk to him. Is he off duty?'

He looked down at me and smiled. 'I would not know. But when we heard that you might have something to tell us, I though it would be better if you and I had a word first.'

I said, 'Who's "we"?'

'Mr Christopher Kennedy is in touch with us.'

I reflected that I should always pick up my voicemails promptly, and at the same moment noticed how he had edged around my question. I repeated it. 'And "us" means – ?'

'Would you like a coffee? Maybe we should go down to the coffee shop so we don't disturb them here.'

I threw a glance at Mr Hull, who glanced back. Barker was probably right. I nodded grumpily and swept past him to the lifts.

The ground-floor coffee shop was half empty at this time of day. I found a small table as far as possible from the other customers; Barker left me there briefly and returned with my large cappuccino, his small espresso, and the casual comment that he was from Scotland Yard.

I said, 'I think Mr Kennedy has mentioned you. Which section?'

'We're known as the Special Projects Unit. That means...'

'Intelligence,' I put in when he hesitated. 'Organized crime.' This would be the man who had warned Chris not to be too communicative with Johnson. He might turn out to be more useful than Johnson, but I needed time to figure him out. I kicked myself again about the voicemail and muttered, 'Let that be a lesson to you.' From the look on his face, I must have said it more loudly than I intended.

'Mr Barker, thank you for the coffee, but Friday is one of the busiest days of my week, especially in December, so would you just tell me why you're here?'

His smile was a little too ingratiating. 'I wanted to meet you. Mr Kennedy told me that you might need help with something. A girl you've met?'

All right. 'Maybe. Her name is Nina. At the moment, she's too ill to be bothered, but...' I was trying to think and talk at the same time, always a dangerous business '...she might need help in a little while. She's an illegal immigrant. She was brought here by traffickers and forced into prostitution, but she got away from them. Basically, she's too frightened and sick to make any sense now, but she doesn't want to go back home. She's going to need a lot of help. In return, I think she might be able to help you – if I understand your concerns.'

'Mr Kennedy knows about our concerns.'

'But I don't,' I said thoughtfully. 'Not all of them. For example, I'm wondering why you don't want me to talk to DS Johnson.'

'There's nothing wrong with you doing that,'

he corrected me. 'Not as far as I know. But we'd prefer that the girl doesn't talk to him. We could probably do something for her. He can't. We want to keep this as quiet as possible and, to be blunt, King's Cross would only have to hand her over to us anyway.'

I remembered what Kennedy had told me about this man. Or his group, anyway. 'You don't trust them at King's Cross.'

He shook his head. 'It's less clear than that.'

'Bad apples?'

'A possible conflict of interests.'

I snapped, 'You lot outrank them.'

'In some respects, but we don't want to make any premature moves.'

'You are investigating them.'

He looked pained and took a long, slow sip from his cup. I wasn't expecting to be enlightened. He didn't disappoint me.

I said, 'What do you want?'

'I'd like you to take me to her.'

I shook my head. 'She's safe. She simply can't help you right now, and maybe she's still too frightened to, anyway.'

'Then somebody will have to persuade her it's the best thing to do. In her own interests.'

I thought about that one and said, 'Actually, I agree.'

'Miss Hoare, I'm being as patient as I can, but—'

'But you'd better not threaten me if you want my help.'

205

That stopped him. He started to drum his fingers on the table top. I'd antagonized another policeman. A little Barnabas-style reasonableness was probably needed at this point. 'I've already said that I agree with you. I will talk to her about this, but if you want her cooperation, you'll have to wait. She's being taken care of by people she's starting to trust, people who can talk to her. She doesn't speak much English, you know.'

'We can get a translator.'

I snapped, 'You'll need to!' Then I took a breath. 'You will also need to offer her a deal, but she'll have to be able to trust you to honour anything that you promise. So if you'll tell me how I can contact you, I will – as soon as possible.'

I gave him what I tried to make a perfectly reasonable, expressionless, unmovable stare.

He didn't entirely give up, but he did blink first. 'You're out of your depth.'

I laughed. 'I know I am! Still – I'm all I've got.'

His lips twitched. 'Not really. Mr Kennedy says you may be the most stubborn person he's ever known. He also informs me that if I arrest you he will break off all communication and ensure that our "heavy-handed police harassment" is splashed all over his newspaper almost as fast as their solicitors break down our door.'

I said, 'Well then,' and a little ball of warmth made me smile. To his credit, he smiled too. He also handed me a card with his name and two different phone numbers, one with his extension at Scotland Yard and one for his mobile.

'Any time,' he said. 'But soon, please.'

I said I'd do my best and got to my feet. I wanted to get out of the building and listen to that message before something else landed on my head. We shook hands and I left, trying to look as though I was thinking about books and business. Trying not to hurry.

In the car park, I stopped behind the second row of cars and switched my phone on.

Kennedy's voice said, 'Hi. Dido, there'll be somebody waiting for you at the hospital. His name is Allan Barker. He's a friend of mine, don't bite him. Sam Johnson and I will be at the shop at ten thirty. If you aren't back by then, we'll go around the corner to the pub and wait for you there. Dido: Johnson isn't a friend, he's a contact. All right? If there's a problem, you can get me on my mobile. Otherwise, I'm assuming you're all right with this. See you.'

I looked at my wristwatch. It was a quarter to eleven. They would be well into their first pints, but I might get there in time for the second round if I hurried.

# Chapter 26

## In the Box

The thing I drive these days – a tall, van-like, purple MPV with space for any combination of passengers, toys, folding bookshelves and cartons of books – is conspicuous enough to draw the attention of parking wardens. I jammed its front wheels into the last metre of space in the residents' bay and left the rear wheels illegally on a yellow line. I'd already had one parking ticket that week, so my actions were simply a plea for mercy. Nobody was waiting on the pavement. I stopped for a moment at the door of the shop to squint through the glass and identify a slew of envelopes on the floor under the letter slot, realized that I didn't have time to go out drinking, and kept on walking.

They were at a table in a back corner: Kennedy, the dark man whom I did recognize from that news programme, and what looked like a double vodka although melting ice cubes might have bulked it out. I slid on to the bench seat beside Chris and upended the mixer into the glass.

'Late,' I said. 'Sorry, there was...' I caught a sudden movement from Chris and remembered '...a lot of traffic.'

'This is Detective Sergeant Sam Johnson.'

We exchanged greetings. He was in his early thirties – brown eyes, short-cut brown hair, clean shaven. Another of those well-meaning suits, with a plain tie. I decided to smile charmingly and thank him for coming, and I thought I caught a friendly, speculative look, so that was all right.

I leaned toward him. 'I need to talk to you about Annie Kelly. Do you know who attacked her?'

Johnson said, 'We don't have any witnesses. Somebody in the building heard the row and dialled 999, but they haven't come forward.'

'What about this friend of hers – Georgie?'

'Wee Georgie McIntyre?'

I let out a snort: he sounded like a character in some kind of Glasgow-gangster soap opera. 'I don't know his last name. He's an old friend of Annie's. I think he sells drugs.' I decided to tell him what he'd probably be hearing soon from other sources if he hadn't already. 'I went to see Annie in hospital today. This man, Georgie, had given me some money to take to her.'

I'd managed to startle them both: four eyes glued themselves on my face, and Chris said,'You didn't tell me – what happened?'

'He was waiting for me in the street when I came home yesterday. He gave me £200 and said to tell her that he'd see her around.'

'A threat?'

I thought about the answer that I'd already heard from Annie, and said that he hadn't struck me as particularly threatening.

Johnson persisted: 'Did he say anything else? Anything about where she can find him, or what he's doing?'

I shook my head. 'You wouldn't expect him to. He just told me he was there when Annie was attacked, and he was the one who called the ambulance.'

Johnson nodded slowly. 'It was a woman who called the police, and a man who asked for an ambulance. Neither of them left their name.'

'Annie had told him about me. That was why he brought the money to me. He wasn't unfriendly, just a bit impatient when I wouldn't agree to do everything he wanted. But Annie mentioned another name this morning. Somebody I saw with Georgie. It sounded like "Andry".'

Johnson thought about it. 'There are a couple of people she could have been talking about. Balkan thugs. Most of the gangs come from over there.' He looked at the dregs of his pint, then at Chris. 'I'd better get back and see what I can find.'

I stopped him. 'This "Andry" was with Georgie the first time I saw them. Big – the muscle-builder type: about forty, shaven head, stubbly face, blue eyes.'

I thought that it rang a bell, but he rose to his feet without comment. 'I'll check. Miss Hoare, if you see this man again, give me a call right away. Either of those men. Chris will give you my phone number. About the big man – if it's who I think, he has a bad record. You should keep away from that one. But I don't really think they'll hassle you. Just keep your eyes open, especially if you're going out alone at night.'

I'd guessed most of this already but I pretended to be grateful for the advice. He looked from one to the other of us, made polite noises, and departed.

Chris said, 'Another?'

I said that it was a bit early for me and thank you, I could manage a single. I had errands to do before the shop was supposed to open, of which the most interesting was an overdue visit to the nearest supermarket; but I also had some things to tell him about Annie and to ask about Barker.

When he came back from the bar I said, 'Annie may be getting out on Monday. I've arranged to phone and find out. Annie was saying she might go stay with friends, but she'll have to go back to get her clothes.'

'Have you told anybody about this?'

'No. But I have Barker's phone number – numbers. I was thinking that maybe I could offer to drive her home. It would be uncomfortable for her to go out alone, looking the way that she does, and she'd be safer if somebody were with her; so she might agree. If she does, I can set something up with the police. I could warn Barker as we're leaving the hospital and let him know what route I was taking, and he could have somebody tagging along to keep watch. If Muscles turned up, they should be able to grab him, or at worst scare him off. If nobody did, there'd be no harm done.'

Chris was looking at the proposal. 'They might like the idea of arresting him on a charge of GBH.'

'You mean, as opposed to...'

'...anything to do with the real investigation. But the question will be, why you?'

'Do you mean, why not you? She's more likely to accept a lift from me. All I'd have to do is keep in touch with the backup. If they're interested. It was just a thought.'

'Give him a ring later today and see what he says.'

I nodded. 'Chris, I need to talk to you, but if I don't get up the road to the supermarket before I open the shop, there will be literally no food in the flat, and then Barnabas will take Ben away for his own good, and Mr Spock will go feral. You couldn't come back later?'

He said, 'If it won't put too much strain on our friendship, I'll come with you and carry bags.'

I looked at him and raised my eyebrows wearily. 'You stereotype,' I said. 'Are you so enthralled by my high-society lifestyle?'

He said that knowing as many policemen as I do made me seem very glamorous to a mere journalist, and that only a classic Jaguar was a worthy shopping vehicle for a person like me. I think we were both nervous about the situation, and probably a bit drunk.

When I hurry, it can take me a very short time to fill a worthy vehicle with baked beans, cat food, milk, oranges, frozen oven chips and bananas. The shop was still locked up when we parked.

'I have to put the frozen food away,' I said unnecessarily, and we loaded ourselves up and struggled into the kitchen.

'I'd better go. You said there was something else?'

I thought about that while I slung some packets into the freezer. 'Johnson: you haven't told me why Barker is worried about him. Is it only him?'

'Remember that our two nasties are just a small part of the picture. Barker has more or less shut me out right now, even though we're old friends. But you're right: they think a gang of traffickers must have had some police in their pockets for a couple of years. It can be turned to advantage if they find out where the leak is; but the one thing that nobody can risk at this point is having it get out that the Yard knows some of the local coppers have been turned.

'About Nina: Dido, you've stumbled into one tiny corner of this picture. Scotland Yard have been after these people for two years now. I know that there are two gangs, one based in King's Cross and the other one over Wembley way. They're in the same business: girls, drugs, illegal gambling, and money-laundering. They cooperate sometimes, if it's profitable. But there have been inter-gang killings, too. We're talking millions of pounds' turnover, as well as the costs of policing their crimes and picking up after them. It's an international problem, and Barker's lot are working with police forces from several countries. But some little accidents have happened here in London. Sometimes they seem to know things that they shouldn't. That's why the central bunch are playing this very close to the chest now.'

Barker must have said that Chris could tell me this much. Or maybe I was just too far out of it all to matter. I said, 'I think I get the picture. So it's not particularly Johnson they're worrying about?'

'It's anybody outside the unit. They've almost certainly wondered whether I've dug up too much and let it slip to the wrong people. Personally, I've never caught a whiff of anything wrong with Johnson. But that doesn't mean anything.'

I could feel my expression growing more sour as he spoke. I was glad this icy place wasn't my world, and I wanted to change the subject.

'Chris...'

'I have to get over to the office. I was supposed to be in an editorial meeting fifteen minutes ago. Promise me that you'll contact Barker this afternoon.'

One more for my 'to do' list. 'All right. When will you—?'

'I'll phone you this evening—'

He was interrupted by a blip of my doorbell.

'That's Barnabas. But do phone me, whatever.'

'Whatever,' he agreed. 'Take care.'

I mumbled something about always being careful.

'Dido?'

I indicated that I was all attention.

'I'm uneasy. You're having a hard time over here. Is it just coincidence, or is there something going on that we haven't recognized yet? And whatever it is, is it possible that *you* are being threatened in some way that we don't recognize? Because there are certainly things going on that we don't understand. Aren't there?'

I listened to noises out in the street. Suddenly it felt as though I was inside a box with darkness everywhere around and the animals prowling. I shook myself: *stop it!*

'Are you saying that somebody might be getting at *me*? Because that's crazy. Yes, of course it's coincidence, bad luck – whatever.'

'Of course it is,' he agreed slowly. 'Anyway – take care.'

# Chapter 27

## Dodgy Dealings

Customers wandered into the shop during the lunch hour. They thinned out in the early afternoon, which gave Barnabas and me a chance to sit down in the office, and exchange information as we divided up the newly arrived catalogues between us and finished off the day's paperwork. That more or less consisted of me apologizing for not keeping him posted from minute to minute.

'If you got a mobile phone—?' I suggested weakly.

'Ridiculous! I do not need to tell anybody that I'm on the bus. I do not wish to download ringtones, play video games or send text messages to my fellow infant-school pupils.'

I almost said, 'But imagine how you could keep track of me.' I shuddered. I shouldn't even dream of reforming his technophobia. Besides, the handwriting of the Elizabethan period is my father's technical forte, and what's wrong with that?

There was silence for five minutes or so while

he finished running his eye down the pages of the new Bernard Davies catalogue. At the end, he placed it neatly at his right hand.

'There is quite a nice-sounding copy of Hogarth's *Five Days Peregrination* here, and it seems underpriced. I shall phone them in a minute. But it occurs to me that you haven't told me about yesterday. You did mention that you had something to show me, I believe. You went to Crow Hall? What happened?'

What had happened was of course that in the press of events I had hidden the book in the filing cabinet and forgotten about it. 'They still had it. I looked it over and of course it was Lewis's copy. When I asked where they'd got it, Mrs Lane shuffled through a ledger and came up with a name I didn't know: John Brown. Her husband thought about it for a while and said that he remembered the man coming in at the beginning of the week and telling them that it had belonged to his mother, but Mr Lane didn't remember much else. The man was middle aged, tidy, ordinary – not a book scout or anything like that. Barnabas, it is the old man's copy.'

'But apparently not sold to them by the old man.'

'Whoever it was, he wasn't memorable in any way. They said that he wasn't crazy or even forgetful, and he certainly wasn't wearing a blanket.'

By this time I'd dug the parcel out,

unwrapped the book, and placed it in my father's hands. He opened it carefully, turned a few pages, and stopped at the picture of a white rose with delicate veined leaves and pink-tinged petals. 'You're sure this is the same copy?'

'Do you see the contemporary signature on the fly leaf? I noticed it when the old man showed me the book.'

'Hmm.'

'John Brown might have come by it honestly. Well, not exactly honestly, but he might have bought it from Lewis, I suppose.'

'What did you tell them?'

'That two months ago the book had been the property of an old man who is mentally un-stable, and who I was sure wouldn't have agreed to sell the book to anybody. Which left the probability that it had been stolen from him.'

'Why is it here?'

'We talked about what to do, and I pointed out that I'd reported it missing to the ABA and the PBFA a couple of days ago, and that they had circulated it. They're PBFA members. In the end, I said I'd take it and see if I could get to the bottom of this; and Lane said that he'd contact Brown – he took down his address when he bought the book, of course – and ask him to provide evidence of ownership.'

'Ah,' my father remarked.

'What does that mean?'

'There was a message on the answering machine when I came in. I understand it now. I made a note on a piece of paper somewhere here. From somebody called "Jeremy". He just said, "The address is a fake". He left his number.'

I shrugged. 'All right.' I'd better think about this. I now had both of Harry Lewis's precious possessions, and maybe I should make a serious effort to tell him so. Pretty book. Funny monkey. Both safe, and waiting for him to claim them – if he could, if he should...

I didn't know what good it could do, but it struck me once again that I ought to visit the old man, wherever he was. Try to talk to him. Find out who was in charge of him, what the prognosis was, what they were thinking of doing about him. I didn't really have time for all of this and I didn't know where to start.

Yes I did: Smiley.

'Barnabas, I might have to go out again in a little while. Do you mind?'

He claimed that he didn't.

'If I do, I'll go almost right away,' I decided. 'I just have to make a phone call. And I'll have a sandwich. Do you want anything?'

'Mr Stanley served lunch before I left,' Barnabas said.

I asked whether Ernie was there, and learned that he had been stepping off the bus just as Barnabas had been getting on. That would make two phone calls.

Upstairs, I pushed some cheese and pickle between two slides of fresh bread and carried my sandwich into the sitting room. Easy things first: I rang Ernie's mobile.

'Hey, Dido,' he greeted me cheerfully.

I said, 'Hey Ernie.' I noticed that mine was no match for his breezy greeting. 'Are you all right there? How is she?'

I was assured that everyone was fine, that Nina was sleeping quietly at the moment and might be getting over the worst, that Mr Stanley seemed all right, and that the monkey was still nervous whenever Ernie came near. 'I guess it just doesn't like me looking at it,' Ernie said sadly. I rang off before he asked about passing the phone to his host.

Then I phoned the police station. Sergeant Smiley sounded as though she was eating lunch at her desk, like me. I made polite conversation for a few seconds, took a deep breath, and asked about the old man.

'Making progress,' she said. Her tone implied that she had some questions for me, too.

'I need to talk to you about him. Could I come over?'

'Has something happened, Miss Hoare?'

'In a way,' I told her and left it at that so as to grab her attention. It worked.

'I have half an hour right now,' she said and offered to meet me at the back door of the building. I waved to Barnabas as I passed the door of the shop, climbed into my MPV – no parking ticket this time – and removed it from its ambiguous position.

It took me nearly ten minutes to get as far as the police station, but she was waiting for me as she had promised.

She said, 'I'm on lunch break. Would it be appropriate to go and get a cup of decent coffee, or do you want something more official from me?'

I told her that unofficial was fine, and we headed back out into the dull afternoon, cut across the street and walked a block south to where a little greasy spoon occupied the corner on the main road. It was between meal times now, and we got a table at the back without any trouble. They even did cappuccino. This is trendy Islington, after all.

# Chapter 28

### Fingers

They had put Lewis into a little nursing unit on the main road between Crouch End and Muswell Hill. If there is a quick way to get up there, neither Smiley nor I knew it. We arrived just after six thirty in the forecourt of a low, long building surrounded by overhanging trees and thick bushes.

There wasn't enough light for me to see whether she looked as fed up as I probably did, but her first words were, 'We'd better make this fast. My husband will feed the kids, but I like to get back to them as early as I can.'

Somehow I didn't associate getting back to the kids with police work. I saw that this was fairly silly and relocated all women police officers, on the spot, into the working-mothers category of the human race. I took my chance to comment that I too had a little boy, whose grandfather was kindly looking after him for the moment. On that understanding, we pushed briskly through the main door, showed a police badge as we hurried past the desk, and walked without a pause down a long, cluttered corridor towards the rear of the building. Smiley had been here before.

I said conversationally, 'You must have been here before.'

'I visit him most days. I'm supposed to try to get him talking and see whether I can get any more from him about what happened. He doesn't remember.'

I missed a step, caught up, and said, 'When were you last here? Does he talk to you? What about his mental condition?'

She slammed the swing door open without slowing down and said, 'It varies. He was almost all right yesterday for a little while and then he glazed over and lost it. I wonder how he'll react to you?'

So did I.

We found an old man alone in a double room at the back of the building, sitting motionless in an upright chair beside of one of the beds. My first thought was that this was a roommate; but when I looked more carefully I saw that the person with the tidy grey hair and clean-shaven face, the striped pyjamas and the plaid dressing grown, was indeed my crazy old Harry Lewis. He was wearing a neck brace, and his right hand was in a kind of metal frame. It looked as though he had broken some fingers. He didn't look at us.

Smiley walked over quietly and leaned down in front of him. 'Mr Lewis? Good evening, Mr Lewis. It's Laura. How are you feeling now?'

I stood back and watched. The old man peered up at her for a moment, and then looked away. He seemed to be watching something on his bedside cabinet. His gaze was so intense that for a moment I thought he was looking at a bug crawling across the tidy surface.

I imitated her quiet approach. His eyes flickered at me, and I smiled at him. 'I've come to visit you too.' Something flickered again, and I thought of the monkey – the day when I had caught his monkey, learning to approach it gently, not staring into its eyes. It felt as though Lewis might jump to his feet at any minute, screeching wildly, trying to escape.

When I had almost reached the bed, he

croaked, 'The book shop. You're in the book shop.'

I heard Smiley sigh.

'That's right.' I kept my voice light, almost singing. 'I'm glad to see you're better today.'

But I'd lost his interest. He repeated, 'In the book shop,' and looked away.

I needed to keep it simple. I looked around, found another chair against the wall, carried it to the foot of the bed – not too close, but watching him. I sat down and waited, noticing Laura Smiley drift away to the other side of the room.

Lewis threw me a quick look from under shaggy eyebrows. 'I went away.'

I nodded. 'When you went away, you left something at my shop.' A frown flickered across his face. 'You remember your rucksack? The sleeping bag? You left them in my bin. Everything is safe. You can have them back any time you want them.' Not that I had them now, but Smiley could get them back for him – that is, if he ever did need them again.

He nodded, bent his head forward and shut his eyes, as though he had suddenly fallen asleep.

I looked at Smiley, remembered to keep my voice low, and asked, 'What's going to happen?'

'He'll get a physical assessment next week.'

And a mental assessment too, I guessed.

'If everything's all right, then we'll have to find a place for him to go. I'll get somebody to start—' She broke off suddenly and felt in the side pocket of her jacket. 'Somebody's trying to get hold of me.' The mobile phone that she pulled out was silent, presumably it was on a vibrating mode, because she pushed a button and read the screen. 'Something's happened. I'll have to take this outside. Will you be all right? I'll be back in a minute.'

I nodded, always watching Lewis, who did not react to her departure. I said to him, 'I'm not going yet. There's something I have to show you. I'll just see whether she's all right.'

And again I moved gingerly. I had barely reached the door when I saw her through the little glass window, running towards me. I stepped outside and pulled the door shut. When I saw her face, I went to meet her.

'I have to go.' She was breathless – she must have sprinted all the way back from the main entrance. 'You'll be all right. He's being good this evening – maybe he'll talk to you. Look: you ring me in the morning if you want to talk to me about what's going to happen. I have to run.'

But she wasn't moving.

'What is it?'

I watched her make up her mind. 'It's another one. A hand in a shopping bag. They say it's the same one, I mean the same person. Somebody noticed it hanging from the railings of a house at the northern end of George Street.'

We looked at each other. My street. She made a little gesture with her own hand, and then

225

turned and ran.

I stood there. Not invisible, not hidden, but hanging from the railings, waving in the wind. Gesturing at everybody. Giving everybody the finger: look, here I am again and you can't do anything about it.

My first impulse was to chase her out to the car park, but there was something I'd come to do, and I still had to do it before I left.

I waited until my breathing grew normal, and then I slipped back inside the room. Mr Lewis was waiting for me. I sauntered across to him and sat down on the edge of his bed, just at his side.

'I have to go home,' I said, 'but I'll come back again. I have something for you. A picture.' It was waiting in my bag: one of the monkey snapshots which I'd kept. I put it into his good hand: the monkey in the cage, the flowery curtains, the window ... At first I thought he didn't recognize it, but when I stood up I saw his fingers tighten on it. 'He's safe,' I said. 'He's fine.'

He didn't speak, so I grabbed my coat and walked out, throwing a backward glance from the doorway. He hadn't moved.

I suppose that sometimes I can be a little slow. On one level I was thinking about Lewis all the way back to the flat; but overall I was worrying more about what I was going to find when I got there. As soon as I turned the corner, I could see the activity up at the far end of the road: cars, a blue light, dark shapes moving around. Presumably DS Smiley was one of those shapes. Some people were streaming up in that direction: the audience for today's show. I parked on the yellow line across from the shop and was at my front door before something else struck me. I'd been thinking about the day when Lewis had found the thing which had started all this, but trying not to remember my brief glimpse of the dead hand; and my mind had drifted back to the way I had left him: sitting, clean and warm, beside a made-up bed. It didn't seem such a bad exchange from his point of view, and his physical condition had looked reasonable.

About the broken fingers, though: I suddenly found myself wondering how that had happened. Would your fingers be broken if you were hit by a car? I couldn't see it. All right, it probably wasn't impossible. If he had been thrown through the air by the impact, he might have held out a hand to break his fall. Or had he been trying to push a hurtling car away from him? Maybe. Maybe, but the picture that had suddenly popped into my mind was of Harry Lewis being held down and threatened and hurt. Somebody holding him, punching him, bending his fingers back, saying *'Give me...'* or *'Tell me...'* I'd probably seen something like that in some gangster movie. I could imagine Vinnie Jones playing the baddie. Maybe I watch too much television.

Hurt. Hurt.

# Chapter 29

## High Anxiety

I said, 'And you too, please – any time I can help out,' leaned down and kissed Ben on the nose, smiled at Jean Smith, whose son Mike was one of Ben's classmates, and said goodbye to all three of them. It wasn't the first time that Ben had gone to visit Mike on a day when my timetable had been too complicated to manage. Mike had been with us once or twice, too, but my emergencies seem to happen more often than the Smiths'. I ought to think of something: maybe a Sunday at the zoo when it wasn't quite so cold and wet. I waved to the three of them standing in the doorway of the Smiths' house, threw a bilious glance at the lowering skies and fled to the van to make another attempt to phone DS Smiley. She had been unavailable all morning. She still was. I left another polite message, switched to standby, and drove back towards George Street.

I was stuck at traffic lights halfway home when my mobile rang. I was interested to notice that what I felt, as I switched it on, was a kind of anxious shrinking: maybe things were starting to get to me.

'Ms Hoare? I've only just picked up my messages. I'm sorry I had to leave you like that yesterday. And I haven't had a chance to contact the nursing unit. I'll give them a ring when I have a minute and I'll make sure they know you're on the visiting list. All right? If there's a problem, I'll reach you on this number?'

Instead of answering her directly I said, 'I'm just on my way back to the shop. It looked as though you're finished in George Street for this morning?'

'We finished last night,' she said. Her voice would have soured milk. 'There wasn't much to finish.'

'And it really was in a bag hung up on some railings?'

'Nice and high out of the reach of little kids,' she said. There was no mistaking her tone.

'But why?' I hadn't meant to ask that; it burst out.

'You tell me. Somebody's laughing at us.'

I couldn't stop myself saying, 'Is that all? I mean – is it finished now? Do you have the whole body?'

Silence.

There was nothing I could say that would explain why I'd had to ask, so I didn't try. When the silence had stretched out for a while, she said, 'Most of it.'

229

I said, 'So someone is deliberately—' Well, yes they were. That was what she had meant. I thanked her for her help.

I made a little detour because of what she'd said and approached George Street from the north to drive past the railings in question. I could have saved myself the trouble. I caught a quick glimpse of two or three people standing on the corner, probably gossiping, but it wasn't much of a crime scene. There was somebody coming out of the gate of number 21 as I drove past, a man I didn't recognize. I hadn't seen Mrs Acker for a couple of days.

We were supposed to be opening at eleven, and I had to get ready. I was pretty sure that Barnabas wouldn't come in. That was the other problem weighing on me this morning. He had phoned early, while I was still upstairs. There had been a lot of noise in the background. At first I'd thought the screeches were coming from the monkey, but Barnabas had enlightened me, and Ernie had said it wasn't unexpected and that the next couple of days were going to be bad for both Nina and everybody around her. Mr Stanley couldn't be left to cope alone. That meant Barnabas and Ernie spelling one another for the foreseeable future. Hence the rapid ringing around to friends. Now that Ben was sorted, for today anyway, I could concentrate on getting through the next eight hours. It looked as though I owed almost everybody I knew big time.

I unlocked the door without much enthusiasm, swept the morning's mail off the doormat and dumped it on the desk without even looking at it. Then I set myself to shelving books, dusting, and throwing out quantities of rubbish. The floor really needed washing. Maybe on Monday. At eleven o'clock on the nose I hid three dirty coffee mugs out of sight in the wastepaper basket and unlocked the door.

Somehow I must have dealt with things, because the place was full of people coming and going all day, and none of them actually shook me by the shoulders or backed away, looking scared. The credit card slips and cheques in the drawer at the end of the day were evidence that I had sold a lot of books and prints, even though I couldn't remember much about it.

Things were winding down when Ernie turned up. I saw him arrive, withdrew from a chat about the chance of a white Christmas, and sidled around the central row of bookcases to intercept him.

'What's wrong?'

He grinned at me. ''S'all good. She's asleep, so the Perfessor said I should get down here for an hour and help until you close. What d'you want me to do?'

I grabbed his sleeve and pulled him inside the office door. 'Can you take over? I haven't had anything to eat, and I want to walk up the street. Mrs Acker should have come in today, but she hasn't turned up. I hope there's nothing wrong. I'll get back in a few minutes.'

He nodded firmly, dropped his jacket and his bag on the packing table, and marched out to patrol the aisles. I wriggled into my own jacket, made sure that my keys were in my pocket, and ran, thinking food. Food hadn't happened to me all day. I trotted along to the newsagent for some dark chocolate and an emergency Break Bar (breakfast and lunch, between them) and then came back to George Street, munching as I walked.

I had to see Mrs Acker. I'd been counting on her turning up today to give me another £5, because I had her down as the kind of obsessive person who wouldn't miss that sort of appointment unless she was actually on her death bed. I'd spent my rare free seconds drifting over to the door and taking a look up and down the street. I kept telling myself that I'd simply missed her. Then I told myself that she might have been too busy to come in, what with Christmas and everything. Or something might have happened which was perfectly innocent and harmless, and she would turn up tomorrow instead. I repeated all the arguments while I stuffed the empty chocolate wrapper into my pocket and tore open the cereal bar, took a big mouthful of honey and puffed rice, and chewed stickily.

A faint light was on in the upstairs window of number 21 this evening, but there was no other sign of life. I squared my shoulders, pushed the squeaky gate open, and marched up the path to the door. When I pushed the bell, I clearly heard chimes in the hallway, but there was no sign that anybody else did. I rang again, and a third time. After a while I went back down the steps, turned around, and examined the silent face of the building again. The light I had seen was still on, but if anybody was looking out, I couldn't see them. I retreated on to the pavement and turned towards home, looking back over my shoulder every little while. Something was wrong with her, but I couldn't do anything about it.

In the end, I shook myself mentally and told myself to stop this nonsense. She'd forgotten she was supposed to be coming in, and there could be a dozen simple reasons why she hadn't answered the door when I rang. There was nothing to do but try later.

I didn't have to. The phone rang at exactly six thirty, just after the last customer had gone and while I was still explaining to Ernie that I considered he was working for me, whether he was here or up at Crouch Hill, which was why I'd just handed him more cash than he had been expecting. But it was true.

I hoped it wasn't a customer on the phone; even more, I hoped it wasn't Barnabas wanting to tell me about the day's trials on Crouch Hill. But the voice at the other end, though toneless and a little faint, was undoubtedly Mrs Acker's.

By now I was too exhausted to want to say anything except a feeble, 'Oh. Can I help?'

'You know I was supposed to drop in there today, but you may have noticed ... I was very busy. Mr Acker has just popped out, so I was going to come, but I'm very sorry, I didn't get to the cash machine and I see that I don't have any money at all. Will tomorrow be all right, or maybe Monday?'

So, presumably she had seen me at the door after all. I pulled myself together, told her it didn't matter, don't worry, I was quite un-bothered. All those lies.

'I'll drop in tomorrow afternoon,' she said. She sounded as flat as I felt.

Ernie frowned when I hung up, and asked what was wrong. When I admitted that I was so tired I couldn't stand up, he offered to go and get Ben for me. I felt like kissing him. Instead, I accepted his suggestion with dignity, locked up, crawled upstairs, and by the time that they got back I had a magnificent banquet of baked beans and chips all ready for the three of us. At some point, Ernie went home, Ben went to bed, and I lay down for a moment on top of my duvet and fell off a cliff into blackness.

When I woke up it was dark, which was not unusual these mornings, although the silence outside suggested that it was early. I peered blearily at the alarm clock: not quite six o'clock. Early to get up on a Sunday. Then I realized that I was still wearing all my clothes and began to think about washing my face and changing while coffee brewed. I went on examining that plan of action for a little while longer, and had just managed to sit upright when I heard the noises: a car had braked hard in the street outside, and I could hear voices rising. Something about them reminded me of Andry and Wee Georgie, so I slid out of the room, shut the door softly, and ran to the front window.

There were headlights below: a car that I didn't recognize was in the middle of the road, and a man stood – or maybe 'wobbled' was a better description – with one of his hands on the driver's door. When he straightened up and took a step backwards, the street light fell on Mr Acker's face. PC Kenneth Acker was the worse for wear. He pulled a handful of coins from his pocket and threw them at the car. They clattered on the windscreen and the bonnet and showered on to the road, and he was saying something in a low, hard voice. I pulled the window up an inch in time to catch, ' ... all I've got, so sod off!' The driver's door started to open. Acker took a step backwards and kicked it shut. Then he turned and stamped off. You could see that he was holding on to himself and spoiling for a fight. He walked, not up towards his house but off in the other direction. Maybe he was going to walk off his temper before he went home. Maybe he just didn't want the driver finding out where he lived.

After a moment the driver's door opened again, and a man with a long, dark face, probably an Asian, got out. He bent down and looked closely at his door and said something aloud. I wondered what would happen if I leaned out and yelled, 'Be careful! That man is a policeman.' Childish.

The minicab driver – that had to be who he was – started collecting the coins. He reached beneath the front bumper of the car, chased them across the road, searched both gutters. Finally he stood under the street light counting what he had retrieved. It didn't take long. He seemed to shake himself before he got into the car, started the engine, and drove away. I shut the window, feeling dirty. Then I opened it again, leaned out, and waited. It was eight or nine minutes before a dark figure appeared at the top end of the street. He was walking slowly, as though he was tired, stopped, and turned in through one of the gates. Acker was home.

I couldn't swear that it wasn't there already, when I leaned out of the window to watch Acker come home. The angle from my window is quite sharp, and I could easily have missed it; it's just that I don't think so. But it was certainly there by eight or eight thirty, when a few people had started to show themselves in the street and Ben and I were having breakfast in the kitchen. Sergeant Smiley told me afterwards that the newspaper delivery man who works for the newsagent in the cross street noticed it when he walked back down at the end of his round: an old supermarket carrier bag, slightly dirty, dangling high up on the iron railings of the third house to the north of my shop. He didn't even try to look inside the bag, because he had heard about the other one. The newsagent phoned it in to the police.

# Chapter 30

## Questions of Coincidence

When Barnabas arrived at one o'clock and found the shop still locked up, he rang my doorbell. I went to the sitting room to look out and found him standing staring away to his right.

I leaned out the window and waited.

'You slept in?' he speculated loudly. 'And what's that?' His eyes were fixed on the spot a few metres up the street.

I said Ben was with me today, but we'd be right down to take a look.

By the time that we had put our lunch dishes into the sink, grabbed our coats and keys, and gone downstairs, my father had vanished, but the Christmas lights were flashing in the window of the shop. I threw a furtive glance at the police noticeboard and helped Ben to open the door.

Barnabas was hovering halfway along the near aisle, waiting for us. Ben rushed to give him a hug, which brought a smile to his face; but then he raised his eyebrows at me and indicated what we were both thinking of by an inclination of his head.

'This morning,' I said. 'Another shopping bag thing.'

I received a look of sheer disbelief.

I said, 'I know. The police turned up some time before nine, and spent hours out there, but I didn't think they were very happy.'

'Blasé?' my father suggested sarcastically.

I substituted: 'Bored and anxious, all at the same time.' It sounded inadequate, so I tried to explain. 'It was exactly like the one that some-body found yesterday at the top end of the street.'

'Why?'

I knew what he meant and told him what Smiley had said: that somebody was having a laugh at the expense of the police. I didn't mention what was really bothering me: five menacing plastic bags and their contents left in a tight cluster right near my home.

Barnabas said, 'Rubbish!' But the door open-ed then, and the first customer of the day drifted in and stopped in front of the prints cabinet. It was looking empty. I ought to have noticed that. It was just one of the many things that I'd missed.

The afternoon was a juggling act. It was while my father and Ben were out for half an hour to walk off their restlessness that Mrs Acker appeared. I remembered to smile at her. I couldn't make out what was bothering her. If anything. Only her voice still had that flat tone I'd heard the night before.

'Miss Hoare, would you buy my books?'

'You mean all of them?' I searched rapidly for an excuse. I had been selling books to Mrs Acker for something like six years, and if I couldn't remember any of them, that was because they had usually been cast-offs from my 50 pence bargain bin or the folding 'Everything £1' bookcase that I used to leave outside the shop on fine days. I'd stopped doing that over a year ago. I played for time. 'I suppose you must have quite a few by now,' I said.

She nodded slowly and went on watching me. Well, this isn't an unfamiliar situation for any second-hand book shop owner. A few people do think we're lending libraries.

'Mrs Acker, I'd be glad to come along and take a look at them, but you can see I'm fully stocked at the moment, and I don't think I'd have room for so many. What I could do, if you like, is come and see what you have, and then maybe choose a few volumes?'

She said flatly, 'I want to sell all of them right away.'

I hesitated. Of course you do. 'I'll look at

239

them if you like, and I can always suggest a general dealer who'd come and buy the rest.'

'But,' she said reasonably, 'you could buy them all as one lot, and then sell them to the dealer, couldn't you? It's just—' She came to a stop.

I mimed that I was considering the idea and rejecting it regretfully. 'I just don't have the space. Those dealers usually have big storage places, but I don't. But let me come and take a look so I know what there is. When is convenient? I'm afraid it's impossible today until after we close, but I could come this evening.'

She nodded once. 'Between seven thirty and nine this evening, please. Thank you.' She took a couple of steps towards the door and stopped quickly. 'I forgot,' she said, and handed me a new £5 note.

I said, 'I'm a little busy just now. Is it all right if I bring the receipt with me this evening?'

She thought about it, nodded, and nearly smiled at my ear. Then somebody else had a question about some travel books, and I lost sight of her.

At six thirty Barnabas said, 'I want to talk to you. Will you, for goodness sake, lock that door before anyone else wanders in? My sympathy for my fellow man is beginning to run low.'

I looked at him sharply. Maybe it was just the overhead lighting, but I thought he looked grey. This is not good in a man with a weak heart. I announced that we were going to forget about clearing up, turn out all the lights, and go upstairs for a pre-dinner cocktail – Irish for him and me, and chocolate milk for Ben. And we were still slumped in the sitting room at seven o'clock, watching television, when Ben noticed how hungry he was. In fact, he and Mr Spock seemed ready to make an issue of it.

'This, if ever, is an occasion for junk food,' Barnabas commented. 'If pizza were to be delivered—?'

I thought about it: starch, oil, additives – lovely – and found a price list in the top drawer of the desk. I told him that I liked mushrooms and bacon, and that Ben liked chicken.

'And bacon,' Ben added.

'Are you feeling all right?' I asked my father quietly.

He replied equally quietly that he was. It was all that I expected. So I said that if he would phone the order for delivery, I'd feed Mr Spock before anything happened, and get our plates and glasses ready.

'Will Mr Spock really eat us if we don't feed him?' Ben asked. He sounded genuinely interested.

Barnabas said that this particular cat was too small for anything of that kind, but we should not risk it. Then, moving towards the telephone, he added that he and I should have a word quite soon, because he wanted to get to get home early; and everything came sweeping back like a thunder cloud.

We ate the pizzas out of their boxes because it seemed like less trouble, exchanging slices; and when we all had got our fingers greasy, I told Barnabas about Mrs Acker.

He fixed his eyes on his wedge of margherita. 'Sell you her books? Isn't that odd?'

I'd been thinking that too and had a theory. 'He's been hitting her, and he keeps her short of money, so she's going to try to get some cash together and leave him.'

'Possible, indeed commendable.'

'It wouldn't have taken me so long,' I said grimly. 'I told her I'd go there this evening and take a look. It won't be anything we can use, but I'll work out how much she has and give her the name of somebody who might want them – somebody like Book Exchange with big second-hand stocks. I think I've made up my mind, though – if it's too bad to sell, I'll offer her something, even if I have to take it all straight over to the recycling.'

'You've made a certain amount of profit from her over the years,' Barnabas remarked in a measured tone. It seemed to imply approval. 'Dido...' His eyes fell on Ben, and he stopped and started again. 'I've been taking a rational look at that matter again – what you mentioned to me this morning. I am playing with an idea, and I would like to talk to you about it this evening if possible.'

I said, 'If I went down the road now, while Ben's having his bath, then when I get back—'

He nodded. 'Don't be too long.'

So I left the two of them running the bath, stopped off in the shop long enough to write out another receipt for Mrs Acker, grabbed a pen and a big lined pad to show willing, and set off along the street.

The sitting-room curtains were slightly open tonight, and light spilled out in front of the building, where something was going on. In the deepest shadow beside the steps I could see people. Three, maybe four dark shapes. There was something menacing in their stillness. There were no lights in the bottom flat, but it looked as though the door there was open. I manoeuvred myself behind the brick gate post and peered around it. They were so still that I had the sudden strange notion that they were stone figures. Then one of them shifted out of the shadow: a stranger. My eyes must have been getting more used to the darkness, because when I looked again at the fourth shape I saw that it wasn't a man, but a wheelie bin. Somebody had been manoeuvring it in or out the open door. It shifted and its wheels grated.

'Shove off.' That was a low voice, full of controlled venom. Acker? I was pretty sure that it was the voice of the man who had come into the shop talking about the monkey notice he had found.

Somebody guffawed. I pressed close against the brick column and started to feel that it wasn't thick enough to hide me. Then someone else spoke; this voice was very quiet, and I couldn't hear the words, but something made me think, something convinced me that what was happening down there was terrifying and that I didn't want to be anywhere near it.

'Next week,' a voice said more clearly. 'Next week, don't forget, you make the call.' I knew that voice. I knew the accent.

'You do,' another said, 'you got—'

He broke off.

There was a movement, and a boot grated on stone. I ran for it: up the street to the house next door, in through their open gate and into the shadows of the little, wet lawn. They had rose bushes here, and if I ducked down behind the row, they would probably hide me. When I saw figures moving on the path next door, I did just that. I crouched and peered around the thorny branches and watched two of the men step into the street. They turned in my direction, and the headlights of a car coming toward them struck the two of them face on. They must have been partly blinded, but I could see them clearly now. One was a stranger. One was Andry. By the time the car had passed, they were past the gate and had their backs to me. I straightened up cautiously, listening to a grating noise at the Ackers' house. I looked up at that moment. A pale face was at the sitting-room window: Mrs Acker. She looked out, unmoving, until the basement door slammed and then she yanked the curtains shut. Then Acker lurched up the flight of stairs, unlocked their front door, and went in. When I heard the locks grating, I got myself out of there. The front of number 21 was deserted again. Even the wheelie bin was gone. And I certainly wasn't going to try to see Mrs Acker now.

I stood for a long time in front of the shop, trying to understand what I'd discovered. When I finally went upstairs, I told Barnabas that the Ackers were busy. If my voice was strained, he seemed not to notice. He was making tea.

I said that I'd better get Ben out of the bath.

He held up a hand. 'He's all right for the moment. Dido, this business of body parts is incredible in the extreme. The idea that they are intended as a triumphalist message to the local police is simply frivolous. Unless, of course, we are talking about a raving lunatic.'

'None of the parcels was exactly hidden. You said that yourself.'

'They are indeed being – ah – flourished rather than safely disposed of. I might hazard a guess that they are intended as a threat. Wouldn't you think?'

'Who's threatening who?'

'Who indeed?' Barnabas muttered darkly. He poured himself some tea, raised an eyebrow to ask whether I wanted some – I shook my head quickly – and said, 'Nevertheless, it does seem the most likely reading.'

We could agree on that. You would have to be a tired, angry, overworked police officer to say anything else, even as a joke. I was only tired, and as for the last question, I had no answer to it, not even by the time that I had put Ben to bed and my father's taxi had left for Crouch Hill.

When the phone rang, it was a relief to stop thinking about what I'd witnessed.

Kennedy's voice said, 'Didn't Barnabas tell you I rang there more than an hour ago? I wanted you to call me back.'

My heart sank. 'I guess he forgot. Sorry – things have been impossible here and I'm not sure he's very well.' I pushed that thought away. 'Has something happened?'

He said, 'I'm just checking in with you. I heard that you had another one down there today. Are you all right?'

I lied and said that I was. Then I backtracked by admitting what was bothering me: Smiley's flippant remark, Barnabas's comments, my own doubts.

'Shall I drop in? I'm just along the road. Maybe we can figure something out together. And have you heard about Annie?'

'What?'

'She's being discharged tomorrow at about ten o'clock. Barker suggested I should speak to Sam Johnson about your idea and Johnson was agreeable, if not keen. Are you still willing?'

'At the moment, no; but I will be when I've had some sleep. It hasn't been a very good day. Chris, yes, please come.'

He said, 'Hang on, I'll be there in fifteen minutes.'

Kennedy was something real. I'd feel safer with him around.

There are up to a hundred people living in this street, with as many more again in the council estate to the north, and a lot of others around one corner or the other. And the shopkeepers, the people who work around here: don't forget them. My mind hovered over the idea that somebody was trying to set up an old-fashioned protection racket, the way they do all over the world, but here in trendy Islington: Fifty nicker a week, guv'nor, you get our guarantee that nobody will make you into pork pies. Perhaps that would explain what had been happening tonight. Nothing had happened, really. Or they just hadn't bothered to approach me yet.

I tried to find some clarity – without much success. I knew Annie Kelly, whose criminal connections looked pretty genuine and who was responsible for bringing Georgie and Muscles into my life. And consider Muscles, Andry, whatever his name was: dead girls, dead young prostitutes certainly seemed like his kind of thing. Or maybe it could be pointing a finger at me after all. A dead finger. Oh, damn it.

When the doorbell finally rang, I made sure of both the car and its driver's identity before I went down to let him in.

# Chapter 31

### Escape to the Suburban Dream

After I'd driven up and down every row in the car park twice without finding a free space, I followed others' examples and left the car in one of the lanes, lined up with a row of legally parked vehicles. I threw a slip from the nearest pay-and-display machine on to the dashboard, locked up and glanced at my wristwatch. It was nine thirty-five, and by the time I had reached the fourth floor and dashed into St Catherine's Ward I was cutting things fine.

Mr Hull was at the nurses' station again this morning. He looked up and saw me. I waved at him and headed towards Annie Kelly's side room. I could see that he had something to say, but I assumed it would keep. I was wrong. He had probably intended to warn me. When I knocked and let myself into Annie's room, I found her sitting stoney-faced on the edge of her bed with Sam Johnson standing over her. He had been talking when I came in. I stopped short. They both looked at me.

'I was offering Mrs Kelly a lift home,'

Johnson said.

I said, 'Unh-hunh? Well that's why I'm here. We have it all arranged.'

We had, too: even before I'd taken Ben to nursery, I had spoken to Mr Hull, then Annie herself, pretending first that I was phoning to ask how she felt, and then offering to come and drive her home when she told me the news that she was being discharged. Even more significantly, I'd spoken to Johnson and finalized arrangements for him to send an unmarked car after us. So what was the game?

'See?' Annie said to him. 'So thanks but no thanks.'

'Mrs Kelly —'

She turned a blank face to him.

He said, 'If you're sure, I'll say goodbye. Don't forget to contact us if you can remember any more about what happened to you. And good luck.' He nodded to her, and then – only marginally more cordially – to me, and went away.

I decided to get in first by asking, 'What was all that about?'

She made a face. 'He just wants another chance to bug me. I've had it up to here with them going on. I just wanna go home.'

I accepted that without argument and changed the subject. 'Have you got everything?'

'There's nothing for me to have.' She looked down at herself. The knees of her jeans were black with dirt, and they had slit the sleeve of her blue sweatshirt to get it on over the brace. The sight seemed to depress her. 'I just haveta get something clean to wear. Dido, it'll take me half an hour down at the flat to change and pack. Are you sure you're all right? Because that copper seemed to be saying they think I might have some trouble, I mean that somebody might turn up and have another go.'

I said innocently, 'Not unless you're alone, surely? I'll stick around until you're ready to leave, we'll keep our eyes open, and I have my mobile – I'll phone for the police if anybody turns up.'

She threw me another of those Kelly looks that I found hard to interpret. 'I'm surprised you're here alone. Thought you'd have Chris with you.'

'Working hours,' I offered.

She said, 'Oh,' and stopped talking when two nurses arrived to deliver some prescriptions and advice, check around the bed, and drape the coat over her shoulders. The formalities took a little time, but eventually we got into one of the overworked lifts and started down.

There was no sign of Johnson. I didn't know whether to be reassured that he was keeping out of sight. Annie moved stiffly, which gave me a problem. When she caught her breath sharply as she stepped out the main door, I decided to take a chance.

'Annie? Are you all right? Do you want to wait here while I go and get the car?'

'No!' It was quite definite, and it made me think that she too was afraid to see somebody she knew. 'I'll do,' she added. 'Just don't walk too quick.' So we made our way to the car at a convalescent's pace. When I turned into the road, there was an unmarked and unremarkable car waiting at the kerb which pulled out a few metres behind us. Only the driver was in it – I couldn't see his face. It stayed with us, nearer or farther away, for more than a mile before I lost sight of it.

Following Annie's directions, we went down to the City Road and then turned off, ducking and weaving through the side streets. As far as I could see, we weren't being followed. But when we drew up outside a low block of refur-bished council flats, there was a car parked across the street with its driver sitting inside, and it looked like the same one. I reminded myself that the police already had this address.

I said, 'Stay inside,' and climbed out to circle the car, keeping my eyes peeled. Aside from a black and white cat balancing on a low wall, nobody seemed to be paying any attention. I opened her door, gave her a hand, and used the electronic central locking. Then I pulled my mobile phone out of my pocket and held it ready while we headed through a passageway in the centre of the building, turned right at the end, and climbed a flight of concrete stairs to the first floor. Once there, we jostled each other to peek around corners and check out the open walkways off which the doors of the individual units all opened. Nobody. I climbed the last step to the landing and checked the next flight up. Empty. Finally, I went and leaned over the railing and looked back the way we had come. There was a woman coming in from the entrance carrying supermarket bags, but she turned towards the other side of the grounds.

At the door of the second flat along, Annie pulled out a key and raised it to the lock.

I grabbed her wrist. 'Wait! Will anybody be in there?' She blinked and hesitated, and I persisted: 'Whose place is this? Does Georgie have a key?'

She shook her head. 'I borrowed it from a friend of mine who's away for a coupla months, and of course Georgie bloody doesn't have a key! I'm not that stupid!'

I persisted. 'Could anybody have got in?'

We both looked at the door itself and at the window beside it; neither of them showed any sign of tampering. Then she laughed shortly. 'Dido, you been watching too much telly.' She was already turning the key in the lock. I stepped back and positioned my thumb on a button of my mobile: if I pressed it, Johnson's phone would ring and he was supposed to come running. I hoped.

I followed her into a stuffy kitchen. Silence. With a picture in my head of armed men breaking into some dark and dangerous Docklands warehouse, I followed close, holding the mobile in front of me like a gun, ready to fire off an alarm. Cramped sitting room, big TV set, plastic furniture, mess – pillows had been scattered and a chair overturned, and I realized that this was where Annie had first been attacked. Tiny bedroom – as messy as mine. Nobody jumped out of the cupboard, and there wasn't enough space under the bed even for somebody as wee as Georgie. Bathroom: beige tiles with a brown and orange flower design and a brown suite and nobody lurking. I put the phone away, feeling silly.

Annie sighed. 'All right? I'm going to have a pee and get out of these clothes. I'll meet you in the bedroom.'

We were standing a good five feet from the bedroom at the time. I went into the hallway and left her to it.

Considering the bruises and soreness, however, she moved faster than I'd expected. Twenty minutes later, I was lugging her big old suitcase out of the place and leading the way to the car with the kind of precautions we had taken entering. Thirty seconds after that, we locked the doors, strapped ourselves in, and pulled away from the kerb. I kept my eye on the rear view mirror long enough to make sure that the parked car had pulled out after us. It was still there after I made two right turns and a left, and was heading towards Old Street.

'Where are we going?'

My passenger said, 'Straight on, over the

253

junction. Watch for Sun Street. We'll make a left there. 'S not far.'

When I slowed for the traffic lights a few minutes later, I caught the street sign and made the left. This wasn't an area that I know particularly, and I was taken by surprise a minute later when she said, 'Here, this is it – that's fine. And Dido, thanks. Really.'

I looked up at the big sign just ahead of us: Liverpool Street Station.

'Where are you going? I can drive...'

But she was already dragging her big case out of the side door, moving faster than ever. 'Nah, thanks love, but not all the way to Wanstead. I'll speak to you later, all right?'

I thought fast. 'How can I reach you if I hear anything about Georgie?'

She stopped with her hand on the door. 'I had enough of that man for now. Look, I'll phone you. You're in the book.'

'Yes, of course, but will—?'

She slammed the door, waved cheerily, and dragged the case through the station entrance, vanishing into a surge of bodies just as the familiar, anonymous car pulled up behind my MPV and Sam Johnson emerged from it. He ducked and looked through my rear windows, then came to the driver's door. I rolled my window down.

'Miss Hoare, what—?'

'Catching a train to Wanstead. Why—?'

But he was already sprinting for the train.

254

Presumably. I thought about it all for a moment, gave up, turned around and headed for home. I was way behind with all kinds of things. Some of those things were even, actually, my own business. Unlike this scheme of mine which had just gone off the track. For the moment, I wasn't feeling too clever. And I really ought to have recognized the oldest trick in the book.

But maybe I had just been distracted by surprise.

As soon as I got into the shop, locked the door behind me and picked up the mail, I found the answering machine flashing. There was one message on it, and the voice was Mr Stanley's.

'Miss Hoare?'

There was something wrong.

'Miss Hoare, please phone me. I'm afraid something has happened. I am so sorry.'

I turned into ice. Barnabas!

# Chapter 32

## Wasting Time

I pressed the button to return the call and listened to a phone ringing. And it was my father's voice that answered. I sat down and took two deep breaths before I could identify myself.

My father said, 'Is something wrong?'

I took one more breath and was able to tell him in a steady voice that I was merely returning Mr Stanley's phone call.

Barnabas said, 'He is extremely upset. I've been trying to persuade him that it was not his fault.' It's funny how many catastrophes you can imagine in some circumstances. 'It seems he ran out of milk after breakfast this morning and walked to the shop down the road without bothering to call on me, because she seemed to be sleeping. When he arrived back, he found the door of the flat open. Nina is gone.'

'Gone? How?'

'He was pleased at the improvement she was showing at breakfast time. She drank a cup of tea and ... Well, our friend is deeply embarrassed and wonders whether he should contact the police.'

I thought fast. 'Could she have made a phone call while he was out?'

I heard muffled voices, and then my father returned with the news that there was no way of knowing, but no reason why not.

I gave him a quick outline of my own morning's loss.

'You are wondering whether the two of them might have been been in touch?'

Well, as a matter of fact. I got down to the nitty-gritty: 'What time did he get back?'

Another, shorter, exchange. 'He left at about a quarter to nine and wasn't away for more than ten minutes, fifteen at the outside.'

If Annie had known Mr Stanley's number, there would have been time for her to push a coin into the pay phone in the ward and ring Nina. How could she have Mr Stanley's phone number? Or how could Nina have hers? It seemed more likely that Nina herself had rung a friend, or somebody she believed was her friend, and gone to meet them.

I said, 'Tell Mr Stanley nobody blames him. Did he look outside when he saw she was missing?'

'We both walked up and down the street. He hadn't thought she was strong enough to go far. Of course there is the bus stop just at the corner. But, Dido, I think we should contact somebody about this.'

'I will,' I told him glumly. 'I know who. If a

257

policeman called Barker phones you – I suppose you should tell him anything he wants to know.'

'Barker,' my father repeated in a voice as dry as talcum powder. 'I suppose we should.'

I found the card with his numbers written on the back and dialled his mobile. It was answered immediately with a clipped, 'Barker'.

I snapped, 'Dido Hoare.' Calmly, now. 'Mr Barker, Nina has vanished – possibly with Annie Kelly, who was discharged from hospital this morning.'

There was a silence. Then a very patient voice said, 'You'd better tell me everything.'

I said I'd give him the morning's action in chronological order, and did.

After scarcely any hesitation the long-suffering voice told me that he had some phone calls to make and would contact me soon. I decided to push it and shouted, 'Wait!' Then I told him about the telephone. Nina had been stronger today, but not that much. Chances were that she had phoned for somebody to pick her up, using Mr Stanley's line, rather than catching a bus. If so...

'I'll have somebody check the phone company's records – and the bus drivers on that route: one of them might have noticed her. And we'll get back to you when we can.' Nobody had yelled. That would almost certainly come later.

I was thinking about coffee again, but the

phone rang before I could move. I made myself answer briskly.

'Miss Hoare, it's Mrs Acker.'

I said hello.

'Yes. I was just checking, if you weren't too busy right now, whether we ... About the books, I mean.'

At least it was business, even if it wasn't any business that I wanted. From the business point of view, it was nothing but a waste of time. I looked at my wristwatch and made an appointment for eleven thirty. I could probably stay out of trouble for twenty minutes.

As soon as I had hung up, the telephone rang again. I let it go on ringing, and ran.

There was still some coffee in the machine. I reheated it, poured it, and wandered into the sitting room, resolutely not looking at the mess in the bedroom or the mess in the bathroom as I passed those doors. Mr Spock followed me, and we settled together on one of the sofas for a quiet five minutes. At the end of that time, he was asleep and my own eyelids were trying to close. But the phone rang. I didn't move until I heard Chris Kennedy's voice coming from the answering machine, and then I picked up in the middle of his message.

'I'm here.'

He said, 'Good morning. You were asleep when I left – I had an eight o'clock meeting. How are you feeling?'

I told him that I was gibbering, and in the

soup, and why.

He whistled between his teeth. 'So that's what Johnson was on about. He phoned me ten minutes ago and asked if I knew where you were. He's been phoning the shop and your mobile.'

'Was he in Wanstead?'

'Was he supposed to be?'

I said, 'Maybe. Did he say what he wanted?'

'He wants you to phone him. I hear that Mrs Kelly gave you both the slip at Liverpool Street Station.'

I asked what that was supposed to mean.

'She went into the station through one entrance, carried on straight out the far side, and got into one of the taxis at the rank there. He just caught a glimpse of her taking off. He's phoning around the cab companies to find the driver, but he wants you to contact him if she gets in touch with you.'

Oh. Not Wanstead, then. I noticed that this opened up a possibility that she and Nina really had arranged to meet, though I couldn't quite see how or why. Unless after all Georgie and Muscles ... A deal of some kind with Annie? The possibility made me sick. One way or the other, I didn't think she had any intention of contacting me at any time soon, and that was all right with me. Who was it who'd said I was out of my depth? I should concentrate on other things.

'Chris, I'm supposed to be going up to the Ackers to look at her book collection. I'm due now. But I'll keep my mobile switched on.'

He said, 'I'll phone you later. Don't...' A hesitation. He might have heard something in my voice. 'All right, I'll see you soon.'

Mr Spock's ears twitched. I could tell that he was dreaming of something good: of hunting mice and goldfish, of running along the top of the brick wall among the birds, with beetles scuttling away to the safety of a leaf or crack. I felt a twinge of envy: it must be comforting to be the big predator in your own world.

I left quietly.

I was late arriving at number 21, but despite that I slowed to a shuffle on the front path. Not that there could be anything to see. The wheelie bin had disappeared again, presumably rolled back into the basement; the shutters there were closed; there wasn't so much as a scrap of paper on the path to suggest that anybody might have been having a stand-off there only a few hours ago.

Not quite nothing. I diverged for a second from the straight path and took a quick look at the marks of wheels and scuffles in the grit on the doorstep of the flat, just to assure myself that I hadn't imagined last night. Then I climbed to the upper door and rang the bell. I heard nothing until the mortise bolts suddenly clattered, the door swung inwards and Mrs Acker stood there with a scarf wound round her head, an old-fashioned pinafore apron over her clothes, and shapeless slippers on her feet.

There were bags under her eyes.

I said, 'Sorry I'm late. A couple of phone calls came just as I was leaving.' I waved my notebook and pen to reassure her that now I was here at last, I was totally serious.

She nodded listlessly and stood aside to let me in, turned the key in the locks, and led the way upstairs.

This time we went straight to the back of the house, where a little room was squeezed in beside the bathroom. As she opened the door, I was struck again by the chill of these draughty rooms. She stood back and motioned for me to enter a room the size of a child's bedroom, empty except for a threadbare brown carpet, an old dining chair, and eight unmatched bookcases along two of the walls. They were old, battered things of different dimensions and colours, obviously the product of second-hand furniture shops, and they were full.

I made a rough count: twelve or fifteen hundred books, including paperbacks. Some dust jackets, but mostly just faded cloth or paper spines. I unbuttoned my coat, opened the notebook, and started at the right hand end. In normal conditions it might have taken me ten minutes to give my estimate. But that wasn't the point now. The point was to keep her there, get her talking. To show willing – Mrs Acker was standing in the doorway – I began at the top by counting paperbacks and pulling one or two of the hardcover books off the shelf, opening them, checking the copyright page, and even making a note of one of them. By the third shelf, she was growing restless.

'Is there...? Do you think...?'

'It's all right,' I said. 'I want to be careful about this. You don't want to be cheated.' I already knew that cheating her would not be possible because there would be nothing in this room worth the effort.

She said, 'I didn't realize how complicated it was.'

I pulled down a copy of *Memoirs of Hecate County* – it looked as though somebody had splashed raspberry juice on the front cover – opened it to the copyright page which confirmed that this was a reprint of the 1951 London edition, and wrote myself a reminder in the notebook that this too was not interesting.

'The thing is,' Mrs Acker was saying behind me, 'I didn't realize that it would take you so long. It's nearly noon, and I think that Mr Acker is meaning to come back during his lunch hour, so I ought to go down and make him something.'

I let my voice grow slow and absorbed in my work and said, 'That's all right, I'll be fine. You can keep me company when you're ready.'

She didn't move.

I kept my back turned. You learn things from dealing with monkeys. After a pause I said, 'Mrs Acker, I keep wondering, and I hope you don't mind my asking this, but you keep these books so well.' That was true; there hadn't been a speck of dust anywhere. Maybe the purpose of that old chair was to let her use a feather duster every day. 'You obviously enjoy books. Why are you selling them? I don't think you'll get as much as you paid for them.'

There was a kind of gasp behind me and she said determinedly, 'Half price? I thought they usually give you half price when you sell a book?'

I told her it depended on whether somebody really wanted to buy it. I counted another bunch of paperbacks and pulled out a newish-looking hardback *Portrait of Dorian Gray* – her books were strictly in order of author, and I'd started at the end of the alphabet. Good reading copy. I put it back. I said, 'So you see, unless you're really tired of these and want to get rid of them, this doesn't seem like a very good idea.'

While I was waiting, I counted another ten paperbacks.

'My husband owes somebody some money.'

*My husband owes somebody some money.* I thought about last night. Owes somebody? It would explain this tidy, cold house with nothing in it that wasn't absolutely essential. And the argument I'd watched might have been a demand for payment, in which case I knew one policeman who was going to find himself in trouble. Along with his wife. I remembered something. I gushed, 'Credit cards! It's so easy to let them run away with you, isn't it!' I stopped, mainly because I couldn't think of anything in the house that could account for credit card bills. I counted to ten and said carefully, 'Does he owe a lot? Because I'm not sure about these books – how much it will help him if you sell your books. But I will look at them very carefully and then we'll try to work out the best thing to do.'

I waited. After a while, she said, 'He ... has a problem.' I waited some more. 'He plays cards, just for fun, but sometimes...'

A gambler! It just could explain what I'd heard last night.

'I have to sell them.'

For the time being, I just nodded and counted a batch of paperbacks – Puffin books. She had told me that she read children's books. I heard her shifting her feet. I waited and counted.

'I wouldn't like Mr Acker to find you here. He has a great deal on his mind. Would it be possible, that is, to come back later?'

I ran the tips of my fingers along the next shelf, while I thought about what Leonard Stockton had told me and decided to say, 'Of course. No problem. I do know how worrying debt can be. If you don't mind my saying so, this flat must be worth much more than you paid when you bought it. Couldn't you re-mortgage? You'd get much more that way.'

'Oh, but we don't own it!' She sounded almost shocked. 'My husband hasn't said any-thing, but I think he wants us to move. So selling my books now would, I don't know, make it easier, when we have to go, so it would be the sensible thing to do.'

I reached the bottom shelf of the first book-case without even noticing while I wondered why she was lying to me. Leonard Stockton had assured me that Acker owned the house, not to mention three big debts that were guaranteed by its freehold value. Maybe he hadn't told her about all that? It was actually starting to make a nasty kind of sense.

I straightened up and said I'd better go and look at the morning's mail. 'Shall I come back after lunch? I imagine the rest of this won't take more than another hour. Shall we say two o'clock?'

When I turned around she was smiling tightly. 'Thank you,' she said. 'That is very good of you.'

I got down the stairs fast, because I wasn't in the mood to meet Mr Acker again, and had to wait at the front door until she caught me up, undid the bolts, opened it, and then shut and locked it again behind me. Safe in her castle. I made haste out the gate. There were a few people around, but nobody I knew.

More coffee. More thinking. Maybe even a phone call to check on Mr Stanley before I got down to business.

# Chapter 33

## Too Much Coffee, Too Many Messages

I wound up by carrying the coffee machine and the makings down into the office and setting them on top of the filing cabinet, where they jostled the old electric kettle for space. I needed a coffee machine down here. Maybe I should go out and buy one.

The light flashing on the answering machine claimed priority over the morning's mail. I'd had seven messages already. I pushed the play button and picked up a pen for some note-taking.

One: 'Hey, Dido. D'ja hear about Nina? I wish I was there, but I had a class this morning. Sorry. My last class finishes at three today. Should I come over there?'

Yes, please, Ernie. I stopped the machine to leave my own message on his voicemail and confirm that I'd be waiting at three thirty to let him in.

Two: 'Miss Hoare, this is Sam Johnson. It's eleven thirty. Please ring me.'

Oh.

Three: 'Dido, I shall be there in a little while.'
Barnabas of course.

Four: 'Dido, hi, it's Jeff Dylan. Listen, you know it's my fifty-fifth birthday on the Thursday after Christmas? I'll be in London, and we're having a birthday party at the Old Nepal. Will you come? Phone me.'

Five: a message about a picture book in our last catalogue – was it still available? Business! I made a note to look for it.

Six: 'Miss Hoare? Allan Barker. Can you give me a ring on 7320 1212? Ask the switchboard to find me.'

Seven: 'Hi. I want to say something to you. Phone me when you have a minute.' That was Kennedy.

It's lucky I don't open the shop on Mondays, not even in December. But maybe Barnabas and Ernie between them, when they arrived, could answer the book query and possibly sell something to somebody somewhere. I translated my scrawl about the picture book into something that another person could read, propped the note up against the computer screen and poured myself a cup of fresh coffee before I rang Sam Johnson on his mobile.

When he answered, I identified myself and said, 'What happened? Have you found her?'

He avoided a direct answer by saying, 'I need to talk to you, Miss Hoare. Could you come in and see me?'

'Not without handcuffs,' I said. I heard a

sound which seemed to suggest he had over-heard my words, though I'd moved the mouth-piece away from my face before I spoke. I repositioned it and said, 'I'm sorry, it's impos-sible. I'm on my own here, and I have an appointment to look at a library in a few minutes. What do you want to talk about?'

He said, 'Wait a minute.'

A door slammed in the background, and the noises I'd been hearing were snuffed out.

'Kennedy told you? She didn't go to Wan-stead.'

'I heard. Any luck with the taxis?'

'Yerr,' he groaned. 'Somebody dropped her off on the forecourt of Euston Station.'

I could picture the forecourt of Euston Station. It meant that she had caught a train to somewhere north of London, or a bus going roughly north, south, east or west, or a second taxi, or had been been met by a friend with a car. I didn't say anything because I was sure he had already thought of all these possibilities.

'Mr Johnson, I have no idea where she would go. I think she said that she was going to stay with a friend. I don't really know her, you know. Not the way you people do. I honestly can't help.'

I caught another grunt. 'She'd better be keep-ing her eyes open.'

I thought about that, not for long, and said that I was pretty certain that she would, because it was probably why she had run away. I said,

269

'She'll turn up. She's persistent.' I meant persistent like a bad head cold.

I caught a noise that was almost a laugh, but when he spoke again he sounded serious enough.

'If she contacts you, try to get her to tell you where she is.'

I didn't like it and I said so.

He said it would be in her best interests, because somebody probably did know how to find her, and it would be better if he got there first. It was probably true. I heard myself agreeing, but I still didn't like it much.

Afterwards I consoled myself by ringing Jeff in Swansea and accepting the party invitation. I needed something to look forward to. When I said that I might have to bring Ben, he went on sounding cheerful. I'd find him a book for a present.

I rang Scotland Yard and asked them to find Barker. He came on the line so quickly that he was probably at his desk.

'Miss Hoare.' He waited.

I pointed out, 'It was you who phoned me.'

'I was hoping that you had something to tell me.'

There was something that I didn't want to tell him, and I assumed he was hinting about that. I said, 'How did you know?'

'We're at cross purposes. I think the time has come for me to talk to the girl. I phoned Mr Kennedy this morning, and he said I'd have to speak to you. Fair enough. I don't know what kind of guarantees she wants, but I'll try to help her, within reason. But this has to happen soon.'

I said, 'Wait a minute.' For this discussion I needed more coffee. When my mug was full, I went back to the desk, picked up the phone, and told him what had happened.

I could almost see him trying not to bang his head on his desk. Or maybe I underestimated his self-control. When I said, 'I'm sorry, very sorry, about this whole thing. I thought it was the right thing to do. It didn't turn out the way I intended. The – person who was looking after her thought she was asleep, and left her alone for ten minutes. I guess she's a little less helpless than we thought. I guess drugs make a person crafty.'

During the silence that followed, I waited for another sermon about amateurs poking noses into grown-up police business.

What he actually said was, 'I need to talk to the person who was looking after her. We'll want to search the place and see whether we can get anything that will help us locate her.'

I should have foreseen this. I said, 'You won't, because she didn't have any belongings apart from the clothes she stood up in. And I'm the person who was looking after her, so you can ask me any questions you like.' In a way that was true.

He said, 'Miss Hoare, can you come down here?'

271

I told him not without handcuffs (though I didn't phrase it exactly that way – and I didn't even hope that I'd get away with it).

'I need you to look at some pictures.'

Oh. 'Mus— I mean, Andry?'

'Yes, I hope so.'

Well.

I said, 'I have to wait until somebody gets here to take care of the shop, and I have to make sure that he can pick up my little boy from school.'

'If it will help, I'll send a car. Phone me as soon as you can give me a time.'

I stared into my coffee dregs and said, 'All right.'

'Miss Hoare?'

'Mm.'

'Do you want to bring a friend with you?'

'Do you mean my lawyer?'

'No!' He sounded amused. 'I just meant a friend, some company. I was thinking of Chris Kennedy, if he's free. Or anybody you'd like.'

I said that I'd think about it, broke the connection, looked at my wristwatch, and rang Kennedy anyway. His message had been that he wanted to tell me something. By now, I thought I could guess what.

His office extension was on voicemail. I said, 'Phone my mobile. Something's happened. Chris...' But I left it at that and tried the number of his mobile, which he answered.

'Hi. How are things?'

I started to tell him that everything was all right, but I was due at the Ackers' place ten minutes ago, running out of time. 'Chris, what did you want to tell me? Do you know that Annie disappeared, and so has Nina? Nina walked out this morning when Mr Stanley left her alone for a few minutes. And I'm trying to talk to Mrs Acker – something weird is going on there. And I think they're going to charge me with obstructing the course of justice, and it would be nice if you didn't yell at me, because everybody else is, and your friend at Scotland Yard is obviously thinking about arresting me for messing him up.' I made myself stop. I waited to hear yet another man pointing out that I had made a fool of myself.

He said, 'Dido, would you and Ben like to move into my place for a while?'

Chris lives in a handsome three-bed flat in Swiss Cottage. It seems, every time I think about the place, like a kind of haven, an oasis – there was even a big potted palm in his sitting room. To be more practical, there was also a 24-hour doorman downstairs.

'Dido?'

'Chris, I don't know what to— Can I phone you back? I need to talk, but I'm overdue for an appointment. Are you busy later?'

'If you'd like, I can come over.'

For a moment, I almost asked him to come with me to Scotland Yard after all. Pride inter-vened, and instead I said that I'd ring him at dinner time, or maybe later in the evening. Then I switched off the coffee machine, bundled myself into my coat, grabbed the notebook and looked carefully up and down the street. Neither Barnabas nor Ernie was in sight, nor anybody sinister. I locked the door and hurtled up the road to number 21.

# Chapter 34

## Cold Comfort

The little bedroom was even colder this afternoon, so I made my way around the bookcases as quickly as I could. I could have estimated the value of these books in five minutes, but I wanted to give Mrs Acker time to relax and talk to me. I had expected her to hang around and watch, but after a minute she mumbled something and went away. She seemed restless today. I heard the hoover running downstairs, and then an irregular clacking sound which I decided was made by the edge of a broom knocking against the skirting board. Apart from that, the house was silent. I persevered. But when I had finished the A's and went to find her, she was standing at the bottom of the stairs looking up.

I'd just started to say, 'I've got everything I need now,' when I heard a key in the door behind her and she looked at me in something like panic. I moved backwards, and by the time that the front door was open I had retreated all the way into the little bedroom.

I couldn't see anybody, but I heard them. She greeted him almost pleadingly. 'Is something wrong, Ken? I wasn't expecting you yet. Shall I make a pot of tea?'

His voice was muffled. 'I came back to get something. Don't bother me.' There was a pause. 'What's that thing doing there?'

'It's just the rubbish from the kitchen, Ken. Would you mind taking it downstairs when you go? What is it?'

'What's what? You don't have to hang around.'

She whispered something.

He said loudly, 'What? Now? Come in here.'

The voices became muffled, but I could hear that there was a question-and-answer session going on, though it was too quiet for me to catch more than a few words until he shouted, 'Why are you blabbing to her?' The sound of his rage brought me back out to the head of the stairs. They hadn't quite shut the sitting-room door, and I angled myself until I could see her standing across the room, facing him. Her hands were clenched on the pinafore.

She said, 'I'm sorry. I didn't see...'

They both lowered their voices after that, but

275

I could hear urgency in their whispers. He finished it with an inarticulate shout and lunged forward. I froze; but he turned aside from her at the last minute, raised his fists and pounded the wall beside the television set with another explosive yell. Then there was a long silence.

'I'm sorry,' she said at last. Her voice was soft. 'I didn't mean to upset you. I just told her I wanted to sell the books. Don't you want me to sell the books? If we're moving?'

He said, 'We aren't going anywhere! Have you got that into your stupid head? I don't give a fuck what you do with your rubbish, just get her out of here!' Silence. Eventually I heard him say roughly, 'Come here, come here. I'm sorry.' They seemed to be standing close, just out of my line of vision, for a long time. Then he was coming back towards the door and I ducked out of sight. If he came upstairs I wasn't sure what I should do. But I heard him hit something soft, and then the front door slammed. I waited for a beat and then I slammed the door of the little room myself, making it loud enough for her to hear downstairs. I called her name and walked over to the landing.

I'd thought that the sound had been Acker punching her, kicking her, but when I went down I found her in the hallway, staring at a rubbish sack sitting beside the kitchen door. He must have split it with a kick, and a trail of potato peelings and crumpled packaging had spilled out on to the hall carpet. I got there just

276

as she went down on her knees and started picking it up and stuffing it back inside.

'I'm finished,' I announced uneasily. 'I need to go away and add things up before I go and get Ben from nursery. Shall I take that out for you?'

She looked as though I'd made an indecent suggestion. 'No! No, thank you, our bin isn't— I'm sorry, did we disturb you just now?'

I lied. Then I said, 'I'll give you a written breakdown of the books. Would you like me to bring it up here later?'

'No,' she whispered. She was looking at my right ear, as she usually did. 'Don't bother. I can drop by the shop later to talk to you about it. Or tomorrow?'

I asked whether she was feeling all right. She said that she was, thank you, and went on looking at what her hands were doing. Like her, I pretended that something crazy hadn't just happened, and left. I had time to work out what to do about these books that I didn't want but was going to have to buy while I was waiting for Ernie or Barnabas or both of them to turn up. I'd leave them to get on with something and go for a walk. I'd find something Christmassy to buy. Or something useful. Or maybe I'd just try to forget the erratic violence I'd witnessed. Or maybe I wanted to talk to somebody.

I passed the police notice which begged 'Anybody who witnessed' things there on Sunday morning to phone Crimestoppers and noticed that my Christmas lights were on. So Barnabas had already arrived. I found a loud conversation going on in the office. When I came in, Barnabas was saying, 'But who would have thought she would be able to get up and leave? Mr Stanley is devastated,' and Ernie was telling him, 'I guess maybe she'll turn up.' Then I slammed this door too.

Barnabas said, 'Dido, are you all right?'

I said, 'Tired.' That was true. And perhaps I'd been frightened for a moment. But I made myself walk quietly into the office to leave the notebook and tell Barnabas that I would probably need some babysitting that evening. Then I evaded his questions by saying I was going to lie down until it was time to go and get Ben. I had just thought of somebody who could help with the Acker problem, and I needed the privacy of the phone upstairs.

When I reached DS Smiley, I described the scene I'd just witnessed and told her about the bruises that my father and I had been noticing, and how impossible I found it to talk to the woman involved. 'So I need some advice,' I said. I hadn't mentioned names.

'I've had experience of domestic violence,' she said slowly. 'Women officers are always getting handed that kind of case. If you want the truth, I try to avoid it. It's usually hard work persuading the women to make a formal complaint, even when they've wound up half dead in hospital. And then they'll withdraw it

278

because of their dependency. They go into denial and tell themselves that he didn't really mean it. You say these people have a serious debt problem? The man is probably under pressures that he can't cope with.'

'He frightened me,' I confessed.

'It happened in my family,' she said suddenly. 'I know what you mean; and it isn't uncommon.'

'What do you think I should do?'

'The most important thing is to persuade her to contact a support group. They'll know how to talk to her. There's a project called Hearthstone: I'll get their number and phone you back. And I could try to find out whether the man has a record of violence. That might give us some guidance. If you'll let me have his name and address, I'll check.'

I said all right and told her his name and rank. She muttered, 'Oh, shit.'

'You know him. So – tell me how to do this.'

'Miss Hoare ... I need to think. Maybe he doesn't have a very good attitude toward women officers, but he isn't the only sexist policeman I've ever met. Do you really think he may become violent? I'm putting that badly. What I mean is, he didn't hit her while you were listening? So do you have any impression of the urgency here?'

I hadn't expected to be asked that, and I wondered how to answer. It had seemed terrifying to me, but to judge by Mrs Acker's attitude both today and before, it hadn't seemed so unusual to her, though to me, it explained all the unhappiness in that cold house.

She didn't wait for an answer. 'What I'd like to do is talk to some people. But I'll contact you whether I find anything or not. You know I'll have to speak to her. I'll see whether I've got enough to take up to his superiors, and think how to persuade his wife she needs help.'

I said, 'I hate this,' and changed the subject. She was going to drop in on Lewis again on her way home. I couldn't go. I didn't bother explaining why. I'd try to see him tomorrow.

'Is there something else? Something wrong?' she asked.

Was I really so transparent?

I said slowly, 'These – bits of corpse that keep turning up around here: I think I'm getting into a panic about it. You must think I'm stupid.'

'You're not the only one, Miss Hoare. It's a nasty business.'

'I just wish I could stop thinking about it,' I told her. 'Those last two things at the weekend – somebody is *sick*!' It was a naked plea for sympathy. When she had made professional soothing noises for a moment, I went on: 'Is it still all the same victim? And does anybody know yet why the body was frozen?'

'I can't talk about the case, I'm sorry.'

I adjusted my strategy and said darkly, 'Every time I go out the door, I'm afraid I'll stumble over something. You don't have to tell me this is irrational. Can you tell me one thing at least? Is it finished? Have you got the whole body now?'

She hesitated. She probably wished she could help. 'Nearly all,' she said. 'It's nearly all with the forensic services now, and everybody's working hard. I can tell you one thing, and I hope it will comfort you a little: it looks as though she wasn't killed. Her death was ... almost natural, almost accidental, and there is no serial killer attacking women in the area, you shouldn't worry about anything like that.'

'But there is more still!' My voice rose a little. Maybe that was telling us both what I really felt.

'Miss Hoare, please try not to worry. I'll be in touch with you about the other business as soon as I can.'

We said goodbye, and I hung up thinking about what she had said: that nobody had killed her. What did 'almost natural' mean?

I lay back on the settee, checked the time once more and closed my eyes. When I opened them again, I knew that 'almost natural' meant that the dead girl hadn't been murdered – shot or beaten to death or strangled. The more I thought about it, the more she was identified in my imagination with Nina. The two of them were the same kind of age, both prostitutes, both strangers in London, probably. Both on drugs? Did she mean that the dead girl had OD'd on something – heroin, crack, something that went with that life? The freezing of the body: say that this girl had also 'belonged' to somebody like Muscles before she died. Say that somebody had simply been keeping her body until it could be safely disposed of.

It didn't explain why somebody was scattering the body in pieces around the streets. That didn't fit. If you stick a corpse into the freezer, that means you are hiding it for a while; if you then chop it into parcels and dangle them around, you are calling attention to them and to yourself, increasing the danger of being caught: the two things were contradictory. Something must have changed, leaving a need that outweighs the risks. The contradiction might just be one need outweighing the other.

Barnabas ambushed me before I could get away, stopping me from the doorway of the shop with a magisterial, 'Dido!'

I said I was just going for Ben.

'One thing first! Something I want you to think about. I'm sure that Pat would be glad to have you and Ben to stay until things are cleared up. Ernie and I will manage in the shop. In fact, there's no reason why we shouldn't close until after the New Year.'

The last part seemed like a good idea – or would by the end of the week. In fact, I ought to put up a notice about holiday closure in the morning. A lot of dealers close down between Christmas and the New Year. As for St Albans, I wasn't sure that Pat and I could live in the same house without having screaming matches. The usual sibling thing. Chris Kennedy's palm tree, on the other hand...

'In fact,' I said thoughtfully, 'I've already had an invitation. But closing the shop would be good.'

'An invitation from Pat?' he enquired, pushing to get it all settled.

'No,' I told him. 'Chris Kennedy. He has plenty of room for three over there.'

Barnabas's eyes narrowed. I waved at him and set off. And Ben and I bought a real Christmas tree, sticky with pine resin, and brought it home with us.

# Chapter 35

## Pictures

The lights were on in the flat when I got back, but the place was silent. I entered cautiously and poked my head into the bedroom, where Mr Spock was curled up on my pillow (I made a mental note to turn it over when I went to bed) and Ben was asleep, half covered. I crept over to the little bed, drew the blanket up gently and tucked him in. He sighed but didn't stir. I closed the door gently and crept towards the sitting room. Barnabas, reclining comfortably on the long settee under an open book, watched my approach with eyes that showed no sign of sleepiness and asked whether I had eaten.

'...because,' he said, 'I ordered a takeaway many hours ago, and didn't quite finish it despite Ernie's assistance. I told him to come in early tomorrow, by the by, since I ought to spend a little time with Mr Stanley. And the monkey, of course.'

I said, 'They gave me a sandwich.'

'Then it's up to you. Tell me what happened.'

I sank into the armchair, inspected the Christmas tree – Barnabas or somebody had found the stand on the shelf at the back of the hall cupboard and they had fixed the tree upright at the side of the fireplace, ready for decorations – and said, 'There was a solid traffic jam everywhere. Even with the lights and the siren, it took us ages to get down to Victoria Street. Then I sat in the corner of a big room for two hours and looked at photographs, and every so often somebody brought me some weak Nescafé out of a machine.'

'This is fascinating background colour,' Barnabas observed. 'And?'

'He's called Andrei Barden, they think, but he uses other names, and he probably comes from Moldova originally, but Barker said that he travels a lot. Barker was almost forthcoming when I pointed to him. He said that he didn't care whether that particular man wound up in jail for fifty years, or back in Moldova, or dead, just so long as he did it soon. Barnabas, they had Nina, too – I was almost certain, though she looked fatter in the picture. She was fined for soliciting three months ago, but they don't know anything about her. She gave them a German name. They're going to ask the local police to watch out for her, especially now they know she's being handled by this man. But they said she probably won't be on the streets any more, or maybe even in London. If she's gone back to them, they'll either send her up north or keep her out of sight somewhere like a club or a massage parlour or something.'

Hearing my own voice going on and on made me feel tired. I closed my eyes and listened to my father stir, get to his feet, and come to loom over my chair.

'I shall go home now, but I'll return tomorrow at midday. I want you to come downstairs with me and put the chain up on the door. Then will you go to bed?' It was less a question than an order, but I was quite willing. All of it.

Upstairs, I went around turning off the lights. In the kitchen, the clean plates were on the draining board and there was nothing that needed to be done right away. A hunger pang invited me to open the fridge. There were two take-away boxes on the bottom shelf. I dug the cardboard covers off half a serving of red pumpkin bhaji and a chicken leg in some gloopy orange sauce. It would only take me a minute to reheat them. So I found a knife and fork and ate them cold out of their boxes. Then I brushed the sauce off my teeth and went to bed. I couldn't remember whether or not I'd turned the pillow over when I lay down. It's strange what goes on bugging you long after you should have fallen asleep.

# Chapter 36

## Deals

When the phone started to ring, I turned and went back. I didn't really want to visit number 21 again and any delay was welcome. When I found Annie Kelly on the line, I realized that hadn't thought that through.

'Dido?' Her voice was big and cheerful again this morning. 'I just wanted to say ta for yesterday.'

'No problem,' I said. 'How's Wanstead?'

She decided to laugh. 'Listen, love, I'm sorry about that, but while I was packing up, I thought about everything that happened, and you're safer not knowing where I am.'

So was she. I said, 'Nina's disappeared. Are you in touch with her? Do you know where she is?'

Eventually she said, 'Oh, shit.' Apparently not. 'What happened?'

'She walked out yesterday when Mr Stanley's back was turned.'

'Unh. Well. Well, I hope she's all right.'

'I don't think she will be. Do you?'

The voice grew more reluctant: 'How was she?'

'A little better. Just a bit. But she needed more time.'

'Yes, well, thing is, Dido, it's not that easy.'

'She was on crack, I guess.'

'Yeah, I guess so. You don't just walk away from that stuff, you know. The next time you start thinking you're rubbish, you'll remember how it made you feel about yourself.'

'Does Georgie deal crack? Will she have gone back to him?'

'Yeah, sometimes he does, I guess.'

I growled, 'So Andrei will have got her back by now. Will he kill her?'

I listened to her struggles to speak cheerfully, to reassure herself and me. Her voice trailed away.

'Annie, how do I find her? I want Georgie's address.' At that point I suddenly remembered my instructions, but it was too late to start fumbling for my mobile phone. 'Or at least his phone number. I'm going to find out whether she's with him.' I crossed my fingers.

What came back was a shriek: 'Dido, you silly cow, you don't go nowhere near them!'

287

I said coldly, 'I couldn't agree more. But if I can talk to him, I'll try to make them give her up. How much do they care about her now? They've had her for months. They've made their profit. How much is she going to be worth to them from now on, when she's sick? I might even offer them a bit of money if I have to. Chris and I will work out some way of doing this.' It was hitting below the belt, but I went on. 'You stop and think about this, Annie Kelly: it was *our* doing that she ran away from them and then went back. You understand? Your fault first, and then mine afterwards for losing her. If they kill her, it's our fault.'

'No it ain't.' She sounded like a sulky school-girl.

'Annie – you know I'm right! You did something good for her, and now you're going to have to follow it up. You have to choose.'

I listened to silence on the line for so long that I started to think she had put the receiver down and walked away. I was afraid to speak again.

'Dido?'

'Annie.'

'If he knows you got this from me...'

'Do you think I'd tell him?!'

'No, all right. Got a pen?'

She recited the number of a mobile phone very slowly. I wrote the digits down just as carefully and recited them back. She hung up. I dialled 1471 without expecting anything, but the mechanical voice actually recited a 'last caller' number: the number of an ordinary land-line. And judging by the first four digits, she was in central London and probably not that far away from me right now. I wrote the number down under the one for Georgie's mobile, folded the slip of paper into a little square and pushed it down into the bottom of a pocket so I'd have it ready any time and anywhere. Georgie would guess I'd got this number from Annie. But it was only his mobile. He probably used that for business all the time – probably half the population of London knew the number, and he wouldn't care because it didn't tell me where to find him, and maybe Nina too. The question was how I could use it.

Mrs Acker answered the door so quickly that I suspected her of sitting on the stairs waiting for me. She stood back and motioned me inside, smiled tentatively and waited. I produced the sheet of figures I had just printed out and hand-ed it over. She looked at it. Then she looked at me.

'Miss Hoare, I didn't, I didn't realize how much work you ... Should I read this?'

'You ought to,' I said. I moved around to her side and pointed. 'You see, these are the paper-backs. I haven't really looked at them, but I counted them. There were nine hundred and ten. They're not worth much.'

'Oh,' she said, 'yes. No, I understand. They never are. I mostly got those from Oxfam, so I didn't suppose.'

'You wouldn't like to change your mind about keeping those, would you?' I asked her hopefully. 'Just for reading?'

'No,' she said. 'No, it all has to go. He ... What ... How much would you give me for them?'

All right. I said, 'A hundred pounds.'

'Oh!'

'Now these next ones,' I went on quickly, 'are hardbacks. Some of them are in quite good condition, but they're not – not what we call "collectables". But I could offer you one pound per volume. There are three hundred and thirty-two of them. And then I've listed two books there at the bottom – the old book of landscape engravings, and the one with the pictures of birds. Those are both interesting, and I'm sure I can sell them to one of my customers.' I glanced quickly at her absorbed face. 'The bird book is worth £75, and I can offer you £100 for the landscape book.'

I had been working out my moves ever since yesterday. I was going to do something entirely irrational now, and I just hoped that she wouldn't realize. I took a deep breath. 'So that's £607 for the whole lot. Or say £600, and you can choose all the paperbacks that you want to keep, and just enjoy them.' The figures made no sense, but I thought she might not notice. I didn't add, Please, please keep them all, but I could have. 'I hope that helps,' I said, 'but if you need any time to think about it, that's—'

'Oh, no,' she said quickly. 'I hoped ... But I'm sure that you're being fair. I did have another book that you would have liked. But I seem to have lost it. Ken gave it to me for my last birthday. That was flowers.'

My heart made an attempt to escape from my chest. I was able to say, 'Flowers? Oh, that is too bad.' My voice sounded artificial. 'Collectors always like flower books. Was it an old one?'

She nodded glumly. 'Very, very old. Ken found it in a street market one day, and he only paid £5 for it, but it was really pretty, and maybe you'd have wanted that too. It must have belonged to an art student, I think, because some of the pictures had been painted, with watercolours, you know? And it was so pretty! I loved it.'

My ears were ringing. I said what a shame, and asked her how long she'd had the book and when it had disappeared, and didn't she think it would turn up somewhere in the house if she looked for it, and if it did she should be sure to show it to me.

She nodded. 'My birthday was in October, and I missed it about a few weeks afterwards. Of course it will turn up. I think it will.'

I nodded. There was no way I was swallowing the bit about the street market, because even the dimmest trader in second-hand tat would have noticed the age of the book, and seen the hand-coloured plates, and then sold it on for a lot more than that to a book runner or a second-hand book shop. Constable Acker's story was rubbish, and I wondered whether the records might show something about him arresting a derelict man during the month of October. But he wouldn't have had to arrest him – just a little intimidation would have done the trick, or a couple of cans of lager. The identity of one middle-aged, tidy, ordinary looking man calling himself John Brown had just stopped being a mystery.

I smiled hypocritically and said that if she did find the book, I'd be glad to look at it any time.

'Then,' she said determinedly, 'I think I should sell all these to you, the whole lot. And then I'll pay the rest of the money I owe you for *Winnie the Pooh.* You can subtract that, can't you, and give me a receipt that just says you bought the books for the difference between them? That will make it simpler.'

It only took me a second to work out why she wanted it done that way and to agree to the deal. I'd print out two copies of an offer of exactly £542 for all her books, and she would sign one for me and keep the second one herself, and then I would surrender the bear. And I still had to try to talk to her about her husband.

Now that our business was completed, she was looking stubbornly at my right ear again and a half-formed sentence faded on my lips.

'Will you take them away now?'

I looked at my wristwatch. 'Ernie – you know, my assistant – is due later. I'll need his help to pack and carry the books. But as soon as he turns up...'

'Maybe you could phone me before you come, to make sure it's convenient?'

I remembered yesterday's scene and understood perfectly.

'And Miss Hoare, if it isn't too much trouble, I wonder if you could give me the money in cash? It would help.'

I nodded. I probably had something else to take me to the bank anyway.

I was only halfway down the road when I guessed, with a burst of relief, that I'd been right and she really had decided to leave him. I wanted to be convinced of that because it got me off the hook. I wouldn't have to try to talk to her now, and I could stop worrying. One problem down, and quite enough left still for me to deal with.

# Chapter 37

## Paying Cash

I'd handed Mrs Acker the cash and watched her count it carefully, right down to the last pound coin. She signed the receipt. I produced *Winnie-the-Pooh*, carefully protected by two layers of bubble wrap, and gave her my receipt for its whole price. Now that we were all square, we stood side by side in her front hallway, watching Ernie carry the last couple of boxes down the path and push them into the back of my purple van. There were fourteen of them altogether, so at least I hadn't had to bother about folding the seats. One of the fourteen – the smallest and emptiest of them – held the books that were actually going to the shop.

'Well,' she said suddenly, her eyes fixed on Ernie and the van, 'it will be tidier now.'

'Did you say that you were going to move?' I asked her tentatively. 'I'll miss you – you've been a good customer. Where will you be going?'

She hesitated. 'Not right away, I didn't mean that. Soon. Mr Acker will be applying for early retirement. He'll be fifty-two, you see, and now he wants to go. Then we'll be able to move.'

I pretended to forget what she had told me and said, 'But it will take you a little while to sell this place, of course, so you'll go in the spring, maybe?'

'Oh!' She laughed a little. 'I told you, we don't own it! I wish we did. It must be worth a lot of money by now, and he could pay—' She seemed to remember something and pulled up short.

I said, 'Oh, oh, I thought you did,' and she gave another of her unhappy laughs and shook her head.

'When he retires, we're going to take a holiday. We haven't been able to afford a proper holiday for years, but there'll be a cash payment, and maybe we'll be able to go over to Spain in the spring.'

I said that would be lovely, thinking that she had never said so much to me before in all the years I'd known her. 'What will he do? Fifty-two is young, these days.'

Her smile faded. 'We haven't talked about that. Ken is so tired, he just needs a rest. You know, the Met are so understaffed these days. He says it's all the new paperwork on top of the rising crime rates. Terrible crime in London nowadays. When I read a newspaper, it gives me nightmares. Sometimes he comes home so tense.'

I'd seen that for myself, all right: tension,

rage – not that it excused anything. I wanted to say something to her now, but Ernie was waiting in the van, there was a errand to complete, and it felt like the wrong time to bring the topic up, because she looked almost happy.

So I left it. I stepped over the threshold, stopped, and said, 'I hope you enjoy the book. And drop in to the shop any time, even if you aren't buying. Just say hello.'

When she smiled you could almost see that she must have been quite pretty.

I got into the MPV and switched on the engine.

Ernie was frowning. 'Where we goin' to put this stuff? You think there's room under the packing table?'

I enlightened him: twelve or fifteen books to check and shelve, thirteen boxes that I had already arranged to deliver to the Oxfam bookshop in Marylebone High Street.

He looked hard at me, and then turned away and stared through the windscreen. There are some gestures that Ernie has learned from observing Barnabas. Well, we'd been doing good business this month and I could afford a contribution.

We were back in the shop an hour later and working – on the website in Ernie's case and the mail in mine – when I remembered that the Acker business wasn't quite as wound up as I'd hoped, and that I ought to speak to Laura Smiley. I dug the telephone out from under a paper snow bank and got through to her instantly, interrupting her greetings. 'You remember that business I was asking your advice about? I've found out something about the man. Could we meet? This is information that you really need, and I think that face-to-face is going to be necessary. It's not simple.'

She said, 'That sounds interesting. All right, but you've caught me on my way out. I have to go and ask Mr Lewis whether he's remembered any more. Perhaps we could speak when I get back?'

I said, 'Yes,' but after I'd hung up, turned to a wants list that I was supposed to be going through, and found that I'd read a whole page of titles without taking anything in, I thrust the list at Ernie.

'I have to go out. If you have the time, could you see whether we have any of these?'

He nodded. 'You'll be back to get Ben?'

I said that I would and then spoiled it by adding that if anything went wrong I'd ring here by four o'clock. Then I remembered to add that Barnabas would be arriving soon, and went out to the van. Like Smiley, I had to ask Lewis whether he'd remembered something. I understood that there were days when I might get an answer from him, and others when I wouldn't. I could corner Smiley at the same time: two birds with one stone.

From the look on her face when I walked into the silent room at the nursing home, she wasn't

297

in the mood to be cornered.

I said quietly, 'Hello, Mr Lewis. Hello, Ms Smiley. I was just driving past, so I thought I'd drop in. Were you talking? I didn't mean to interrupt.'

She controlled herself with a superhuman effort and said, 'No.' No, I hadn't interrupted any sparkling and useful exchange of information.

I sat down calmly in the chair beside the window. Mr Lewis was watching me. When I glanced at Smiley, I saw that she had noticed. She hesitated and nodded at me almost imperceptibly.

I smiled nicely. 'Mr Lewis, I hope you're feeling better? How is your hand?'

He looked at it and held it up. 'Better. Not so bad.'

I went on smiling. 'I'm glad.' Should I spoil it by reminding him? 'I hope you'll be well soon. How did you hurt yourself?'

But I'd miscalculated. Or I thought that I had when he covered the brace with his good hand and moaned. But there didn't seem to be any point stopping – that wouldn't make it any easier. I said tentatively, 'Did some men hurt you?'

When he didn't speak, I threw a quick look at him. There were tears in his eyes. 'Did it happen when the car hit you?'

He answered me with a string of profanity that could have buried the whole room in sulphur. When he stopped, he threw me a quick glance. It seemed to me that his look was sharper, and he said distinctly, 'Big bastard.'

One man?

I said, 'Did you know him? He should be punished for doing that.'

'No, no, no,' he said rapidly. 'They can't.'

Smiley said suddenly, 'They can't let him hurt people, you know. It's not allowed.'

I said, 'Can you tell me his name? I'd like to help you. Will you tell me about him so that I can help?'

He said, 'There was a car.'

Smiley said, 'Were you riding in the car?'

What was going on here?

Lewis nodded. Then the intelligence, the focus faded from his eyes. He hunched his shoulders and looked down at his hand, and cried.

Smiley whispered, 'I'd better tell the nurse we've upset him. He may need medication. Then I want to talk to you.'

She got up and crossed to the bed, put a gentle hand on his shoulder, and whispered, 'Goodbye.' He could have been made of stone. I stood up and said more loudly, 'I'll come back and see you again soon. I'm going to bring you a present next time I come.' He ignored me. We left quietly.

Out in the corridor, she sped up and delivered her message at the reception desk, then almost pushed me out the main doors. It was drizzling.

We looked at each other.

'My car's right here.' She had left her little silver Nissan in a slot marked 'Reserved for Doctor': police privilege. I slid into the passenger seat; she got behind the wheel and turned to stare at me.

'What happened in there?'

I shrugged. I wasn't sure. 'What happened,' I said tentatively, 'was that he started talking about the accident because I asked him about his fingers. I was wondering the other day how they'd been broken when he was hit by the car. I'm no doctor, but—'

She said bluntly, 'The doctor was wondering the same thing. That's one of the reasons I'm up here now.'

'And he said that he was riding in the car. Not hit by it. But when he remembered, he switched off again.'

'Yes. He does that when he thinks of something that he knows he can't handle. It was a bad memory.'

'He was in somebody's car, and—'

She said, 'That's the other reason why I'm here. Somebody came forward – a teenager who saw the accident. She hadn't contacted us before, because her parents thought she was at home when she was actually hanging out with a boyfriend. Her mother found out, and she made her daughter ring us.'

I waited.

'This is absolutely confidential, you understand? It has to stay that way until the investigation is completed.' She waited for me to agree, looked at me meaningfully – I'd be expected to stick to what I said – and came to the punchline: 'The girl saw him being thrown out of a police car. The silly brat didn't do anything as clever as getting its registration number. She was probably falling-down-drunk. The thing is ... she's sure it was a police car.'

'Did she see anyone's face?'

'She says not.'

'A patrol car? A real...'

'Oh yes,' Smiley assured me. It sounded like a small growl.

I was gathering my thoughts. Yes, it fitted. I said, 'I'm going to tell you something. I can't prove anything that I'm going to say, but you might be able to. And incidentally, your source is also confidential for the moment.' I did the staring trick that she had used on me until I made her blink.

'Last autumn, the old man was carrying a book around with him. He saw that I sell books, so he showed it to me one evening.' I told her about the book, its value, and the identifying signature on the flyleaf. 'I never tried to ask him where he got it. But when I went through the things that Lewis left in my wheelie bin, the book wasn't there. I assumed he must have sold it. Or lost it, in one of his vague periods.

'But then I discovered it was on sale at a bookshop down the Charing Cross Road. They said they'd bought it from somebody who gave the name of John Brown, who said it had been his mother's. Only I recognized Lewis's copy. And the address that this man had given them was fake.'

She narrowed her eyes at me and waited.

'Yesterday I went to buy a library...' It was such a ridiculous description of Mrs Acker's books that I almost stopped right there. 'The woman who was selling the books said that she'd had another book that I might want, but she couldn't find it: a book of flower paintings which she'd been given for her birthday. Her husband had told her he'd bought it for £5 in a street market. And now, remember, it's missing. It was the same book.'

'Is her husband called John Brown?'

'No. But the description fits him.'

'And?'

I said, 'Wait. The other thing I found out was that her husband is deeply in debt. She said it's gambling debts. She said a lot of things while I was packing up her books. She talked about him retiring, taking a holiday in Spain. She talked a lot about how tired and tense her husband was, and under what pressure.'

She said, 'As you'd already noticed? Right: are you going to tell me what I think you are?'

'Mrs Acker is an old customer; I've known her for years, and I don't think she was making it up.'

Her face was a picture – not a picture of

delight – but she didn't miss a beat. She said, 'I'm going to need a formal statement from you. Just what you've told me, nothing else – unless you can remember any other relevant facts. I have to take this to the Super as fast as I can, and I'd like your statement to back me up. He's going to hate this.'

I said, 'No.'

She stared at me. 'What?'

'Because he'll hear about it, won't he? Be honest. It will leak out. Mr Acker is violent. He loses his temper – I've seen him in action. He beats up his wife. He lives in my street and he knows me. And I live alone with my three-year-old son.'

She stared at me, hesitated and sighed, 'I understand, but I must do something, and I go by the book. Well, will you talk to somebody informally, to begin with, and then we'll see about the statement? Whether or not Mrs Acker makes a formal complaint, you'll have to make one sooner or later if we aren't going to let the whole thing drop. If he's going to put in for early retirement, they might decide to let it go for lack of evidence. They can do that, you know.'

I was beginning to realize that I'd put myself in line for some heavy pressure. I said, 'I'll meet somebody, if I can't just talk to you now. Unofficially. Not at the station, not at my place.'

'Where?'

I looked at her. 'At the offices of my solicitor, and in his presence.'

A grin slowly broke over her face. 'That's not a bad idea. I'll tell the Super. He'll hate it. Miss Hoare —'

I said, 'Call me Dido. There's something else you should do: look through old staff records. When Acker transferred to Islington, there were some rumours about him. Maybe drinking, maybe gambling, maybe a bit of heavy stuff.'

She stared at me. 'You have contacts in the force?'

'Just a detective who was stationed in Islington when Acker first turned up there. I'll give you his name, if you like.'

She breathed out. 'Later. I have to go back to the station and do a little digging; this shouldn't wait.'

I got out into the rain and said over my shoulder, 'I'll give you the number of my mobile, and I'll keep it on standby this afternoon.'

She laughed and wrote the number in a conventional little black notebook. I was watching, and when she started to write my name beside the number, I stopped her. We looked at each other.

'There've been too many dead women around here this month,' I said. When I heard myself, I really started to wonder again.

# Chapter 38

## My Father's Razor

I shouted, 'See you at two thirty!' at Ben's back and watched him run up the walk and vanish through the door of the nursery. Then I got back into the van, buckled myself in, and checked the street around me and the clock on the dashboard: five to nine. Not bad.

I'd arranged with my father to come and pick him up at home, and use that excuse to call in upstairs. Mr Stanley was on my conscience. It was time to thank him for letting me turn his life upside down and land him with an uncontrollable monkey and an even more uncontrollable teenager. I even thought about stopping to buy him some flowers.

I parked the van by the post box, walked a short distance downhill to my father's place and rang the bell. When nothing happened, I tried the upper bell and was rewarded by the sound of footsteps. The chain rattled, and Barnabas opened the door.

'I'm upstairs,' he said inaccurately.

'How is he?'

'More cheerful. We have been discussing the

effects of hard drugs. He's a little inclined to think that it was a bad idea for us to attempt to deal with her ourselves.'

I squared my shoulders in preparation for another lecture and followed him upstairs.

They were in the sitting room. Mr Stanley, wrapped in a grey cardigan, was holding a tea-cup and saucer. Charlie stared at me sharply from his shoulder, but decided that I was harmless when I ignored him and crossed to one of the settees. My father joined me there.

'Tea, Miss Hoare?'

I said, 'Thank you, but I've only dropped in to get my father. It's going to be a busy day – we have a school carol concert this afternoon. Mr Stanley, I just wanted to say—'

He shook his head. 'No need. I am sorry for the poor girl. It wasn't her fault. I don't believe she could help it, not anything she did. She turned sixteen last week: did you know that? When I was sixteen, my parents allowed me to cycle to and from school, but if I went out in the evenings, they always asked where I was going and why. It's another world now, and not a better one.'

There were a lot of things I might have said, beginning with the thought that when Mr Stanley had been sixteen, Hitler had only recently been removed from power, and a couple of cities in Japan had just been nuked out of existence; but I couldn't, so I changed the subject by asking, 'How is Charlie doing?'

306

A smile struggled on to Mr Stanley's face. 'He's an interesting little creature. He picks up things surprisingly quickly. And yet he is just an animal.' He must have felt a movement then, because he stopped and waited. Charlie had decided that Mr Stanley needed grooming and turned his attention to the head beside him. He stared hard and slid his fingers carefully into the man's hair to tease out the strands. When his hands came away, he was looking closely at something invisible between his thumb and forefinger. He popped it into his mouth. Then he stood up slightly and went back to the search.

Barnabas cleared his throat and got to his feet. 'I will drop in this evening,' he said to his neighbour.

Mr Stanley smiled sweetly, and we left the two of them there.

As he was shutting the front door behind us, my father said, 'The animal still smells. Inevitably.' Then he lapsed into silence for the whole journey.

Back in George Street, I headed to the shop but Barnabas diverged towards the flat. 'Upstairs, I think?'

'I could make another pot of coffee,' I offered uneasily.

He nodded. I obeyed. In the sitting room, facing one another across the low table, I said, 'Barnabas, what is it?'

'When we got out of the van just now – were

307

you aware of what you did? You unbuckled yourself very, very slowly, staring into the rear view mirror. Then you examined the road ahead equally carefully, and leaned forward to peer into your little bin area. As you finally got out, you appeared to be interested in the interiors of the cars parked down the road. A grey car turned the corner rather abruptly, and I noticed that you jumped. Then when you—'

'Barnabas, I was just being careful! Are you *complaining* about my being careful?'

'No,' he said, 'of course not. But you were acting in a manner that is, you know, somewhat paranoid.'

I said, 'I'm all right.'

'I happened to be speaking to Pat on the phone last night, and she said again that of course you and Ben would be very welcome for the holidays. Her au pair has gone home for Christmas so there is a spare room, and Ben would have playmates during the nursery break.'

'Twelve-year-olds don't play with three-year-olds,' I told him. 'They think the little kids will tell on them when they smoke cigarettes and spray graffiti on walls.'

'Pat's sons—!'

'Would never be allowed to do that kind of thing,' I said. 'I told you, I'm just being careful. Following orders.'

'Whose orders?' Barnabas demanded.

I recited a list of names, starting with his, and

added, 'Right now, there are things going on around me. I am... ' I looked at him solemnly, 'in the soup. The mess needs to be cleared up, but until it is...'

I was going to say, Until it is I'm going to go on feeling nervous, but I stopped myself and took refuge in staring at my coffee.

'Perhaps we should examine this?'

I said, 'I don't even know where to start.'

'Start with the facts.' Barnabas ordered. 'Not with what you imagine, but only what you've witnessed for yourself.'

'Bodies,' I said. I did it carefully: Lewis finding the black sack across the road, and the subsequent appearance of other parts of the same body. It was mostly hearsay, but my source was the police, so it was pretty factual. As was the fact that the body had been frozen before it appeared.

'Scattered and mostly in very obvious places,' Barnabas summed up. 'Ergo, intended to communicate something. Perhaps frozen to make disposing of it easier, but then used for a threat?'

'All in this street, or nearby.'

'Because this was convenient, or rather as a message to someone who lives here?'

'How, convenient?'

'Well,' Barnabas said drily, 'let's say this person is a one-legged centenarian who is too feeble to carry them far?'

I held my tongue.

'Or is it rather a threat of violence? "Do you want to end up like her?" That sort of thing.'

'But she didn't exactly end up,' I said. 'I forgot: she wasn't murdered; one of the detectives said she died of natural causes.'

Barnabas had picked up a discarded book catalogue, opened it to a blank back cover, and was writing small, neat, disjointed words. When I twisted my head around I could see that he had covered the first inch or two with scribbled and disjointed thoughts: parts – ? purpose? where? almost certainly threat – to? ?? more to come?'

Then he looked at me encouragingly. 'Who is threatened, then? And why?'

I said, 'All kinds of reasons. Somebody who *didn't* kill her is being threatened with a false accusation. Or a woman, probably it would be a woman, is being warned to behave or she'll wind up the same way. Barnabas, this is guess-work, and you said we should keep to the facts.'

'But then we leap forward as over stepping-stones! Dido, let us find the simplest explanation. Occam's Razor, which – as I keep explaining to you – is the principle that all unnecessary facts in an investigation should be eliminated at once.'

'The vegetable soup principle?'

'What?'

'It was just an image.'

Barnabas frowned at me and abandoned that. 'The relevant facts are, I believe, these: the

310

dead woman was not murdered, and her remains are not hidden, but rather being displayed in public, therefore they are probably a warning. To warn, the meaning must be obvious to the person warned: this is relevant to the local occurrences of the body parts. The first – assuming that the one Mr Lewis found that day was first – was found in this street; then one in Upper Street to the west, and one on the council estate to the east. The next two were again in this street, both positioned on the railings on this side, north and south. Ah. I wonder whether there will be anything else? It seems almost like encirclement.'

I said frivolously, 'Then there will be one last thing, won't there? It will turn up, super-glued to the target's front door.'

'Or sitting on top of their rubbish bin one morning when the dustmen are due.'

I said, 'Oh.'

'Oh?'

'Yes, oh.' It was perfectly clear. 'What would you say if I told you that I know somebody who is keeping their wheelie bin locked up indoors these days?'

'Mr Acker, you mean? I would say it would be unhygienic.'

'Awkward, too. Those things aren't easy to move through doorways and over steps. But you'd do it if you were afraid somebody was going to leave something incriminating inside to be found by anybody who happened to look.'

311

By Harry Lewis, who had been thrown out of a police car after somebody had finished 'persuading' him to do something, or keep quiet – no, not keep quiet, who would listen to his gibbering? – or hand something over or ... Mr Lewis had been going through dustbins as usual when something had caught his eye: the earring belonging to the girl who had died, the monkey's ornament. It wouldn't have been there all on its own, either. Maybe there had been an earlier message which everybody had missed. Or maybe the remains which the old man had found across the street were the first 'message', carried there by Acker himself after they had appeared on his own premises?

I said, 'Ken Acker. The policeman up the street who has a dodgy reputation and a vile temper, and is deep in debt because, Mrs Acker told me, he loses money at cards. Barnabas, you know I saw him the other day, very early. Sunday morning. I was awake, and I saw him coming home by minicab. He didn't have enough money to pay the driver, and he threw a bunch of coins at the car and stomped off. He's a gambler.'

'Policeman,' Barnabas said. 'Would he not expect to be disciplined if they found out about this? Presumably investigated, even prosecuted. Finished.'

'So he's stressed out by what's happening, and he must get out of trouble. Barnabas, he's been saying that he's going to retire soon. Laura

Smiley told me that he might be able to get out of trouble with the authorities if he got out of the force. If he's cornered ... Of course a pension income wouldn't be enough to pay off big debts.'

'Nor would a police constable's salary be adequate, if that's what we're talking about,' Barnabas added.

'He might have won sometimes.'

Barnabas raised an eyebrow. No. The punter never wins in the long run, or nobody would ever bother to run a casino, much less an illegal game.

'They must know how much he earns.'

'Then why did they allow him to run up such a debt?' Barnabas mused in the tone of one who is allowing a child a chance to shine, although he already has the answer.

'Because it's worth a lot of money to have policeman in your pocket? Of course, he's in the uniformed branch, and he's only a constable, but he might be able to tell them if they're under investigation.'

'He is on the inside, at least! He hears and passes on all kinds of inside information. Just one phone call to somebody every week in exchange for—'

'Barnabas! That's what they were saying to him. I heard: they threatened him, something about "making a call" or else.'

He looked at me and nodded. Else they would break his arms and legs. Make sure that his

313

superiors discovered what he was doing. Ruin him.

'Barnabas, I already knew this. Not the gambling link, but – Lewis.'

My father focused on me.

'It must have been Acker who attacked the old man. Laura Smiley and I worked that out today. She's investigating Acker's record now. I think I should phone her.' And Barker, too. Unless he already knew all this. It's hard to see through a situation where the people you're trying to help won't share what they're already thinking.

Smiley's mobile was off, so I left an urgent message for her to contact me. Perhaps she was already on the problem.

More. I said, 'Andrei and Georgie only came into the picture because of Annie, and Annie came in because Chris Kennedy was doing a report on traffickers and a police contact in King's Cross had put him on to her? And Nina was just an accident.'

'She resembles, in many ways, the dead girl whose body is haunting you. One might query the coincidence. Furthermore, one should not forget that the two—'

'Georgie.'

'What?'

'When he was waiting outside to give me the money for Annie—'

'Stop there. Why was he waiting? He could have posted an envelope through the door if we

314

were closed. At a pinch, he might have come in. Was anybody here at the time? Yes, of course, I was. I wouldn't have known him. Just a man leaving you an envelope.'

'He wasn't exactly outside. He was waiting a little way up the road.'

'Outside Acker's house?'

'Across the street and a few doors down, but he could have been watching their door.'

'Perhaps he had a message to deliver there as well.'

'Barker said—'

'Barker?' Barnabas's voice was sharp.

'The policeman I saw yesterday.' Barnabas nodded and waved me onward. 'Barker said they've been investigating a couple of big gangs who smuggle people and drugs, do money laundering – and run illegal gambling, Barnabas. They've been thinking that a policeman has been leaking information to them.'

'I am relieved that things may be less random than they appeared. Coincidence is perfectly acceptable in an imperfect world, but too much leads to superstition. As one might say, Eureka!'

I reminded him again that we were supposed to be considering only the facts, and he said that we were allowed to associate facts and draw the logical conclusions; and then I tried to phone Smiley again. The switchboard said she was unavailable and asked whether I wanted to speak to anybody else, but I didn't.

# Chapter 39

## Don't Look Back

There's never one around when you need him. When Kennedy rang, I told him that I needed a policeman. 'Annie phoned me, and she slipped up. I got the caller number, and what I want to know is where she was phoning from.'

'BT know where the phone is installed, but they won't tell you.'

'Which is why I need a policeman. Do you think Sam Johnson could find out for me?'

He considered it. 'I'd say Barker's people would be better. Do you want to contact him, or shall I?'

I wasn't sure. It was important not to have Annie raided and carried off, because if anybody noticed that, they could quite easily decide to disappear Nina. I thought it was more likely that Scotland Yard would know how to handle this. 'He's your friend,' I said, cowardly.

'I'll get back to you. Are you at the shop?'

'For now, but Ben's carol service is at two thirty.'

'Do you think I might come to that?'

I blinked and commented, as I hung up, that I

didn't suppose the nursery would object to another man swelling the audience numbers. Most of the parents are working mothers and absentee fathers, and an extra body in the room would encourage the children. And I had some things to say to him. It would be a good chance.

Then I went back to fiddling about. It was a long time since I'd concentrated on business, and if my father hadn't been there I would probably have given up. As it was, a trickle of customers bought books, or left their addresses for our next catalogue, and the ordinary process was comforting. At one thirty I tried Smiley's mobile again and left another message before we put a 'Closed' notice on the door and went upstairs for lunch. When Kennedy arrived, we left in his Jaguar. Very high-class group. I was the little one with short legs who had to squeeze into the rear seat. That reminded me of our escape from Andrei and Georgie a week ago, and left me a little out of the conversation, with the chance to worry about what to do when I found Annie, whether Nina was still all right, and what Smiley was playing at, not getting back to me.

The concert was ... sweet, though slightly out of tune. Afterwards there was a tea with mince pies, and an injection of the ordinary life. We came away with Ben carrying his Christmas present from the nursery and fizzing with left-over artistic excitement. He and Barnabas made for the door to the flat, but Chris stopped me

317

when I went to follow and held up his mobile.

'There's a message here from Barker. The address. What do you want to do?'

'Where is it?'

'Wait a minute.' He pressed a couple of buttons, looked at the screen and shrugged. 'Looks like St Pancras. I'll need to check my *A to Z*. I wonder whether she's gone back to her old flat?'

I said, 'St Pancras is only a mile away. The important thing is to find her.'

'She might not want anybody to know she's there.'

I said that I'd look anyway, as soon as I got Ben and Barnabas sorted out.

'I'm coming with you,' he said quietly, 'all right?'

I told him it would be very nice.

The address belonging to the telephone was in a battered-looking council block five minutes' walk from Euston Station; that explained why she had got out of the taxi there. The flats opened off high concrete walkways. We located 138 with difficulty because of the darkness: somebody had smashed the light on the wall by the door and I could feel shards of glass under my feet. The curtains were pulled across the window, and I couldn't see any lights inside, so I pressed my ear against the pane. There were voices somewhere, very quiet, and a whisper of laughter and applause.

'The television's on.'

'It might be next door.'

But I could understand Annie hiding out in the dark watching the television with the sound turned down and one ear peeled for trouble. It was probably what I'd do.

When I pulled out my mobile and rang the number Annie had used, a telephone rang inside. It went on ringing. If she was out drinking with friends in her favourite local, I'd just have to freeze on her doorstep until closing time. But I wanted get this over with. The solution was to make it impossible for her to ignore us. There was a bell push on the door frame, but that wasn't what I wanted. I pushed it first, just to get her attention, and then shouted, 'Annie? It's Dido. Open up!' To reinforce my request, I grabbed the tinny little door knocker and clattered it as loudly as it would clatter. Then I shouted, 'Come on!' through the letter slot at the top of my voice. It seemed likely that everybody in the building could hear me.

The door jerked away from my face, and a familiar voice whispered through the crack, 'Dido? For crying out loud, you shut your gob! Who's that with you?'

I said, 'It's Chris. Let us in, we need to talk to you.'

I heard a dramatic groan, but the chain clattered and the door opened on darkness. Not quite darkness. There was a flickering blueish light at the end of a dark hallway. We stepped inside, and she closed the door with a small click and put the chain up again.

'How'd you find me?' she hissed.

'Sam Johnson told us where you are,' Chris said suddenly.

I'd opened my mouth to say something else, but I closed it again when she groaned and said, 'Mighta guessed. They don't never leave you alone. Come in, take the weight off your feet.'

I didn't want to, but when she moved away in the darkness there was no choice. I bumbled down the hallway after her, banging my elbow on an open door. When we reached the room with the TV set, the screen and the two little tea lights on the table illuminated the little room enough for me to see her face. She looked tired. We found seats on a low settee while she returned to her chair and switched off the sound.

'What do you want?'

I said, 'Nina.'

'Dido, she isn't here. You can look, if you like. I haven't seen her since I left her with you.'

'Have you heard anything about her?' Chris asked, all stern and trustworthy. 'Anything at all?'

I jumped in. 'Is she with Georgie? Or Mus— Andrei again?'

'I dunno, because I haven't talked to them.'

'Then all you have to do,' I pointed out politely, 'is give us their addresses. We won't say we got them from you.'

'Dido,' she said, 'who else would it be? They ain't idiots.'

Chris said, 'Maybe Dido's expecting too much.'

She muttered something about 'winding me up' and we sat in silence for a couple of minutes before I put in, 'She's going to die.'

Somebody in the room let out a huge sigh, and Annie's voice came sulkily: 'I'm gonna die too. Nobody's looking after *me*.'

'You?' Chris snorted. 'You're tough as old boots. And clever.'

'I'm clever enough to know that your police friends are going after them. I tell you anything about Georgie and I'm dog meat.'

'Then you ought to go away,' Chris said. 'Just until this is finished. Let us know what you know, and then take a holiday. You'd never have to testify about just handing over an address.'

'And what do I use for money?' she asked triumphantly. I got the feeling that we were reaching the nitty-gritty. 'Listen, if I hadda few quid, I'd go off and spend Christmas with my cousin, runs a B and B in Weston-Super-Mare. But I've gotta pay my way, she's not rich.'

'Would three hundred do it?' Chris enquired.

'Four,' she said and Chris said, 'Done!'

She muttered under her breath and then said loudly, 'I'm not gonna give you the address in Weston.'

How many B and Bs were there in Weston-

Super-Mare? I asked myself rhetorically. Well, I'd been there: quite a few. But the local police would find her if they had to.

I said, 'Have a nice time. Stay safe. Georgie's address?'

'Money first.'

I thought frantically about the mess in my shoulder bag, where I probably had as much as twenty pounds. I was about to offer to go to a cash machine when Chris pulled out his wallet and counted eight fifty-pound notes on to the table.

Annie put her hand near them and said, 'I don't know about Andry, you know – where he stays – but Georgie's staying in a place just north of here. Wait.' She had a television guide with a ball-point pen at hand, and she tore out a page and scribbled a few lines in the margin. They made the exchange.

Chris angled the paper to the candles so he could read what she'd written. He looked at her. 'He's there now?'

'He was this afternoon.'

'All right, then. Just one thing: whose flat is this?'

'It's mine!' she said indignantly.

'Behind on the rent?' he asked.

'Housing benefit!'

'That's nice,' he said. 'Mrs Kelly, if we go over there and find you've given us the home address of a nice Chinese married couple, I'll shop you to the social services. No more flat.'

It was touch and go, but in the end she decided to laugh, though it sounded sour. 'Deal,' she said. 'But don't go over there alone. With Georgie, you never know what you'll find.'

'Wouldn't dream of it,' Chris said, sounding as cheerful as she did.

At the door, she touched my hand. 'I'll ring you some time. I'd like to know if you find that girl.'

I nodded, and she shut us out.

Chris was standing a few yards away with his mobile phone. He was holding the paper up to the nearest light and reading out the address she had given us. I mouthed, 'Barker?' at him. He nodded. I held out my hand, and he said, 'Wait a second,' into the phone and handed it over.

I braced myself and said, 'I need to tell you about something I saw up the road, in PC Acker's front garden. Andrei Barden was there.' It took a couple of minutes. At the end of my confession I switched off and handed the phone back. We exchanged a thoughtful stare.

'Time to go and relieve your father?'

I said, 'Yes. I'm feeling a bit flat.'

'You wanted to go on a raiding party? There isn't going to be one tonight, though they'll get surveillance started.'

'What about Barker's big project?'

'Finding Georgie again will help him. But they won't do anything until they're ready for the final haul.'

I hoped so – I hoped that everything would work out all right, because I'd tried, and there was nothing more I could do. What I wanted now was to stop thinking about it, have an early night, and wake up in the morning with Ben, and decorate the tree.

# Chapter 40

## A Man Running

It seemed like the middle of the night when the doorbell woke me, but the clock on the bedside table said it was only a quarter past one. The first thought that surfaced in my muzzy brain was that some passing drunk was being a nuisance. The second was that I'd be lucky if that was all. The third was that I didn't want Ben to be woken. I rolled over and fell out of bed, dragged myself to my feet, and staggered out, shutting the bedroom door. The bell rang again as I reached the sitting room. I flung up the window and leaned out. For a moment I didn't recognized her. She didn't look up when I called, 'I'll be right down.'

It was freezing outside. I grabbed my coat as I passed the hook in the hallway and crept down the stairs gingerly in my bare feet. Door. No –

the chain – I still wasn't awake. Chain, door...

Mrs Acker stood some meters away, wearing slippers and a dressing gown, holding her right hand in her left, looking back up the street. Even in this light, I could see splatters of darkness on her hand and her face. Everywhere.

'What's happened?' I called. 'Come in! It's so cold, come in!'

She turned from me and took a few more steps.

I called, 'Wait! What's wrong?' – not that I couldn't see what was wrong.

She turned and looked back and said dully, 'I left our door open.' Then she started to walk in the direction of number 21.

One bare toe on the pavement persuaded me that I'd develop frostbite if I went on. I left the door open in case she changed her mind and ran upstairs, wondering what to do. I opened the bedroom door a crack and listened to Ben's regular breathing. Then I closed it again. No choice. There was an old pair of trainers sitting beneath the coat hooks. I stuffed my bare feet into them, grabbed my mobile phone and keys, and slipped back downstairs. She hadn't come back. I rang Barnabas's number, wondering how quickly I'd be able to wake him; but he answered almost at once, and he sounded more awake than I was. He must have been reading.

'Dido? What's wrong?'

I said, 'Ben and I are all right, but something's happened to Mrs Acker. She just rang my doorbell. She's been attacked, I saw blood, and she's in shock. She's gone back up the road. If he's waiting for her ... Barnabas, I'm calling the police as soon as I catch her up, but I'll have to leave Ben alone. He's asleep now, but can you call a taxi and just put on a coat and get down here?'

He snapped, 'Be careful!' and hung up. I kept the phone in my hand, and concentrated. I could see her ahead of me, walking like an old woman, but she turned in through her gate almost at once.

When I got there, the front door was ajar. Bad. If there had been anybody passing, anyone at all, I would have asked for help; but there wasn't. I looked down. An edging of half bricks divided the slabs of the path from the short grass of the tiny lawn, so I stopped and tugged at one of the bricks until I had loosened it. It wasn't much, but it seemed better than an empty hand. I stopped just outside the open door and called out.

'Mrs Acker? *Mrs Acker*?'

No answer, no sound. I needed some response so that I could get an idea of the situation.

'*Constable Acker*?'

It was so quiet inside that I could hear a tap dripping. The only light I could see was up-stairs.

I stopped long enough to programme the number 999 into my mobile. One single push would connect me to the emergency services.

Then I pressed the light switch inside the door and stepped forward. I didn't call out again. Holding the phone in my left hand and the brick in my right, I crept to the top of the stairs. The light was coming from inside the bedroom. I crossed to the door and pushed it open.

Mrs Acker faced me, sitting on the edge of the double bed. Her husband lay behind her, half on the bed and half off. The sheets were red.

'He was going to leave me,' she said suddenly in her monotonous voice. 'He told me so. He was going to leave me here. I stabbed him when he fell asleep, because I couldn't let him leave me. I love him. I couldn't let ... It's the only way.'

My thumb pressed the button. When I heard a little voice, I raised the phone and gave them the address and said that a man was dead. Then I went over to the bed and tried to make her stand up and come away downstairs with me, but she wouldn't, and she was as heavy as lead; so I had to sit down beside her with my back to the dead man and hold her hand.

# Chapter 41

## Monkeys

On Christmas Eve we closed the shop early. I took myself out to the van. There was one last errand to be done, and this was as good a time as any. It took me less than an hour, and as I came back and opened the door of the flat there was a shriek from the sitting room: 'Don't come in! Mummy, you can't come in here! We're wrapping your presents!'

I said, 'I'll be in the kitchen, then. Hurry up!' and went to discover that there was still a small cup of coffee left. Maybe I drink too much coffee. Maybe that's what makes me edgy.

After a few minutes there was a scurrying of feet in the hallway, then the bedroom, and finally Ben appeared.

'It's all right now,' he said, 'but you mustn't look for them.'

I promised, picked up my mug, gave him a hug, and followed him into the sitting room. They had the tree lights on, a carpet full of bits of wrapping paper and ribbon ends, empty carrier bags and two empty rolls of tape, and looks of mutual satisfaction. I said thoughtfully, 'You people have been doing a lot of wrapping. But I think that when I pick all these things up, I might be able to guess about some of my presents.'

Ben looked at Barnabas and flung himself to the task of tidying up. I joined my father on the settee.

'I went to see Mr Lewis.'

'How is he today?'

I thought back to the old man I'd just left sitting hunched at the side of his neat bed. There had been two Christmas cards on his bedside cabinet. I sneaked a peek when I propped my own up beside them. The little holly twig was from the nurses. The children beside the Christmas tree came from Laura Smiley. Mine was an unlikely scene of Big Ben under a heavy snowfall; well, the way it was going this year, that might not be so ridiculous. I'd sat with him for a minute or two, but he wasn't talking and I wasn't doing any good. In the end, I got up and said, 'I've brought you something for Christmas,' and handed him the book. Something flickered in his face then, and he opened it and started to turn the pages, stopping at the pictures, the beautiful flowers, one after another. I said goodbye, but I don't think he heard me. His fingers were long and thin, like the monkey's.

I told my father, 'They'll have to find him a permanent bed somewhere.'

Barnabas said, 'Yes.' He cleared his throat

and changed the subject. 'That red dress you have hanging on the wardrobe door: is that—?'

'Tomorrow,' I said firmly. 'Red. Just right for Christmas dinner.'

'It looks a little – should one say "festive"? – for a family gathering. You might feel cold in it.'

'It's very cheerful,' I said, trying to be cheerful, 'and Pat's house is always too warm.' My hospital visit had depressed me.

He changed tack again. 'I would have expected Mr Kennedy to have phoned you about the news.'

'Chris is spending a few days in Kyrenia over Christmas. He flew out last night.'

Barnabas blinked at me. I refused to meet his eyes. I know that sooner or later he will decide to ask questions about Chris and me, but he hadn't got there yet. When it happened, I'd just tell him that Chris Kennedy had only ever been in love with one person in his life and that person wasn't me and it made a difference.

Then I remembered. 'What news?'

'I just heard it on Radio 4. Something about dawn raids at over twenty addresses in north and west London. The police have arrested a number of persons who will be charged with trafficking in people and drugs. You should remember to turn on the television for the early evening news.'

I almost went and rang Barker then, but I doubted that he would be free for a day or two.

I had no doubt that this was the big move he had been working for. I hoped it had been a roaring success. Now I just wanted somebody to tell me that they had found Nina. Until she reappeared, things would still be up in the air. The thought of her wandering the streets like a lost monkey, looking at the Christmas lights, looking for a place to sleep, for money and drugs, was depressing. Better to be in jail – I was almost sure of that.

'Dido?'

I said, 'Sorry. I was just thinking about Nina.'

Barnabas said, 'In all probability they will have found her in one of the raids – that, is, if she had gone back to them – in which case she will at least be safe. If she did not go back, then you might hope that she possesses more common sense and a greater degree of self-preservation than you give her credit for?'

I said that I hated not knowing. But I've grown up enough now to know that there are some things that can't be mended.

'And Mrs Acker?'

'Laura Smiley says she will be prosecuted, and she'll plead guilty with mitigating circumstances, and the sentence will be light. The courts have been taking abusive situations like hers seriously, these past few years. She'll get help. Barnabas, can we drop this and talk about tomorrow instead? Christmas Day, remember? We'll pick you up and bring you here for breakfast and the great present opening.'

'I shall probably breakfast with Mr Stanley before he leaves to spend the day with his daughter-in-law in Richmond. That will be quite early. Perhaps I could have a cup of coffee with you afterwards?'

'It will do Mr Stanley good to have a day away from the monkey,' I said heartlessly.

Barnabas shrugged. 'Mr Stanley has informed me that he intends to alter his will. He is leaving me the monkey and the sum of £500 in the event of his untimely demise.'

The two of us sat in silence for a moment, watching Ben pick up the last slivers of coloured paper and deposit them in the last of the plastic bags. We were probably both picturing Charlie rampaging through my father's flat with its shelves and piles of valuable old books, academic journals and notes.

I said, 'What did you say to him?'

'Nothing.'

'But Barnabas!'

'If it ever happens,' my father said in a tone that allowed no argument, 'Charlie will remove to Gerald Durrell's zoo with £500 in his rucksack, where he will live out an appropriate and exciting life as a wealthy monkey amongst friends.'

I started to say what a good idea that was, but another memory interrupted my speech.

'Barnabas! Do you remember? The day that it turned up here, I asked you how you knew about catching monkeys, and you said you'd tell me the story some time.'

Attracted by the word 'story', Ben stopped working and flung himself on to the settee close beside his grandfather.

Barnabas said, 'Ah, indeed.' His voice switched to the storyteller's singsong. 'Well, this was just after the war. Your mother and I were on our honeymoon in Marrakech, and...'